"I'm expecting company for dinner," Robin lied.

"Is that right?" Deetz smirked. "You need to work on that lying stuff. You're no good at it." He reached for the porch light switch next to the door, turned off the light, then shoved the door so hard it bounced off the wall then slammed closed behind him. He ambled toward Robin.

Other Wild Rose Press Titles by Olive Balla:

An Arm And A Leg
Jillie
Code Murder.

Paint Me a Murder

by

Olive Balla

Paint Me a Murder

Cover Art by *Debbie Taylor*

The Wild Rose Press, Inc.
PO Box 708
Adams Basin, NY 14410-0708
Visit us at www.thewildrosepress.com

Publishing History
First Edition, 2022
Trade Paperback ISBN 978-1-5092-4273-3
Digital ISBN 978-1-5092-4274-0

Published in the United States of America

Dedication

For Christine Munsey: Criminal Investigator and close friend without whose police procedural expertise this book would not have been possible.

Acknowledgments

Dennis Burns, M.D. Professor of Pathology
Virginia Hutson – Beta Reader, Critique
Christine Munsey – Criminal Investigator for the state
of Montana
Juanice Myers – Beta Reader
James O'Donnell – Creative consulting, Tech and
Software Resource
Kevin O'Donnell – Creative consulting and
Brainstorming
Ally Robertson - Editor, The Wild Rose Press

Chapter One

Robin Marcato eyed the jagged stumps on her rose bushes and ran a thumb along her dulled shears. She positioned the blades to lop off the final deadhead, when voices drew her attention across the street where her neighbor Vince Banda and his employee stood nearly toe to toe, arms gesticulating, faces red.

"Yeah, that's right," the employee said, teeth bared, dark hair blowing in a stiff winter wind. "Blame the ex-con. Some old biddy misplaces her necklace, and the ex-con must be up to his old tricks."

"Lose the attitude, Deetz," Vince said, waving a hand dismissively. "I believe everyone deserves a second chance, but I'll drag you to the police myself if I find out you've gone back to thieving. Get the equipment ready. We're due at the job site in an hour." He muttered, shook his head, then walked up the driveway and into his house.

Deetz glared after his retreating boss, his lips thin and brow furrowed. He climbed into the back of Vince's pickup and began fussing with a huge horizontal canister Robin recognized as an air compressor. Something about the furtive looks the guy kept shooting toward Vince's house seemed off.

The employee picked up what looked like a wrench from the pickup bed. Between glancing toward his boss's house and scanning the neighborhood, he made

1

some adjustment to the motor atop the air compressor, his actions jerky and hurried.

Suddenly, the young man turned his head and looked squarely at Robin. Embarrassed to be caught watching, she returned to pruning her rose bushes.

Robin's last piano student of the day arrived just as she finished with her garden work. She escorted her student through the front door and into the music room, the drama across the street temporarily forgotten.

Chapter Two

After her student left, Robin prepared a late dinner. She carried her food to the kitchen snack bar then turned on the small, table-top television to catch the evening news. While she rarely listened to the mostly depressing reports, the newscasters' voices filled the otherwise silent kitchen.

Something in the young female newscaster's voice caught Robin's attention, and she studied the small screen.

"Vincent Banda, owner of Banda's Quality Painters, was killed this afternoon in a freak accident," the newscaster said. "According to the police report…"

Robin choked on a sip of coffee. She wiped the dribble from her chin then picked up the remote control and increased the television's volume.

"According to the police spokesperson, Banda's air compressor exploded as he prepared to paint a customer's house. The exact cause of the accident is under investigation."

The young reporter's face was replaced by a view of the rear of Vince's pickup parked in an unfamiliar driveway. Two or three large, twisted chunks of silvery metal lay in the yard, pieces of the destroyed air compressor, according to the reporter. Splashes of yellow paint dotted the ground around the pickup's open tailgate upon which sat the bottom half of what appeared to be a mangled five-gallon paint bucket.

The camera panned back to the reporter who stood beside the young man Robin had seen arguing with Banda earlier that day.

"We're here with Mister Banda's employee Ronnie Deetz." Pointing her microphone toward the man's face, she added, "Can you tell us what happened, Mister Deetz?"

Deetz shook his head, a convincing look of bewilderment on his face. "One minute we're getting set up to paint this house, and the next thing I know, the compressor blows. Just yesterday Mister Banda said he needed to buy a new one." The young man shrugged, a sorrowful look on his face. "I guess he waited too long."

"How did that make you feel? Did you fear for your own life?" the reporter said, the self-congratulatory expression on her face declaring herself the next top reporter.

After Deetz's mumbled response, the reporter took a couple of steps to her right and pointed the microphone toward a uniformed man. "What can you tell us about the explosion?"

"Only that air compressors should be drained of accumulated water after each use and safety tested periodically," the man said. "While a catastrophic air compressor explosion is unusual, it can happen."

…a catastrophic air compressor explosion…

Robin swallowed hard against the lump in her throat. Propelled into some strange, alternate reality, she sat staring at the television. Tears welled in her eyes as a recent photograph of Vince's smiling face swam onto the screen.

A widower of several years, Vince had been a kind and generous neighbor. After Robin's husband John died, Vince mowed her lawn and did odd jobs around her house. He showed up with coffee and pastries at least once a week and sat at her kitchen table chatting away about business and his two grown children, refusing to allow her to wrap herself in a cocoon and fade away. It was at Vince's suggestion that she began offering piano lessons.

"Most kids don't learn music in school nowadays, and that's a loss to humanity." He had said. "You have the piano, you have the space, and you definitely have the skill."

Memories of the argument witnessed earlier that afternoon pushed into Robin's thoughts, and something cold skittered through her insides. She reached for her cell phone.

At the risk of appearing to be nosy, she needed to tell her detective friend Petra Rooney what she saw and heard. Maybe the disagreement between Vince and Deetz had quickly blown over, or maybe Robin was overreacting. But she couldn't shake the feeling that she needed to let someone know. She owed Vince that much.

Robin started to tap Petra's number onto the tiny screen, then stopped. The phone's nearly empty battery icon testified that any conversation would have to be fast.

She sighed and turned the phone off, planning to charge it overnight.

"And that, as my John would say, is why we chose to keep our landline." She stuffed the offending cell phone into her bra and walked to the phone stationed on

5

the kitchen counter. But before Robin could punch her friend's number onto the phone's keypad, the doorbell rang.

She headed for the front door fully expecting to spot a neighborhood kid sprint across the yard after doing what kids have done since the first doorbell was invented.

Squinting through the peephole, Robin was surprised to see Vince's employee Deetz on her porch. Wearing the same work clothes he wore earlier, the man stood energetically chewing gum directly in front of the aperture. Highlighted in the porch light, his face appeared so near it blotted out everything else.

Ignoring a whispered warning from the back of her brain, Robin opened the door.

"Yes?" she said.

"I'm sorry to bother you," Deetz said, "but I worked with your neighbor." He jerked his head once toward Vince's house. "Mister Banda?"

"Oh yes, I've seen you around." Robin nodded.

When the man seemed careful to keep both hands behind his back, the tingle at the base of Robin's neck intensified.

"He talked about you a lot, so I figured you were close." Deetz looked into Robin's eyes. "He said you were like another daughter to him, especially after your husband died and all."

Robin nodded but remained silent.

"Did you hear what happened?" Deetz surreptitiously moved his gaze around the neighborhood, then looked beyond Robin's shoulder and into the house as if making sure she was alone.

"I just heard it on the news," she said, trying

unsuccessfully to calibrate her voice to a normal pitch while tiny hairs at the nape of her neck shifted position.

"Yeah, it was a terrible accident, you know?" A quizzical look flashed across the man's face, and his eyes bored into hers. "It was my job to keep the machinery running." He shrugged and squinted at Robin, a look of indecision on his face.

"I need to go. I have something in the oven." Robin's voice trailed off when the warning claxon at the back of her brain grew too loud to ignore. She took a step back and made a move to close the door.

"So, it *was* you watching me," Deetz said. Something in Robin's expression must have given her away because his lips thinned. "That's too bad."

Adrenaline pumping, Robin shoved the door closed. But the rational, this-can't-be-happening part of her brain slowed her reaction and before she could shoot the deadbolt home, Deetz had twisted the knob and forced the door back open.

"I'm expecting company for dinner," Robin lied. "My friend is a detective with Albuquerque Police, and she'll be here any minute."

"Is that right?" Deetz smirked. "You need to work on that lying stuff. You're no good at it." He reached a hand toward the porch light switch next to the door, turned off the light, then shoved the door open so hard it bounced off the wall then slammed closed behind him. He ambled toward Robin.

Robin's fight, flight, or freeze instinct kicked in, and she made a run for the upstairs bathroom with its locking door. Too late, she realized her mistake.

The man could easily break the flimsy door down. She should have run through the back door and into the yard. Then she could have used the last bit of her phone's charge to call the police. Or she could have screamed for help. Someone would have heard.

"Didn't anyone ever tell you it's bad manners to spy on your neighbors?" Deetz's voice hissed through the locked bathroom door. "None of this would be happening if you weren't so nosey. This is on you."

As Robin expected, one well-aimed kick shattered the doorjamb and sent splinters caroming off the wall behind it. Smiling, his eyes bright with excited anticipation, the man strode into the small bathroom.

"I spy with my little eye," Deetz said.

In unreasoning, unthinking panic, her body adrenaline-infused, Robin tried to bolt around the man.

"Red rover, red rover," Deetz said, "let nosey bimbo come over." He chuckled and spread his arms to block her escape. A silvery two-foot galvanized pipe in his right hand bumped against the shattered door jamb.

Robin took a step back, and her calves bumped the bathtub. With nowhere to run, she bunched her shoulders and doubled her fists. Whatever her attacker had planned for her, she would not make it easy. She martialed her courage and stared into Deetz's eyes.

"Whoo-ee, just look at you," the man said, every word dripping mockery. "Who do you think you are, Bat Girl?"

Sneering, Deetz stepped closer to Robin.

Without warning, she jabbed her fist into his solar plexus, grimacing at the resulting pain that shot through her fingers and up her arm.

A look of surprise replaced the impatience on the man's face. Air exploded from his lungs, and he doubled over. Instinctively, Robin shoved his head downward and brought her knee up into his face.

He growled and fell to the floor, his body blocking her escape. The metal pipe clanged onto the bathroom's tile floor and blood dripped from the man's nose.

Robin tried to leap over her assailant's huddled body, but he grabbed one of her ankles and pulled her leg backward. The white bathroom rug slid out from under her, causing her to lose her balance and fall. Her tailbone smacked against the ceramic tile, shooting electric flashes up her spine. She crab-scooted backward and kicked at her attacker's head with her free foot, but her blows glanced off his shoulder.

"You shouldn't have done that," Deetz said. Bloody bubbles gathered like tiny grapes under his nose. He chuffed a couple of times and swiped at the blood, smearing it across his face.

Gripping Robin's ankle in one hand, he retrieved the pipe with the other. Kneeling, he straddled her abdomen and ground one knee against her shoulder, pinning her to the floor.

His lips pulled back over clamped teeth in a death's head grin, Deetz lifted the pipe, grunted, and brought it down.

Robin screamed and instinctively jerked her head to one side. Then everything went black.

Chapter Three

Robin woke to darkness thick enough to chew and the feeling of being shrink-wrapped in something soft from head to toe. A blinding headache, unlike any she had ever endured, pulsed with every heartbeat. Her mouth dry, and tongue gummy, she tried to lift her arms. But whatever encircled her body prevented all but the slightest movement.

Claustrophobia that Robin had fought from childhood tightened her chest. Gasping for air, unable to think or reason, she thrashed, struggling to free her arms and legs from the wrapping. Heat from her raspy breaths warmed and moistened the fabric around her face. With every jerky movement, her body noisily thumped against the sides and top of a metal enclosure, the sounds reminiscent of the ones made by tennis shoes inside a clothes dryer.

Eventually, she managed to pull her arms from the folds of fabric then disentangled her head and upper body. Once her face was freed, she took in grateful gulps of cold air.

Dizziness kicked up waves of nausea, and she struggled to tamp down mindless panic at the closeness of her prison walls. The utter darkness seemed to drag and suck at her eyeballs, seemingly determined to pull them from their sockets.

Had she been buried alive?

Robin's memory flashed on the image of Vince's employee standing on her porch, his hair whipping in the blustery New Mexico winter wind. She again saw the calm look on his face, as though he were idly cleaning mud from his shoes rather than setting himself to kill another human being.

Robin raised fingers to her head, gingerly touching what must have been dried, encrusted blood which plastered hair against her skull. Sweat generated by her earlier thrashing sent stinging saltiness into the gash above her temple, and she jerked her hands away.

It occurred to her that had she not twisted her head to one side the instant before Deetz struck with the pipe, he could easily have crushed her skull.

Words from a recent documentary about concussions and traumatic brain injury sounded in her head.

Symptoms of a concussion include a headache that doesn't go away.

"Check," Robin whispered.

Memory lapses, slowness in thinking, light-headedness, nausea.

"Check, check, check, and check."

In case of a concussion, take care not to engage in excessive physical or strenuous mental activity.

"Happy to oblige," she murmured, envisioning herself inside a metal cocoon.

Uncomfortable she might be, but she was lucky to be alive. What if, instead of just hitting her once, Deetz had decided to bash her brains out?

Perhaps the reason he had not taken the time to do more damage was simply that he was in a hurry. While the guy had not seemed overly anxious during the assault, he must have been terrified of getting caught.

Based on the amount of blood that must have come from her head wound, maybe he thought one blow had killed her. According to a recent documentary Robin had watched on violent crime, scalp wounds bleed profusely, even when not life-threatening.

Or, and this thought nearly sent Robin spinning off into a mindless abyss, perhaps it had not mattered whether she was dead *or* alive since he planned to put her some place she would never be found, someplace where no one could hear her scream.

Robin's breaths came in quick, short gasps, and her heart raced. She commanded herself to breathe slowly and calm down. Loss of control and dwelling on hideous possibilities would not only be unhelpful but could poison her ability to reason as well as deplete precious energy.

Scenes from old western movies watched with her mom came to mind. Again, she heard the disgusted snorts her mom made when the actresses either fainted or stood safely rooted some distance from the action. With palms pressed to their faces like the character in Munch's *The Scream*, they stood by as their men were beaten unmercifully.

What useless females. They give the rest of us a bad name. Fat lot of help any of them would be in a life-and-death crunch.

Incensed, her mom would proceed to talk above the television throughout the rest of the movie, offering searing commentary and leaving Robin to wonder how the story ended. Then followed a lengthy discourse on pioneer women and their lives.

Those early women were tough as hobnail boots,

her mom would say. *Not simpering, mealymouthed hothouse plants. Their survival, and sometimes the survival of their families, depended on their being strong.*

A surge of images from Robin's assault and its aftermath bubbled up in her memory.

After her initial period of unconsciousness, Robin had floated in and out of awareness. She remembered Deetz grunting and cursing as he dragged her from the bathroom and into her bedroom, where he spread her comforter on the floor then rolled her into its center. She remembered warmth from her breath against the fabric tightly covering her face. She recalled the pain in her hyper-extended knees and the muffled *plop-sss-plop* made by her heels as Deetz dragged her down the wooden stairs. She remembered the crushing pain in her ribcage when he dropped her onto something hard in the back of his pickup, then nothing more until waking inside her tomb.

Perhaps she should have fought Deetz during her periods of consciousness. Maybe she should have kicked and screamed her lungs out. Someone might have heard and called the police.

But at the time, she feared the comforter wrapping her head would dull her yells, ensuring they were heard only by Deetz. That, and the fact that the tight fabric covering the rest of her body made all but the slightest movement impossible had prompted her to play dead.

Robin ran shaking hands along the perimeter of her prison. Rather than the right-angled sides of a casket, or the smooth, rounded sides of the fifty-five-gallon barrel she had envisioned, the portion above her head was uneven with ridges. The sides sloped toward one end, describing a slight wedge.

She scooted as far to one side as the enclosure would allow and moved her hands along the floor. Short, spikey carpet pile reminded her of the horsehair brush she inherited from her grandmother years earlier.

The smell of ancient fabric and rusted metal resurrected images of the nineteen-forty-nine Ford her dad refurbished when she was eight or nine years old.

That old car's trunk had been the perfect fort for her and a friend, until one morning the lid closed with them inside. The girls spent several hours in darkness, crying and screaming. By the time Robin's dad found them, they had curled into fetal knots. His hands shook as he pulled them from what could have been their final resting place.

The memory floated away, replaced by a recent local news report of a young man who had been beaten and locked inside a car's trunk which was then set afire.

Robin's breath caught. Had she been dumped in a trunk? Was Deetz even then preparing to douse the car with gasoline and toss a lit match onto it?

Against her will, she envisioned her prison engulfed in roaring flames.

She shuddered and gulped for air. Lightheaded and threatening to hyperventilate, she struggled to gain control.

Deep breaths in through the nose; exhale through puckered lips.

Robin closed her eyes and tried to mentally remove herself from the flood of horrific thoughts. Using a technique from a televised tutorial on meditation, she pictured herself in the woods surrounding a cabin her parents built in the mountains when she was ten. She smelled the clean air heavy with the scent of pine and wildflowers. She heard the birds call to each other and felt the light breeze that sifted through the trees. She caught a glimpse of a doe with her new fawn, their heads raised, gazes riveted on her an instant before bounding away.

Robin opened her eyes, and the warm, peaceful images vanished, replaced by frigid cold, and stygian darkness.

Her father once said that around the turn of the millennium, automobile manufacturers were required by law to install a safety device that would allow trunks to be opened from the inside. If Robin *were* inside a trunk, and *if* she were lucky, the car might be less than twenty years old. If so, all she had to do was find the safety latch.

Slowly, eyes straining in the darkness, she moved her gaze around the enclosure, hoping to spot the green glow of a safety latch. But she failed to find anything remotely suggestive of a phosphorescent glow. Telling herself that the latch might have lost its glow capability over time, Robin ran her fingers along the strip of metal just below the trunk's latch.

While she encountered tangled wires and various protrusions, all of which she tugged or pressed, nothing moved. No satisfying click was followed by a rush of fresh air.

During her search, however, her fingers periodically dislodged thumbnail-sized bits of flakey, scab-like pieces, the largest of which landed with a soft *thup* on the carpeted floor. She picked up a piece and tasted it.

"Rust," she mumbled.

Wherever she had been dumped, it wasn't new, or even relatively new. That level of oxidization did not happen quickly; it took time, maybe decades.

Scattered around New Mexico, Robin had seen old cars and pickups rusting away in isolated, open fields. While she might have been placed inside one of those deserted vehicles miles from anywhere, the idea seemed incongruent with what she was experiencing. If she were in a field, she would smell dried prairie grasses or tumbleweeds, wouldn't she? The occasional, tiny puffs of air coming from somewhere to her right would smell clean instead of mixed with the heavy odors of dirt, old motor oil, desiccated fabric, and rusty metal.

Maybe Deetz had put her in an old car in his garage, some vintage wreck he planned to re-build. If so, he likely lived in the sticks where she could scream to her heart's content without being heard, and where she could decompose without detection.

However, that scenario did not feel exactly right either. The air in a garage would be still and silent, whereas the cold winter wind hissed and moaned around her prison.

Pain in Robin's right hip intensified from lying on the hard surface, and she shifted her weight onto her left side. Something hard pressed against her ribcage.

With a nearly incandescent flash of gratitude for her attacker's lack of foresight, she reached inside her bra and retrieved her cell phone. Visions of a speedy rescue leap-frogged through her mind as she powered on the technological miracle. The phone booted up, and the normalcy of its glow offered a measure of encouragement.

The lighted time and day announced it was nearly

midnight on Friday. A mere four hours ago she had been enjoying supper. It seemed more like a week.

Impulsively, Robin turned on the phone's flashlight app and panned the resulting beam of light around the enclosure. Monster-dispelling LED light verified that her jail was indeed the trunk of an old car.

Light reflected off rusted steel girders overhead and rounded metal sides. It lit her newly purchased, purple and white comforter in which she had been wrapped, the sight somehow reassuring.

She touched the raw wound at her temple then peered at her fingers. The absence of fresh blood elicited a grim smile. At least she would not bleed to death.

Reluctant to turn off the light and return to absolute darkness, yet recognizing the built-in app was ravenously depleting the phone's already minimal power reserves, Robin sighed and clicked off the flashlight. She squinted at the phone's screen, and her heart sank.

While the battery level still showed a fifteen percent charge, the signal strength reflected only one bar. Based on something remembered from one of her favorite tech documentaries, she could be anywhere from twenty to forty miles from the nearest cell tower. Equally possible, however, was that the weak signal strength was due to her being encircled by steel.

Hoping one bar would be enough to meet her needs, Robin punched nine-one-one onto the keypad.

"What is the nature of your emergency?" the dispatch operator began, her voice loud in the tiny space.

Robin gasped and shut down the call. If her

abductor was close enough to hear her talking on the phone, he would most certainly hustle over and finish her off then and there.

On the other hand, a text would be silent. Perhaps it might even use less power than a call. She could text her friend Petra. She would tell Petra about Vince's argument with his employee and the guy's subsequent tinkering with the air compressor. She would describe her attacker and give details of her abduction.

As a detective with the Albuquerque Police Department, Petra would track the man down. She would make him confess to Vince's murder and to Robin's attempted murder and kidnapping. Then she would make him tell her where to find Robin.

Robin could soon be sitting in her green leather overstuffed chair sipping hot cocoa and snacking from her stash of Girl Scout Thin Mint cookies. Deetz would find himself rotting in jail.

Squelching the excitement that threatened to erupt into a full-throated *woo-hoo*, Robin dragged her finger across her phone's tiny screen to open its list of contacts. Her vision blurry in the absence of her reading glasses, she searched through the list of names.

"Albertson, Bartlett, Chad," she whispered, noting that her not-so-smart phone had kept the contact information of everyone to whom she had ever spoken, worked with, or with whom she had enjoyed even minimal interaction.

"Petra, Petra," Robin whispered as she scrolled down the list.

When her finger approached what appeared to be the detective's name, she punched the screen to open the link. With trembling fingers, she typed: *kidnapped.*

trapped in old car trunk. Low batt. She sent off the text, then waited for a response.

Seconds dragged by, and there was no answer.

Perhaps Petra's phone was on vibrate, and she was too deeply asleep to hear its text notification. Or maybe she turned it off while it charged overnight, as Robin usually did.

Robin's phone tinged, and its screen glowed. Barely able to contain her excitement at the sheer marvel of making human contact, she stared at the screen and pulled up the text.

Fantasies of being quickly rescued faded as she squinted at the tiny print.

Right. And I'm sitting in an oasis while my camel's getting her nails done. Does your auntie know you're playing with her phone?

Chapter Four

Unable to believe what she was seeing, Robin re-read the response to her text. She tapped the screen as her vision cleared long enough to make out the name of the recipient.

Instead of *Petra,* her shaking sausage-finger had hit the name *Quillan O'Farrell,* a man with whom she once served on a church finance committee, a man to whom she had hardly spoken for well over four years.

Robin's shoulders sagged, and she quietly sobbed. Of course, Quil wouldn't believe the text. Had their situations been reversed, neither would Robin.

Her phone pinged again.

Tell your auntie I said Hey.

Robin typed: *Quil, it's me. Call Petra Rooney in APD. No gag. Saw a murder.*

The screen went black. When repeated efforts to reboot the cell phone yielded no results, Robin choked off a moan and hugged the dead phone to her bosom. She bent her knees and drew her legs toward her chest. Like a television screen that suddenly went offline, her brain churned out staticky, white noise.

A sound immediately outside the trunk jerked her back from a dark emotional cave. The flesh on her arms rucked up at the hissing, *schwish, schwish* sound reminiscent of someone slowly moving through tall, dried grass and weeds.

Robin froze, barely allowing herself to breathe. Had the man returned to make sure she was dead, or horror of horrors, to torch the car?

She tasted blood and realized she was chewing her tongue.

For several heartbeats, the sound of approaching movement alternated with periods of silence, each step slow and deliberate.

Schwish. Pause. *Schwish.*

Roiling and thrashing thuds erupted beneath the trunk, followed by a deep-throated growl and something like a cat's hiss. An extended silence culminated in the sounds of leisurely retreat.

A feral mama cat foraging for her kittens?

Robin took a deep breath and blew it out. The upside of the interlude was that it meant the kidnapper was nowhere near, or the animal would never have approached. It also meant, however, that whatever creature was in the process of being devoured probably either made its home somewhere inside the car or had a nest nearby, a nest in which God only knew how many more of its family members resided.

The thought of rats or other vermin seeking warmth from the winter cold by wending their way into the folds of Robin's comforter made her flesh crawl. However, she took solace in the knowledge that New Mexico's sizable snake population would be hibernating rather than searching for a cozy bed and breakfast.

She would allow herself no more daydreaming. Instead of mentally flying above the clouds, and although her pounding headache made it hard to focus on anything but waves of pain, she had to come up with a plan of action.

Robin recalled a televised documentary about brain activity that indicated parts of the human brain can generate bursts of electrical energy at nearly fourteen million volts per meter. More powerful than a lightning strike, pulses of energy that strong could potentially be sensed from miles away, at least, in theory.

With every fiber of her being, Robin focused her thoughts on Quil. She visualized glittering waves of thought shooting through the air and ending in a golden force field around his body. She heard herself commanding him to call Petra and tell her about Robin's texted plea for help.

After sending several bursts of what some televangelist had years ago called *mind power*, Robin snorted and shook her head. She was clutching at straws. Her time and energy would be put to better use in finding a way of escape instead of wishing on a star.

Would Quil follow up on her texts, or did his snarky response mean he had written them off as pranks by one of her nephews, therefore not worth pursuing? He had always struck Robin as level-headed and thoughtful, so it seemed reasonable to hope he might take her texts seriously.

The proverbial mealworm in her hopeful porridge, however, was that even *if* Quil decided to call Petra, she would have no idea where to search.

Sadly, the police would be unable to track Robin using her phone's GPS. That only worked if the phone were on, and that lying piece of technological wizardry was well and truly dead. Fifteen percent charge indeed.

The stark truth was that by using the power-sucking flashlight app, she had thrown away what could prove to be her only lifeline. Had she controlled her panicky need for light, her phone's battery might have been strong enough to send several texts to Petra. She could have even called emergency again since she no longer feared being heard.

The thought that she had squandered her only chance to hear a friendly voice while keeping the line open as the police honed-in on her GPS threatened to send Robin further into a downward emotional spiral. She had even lost access to the phone's dimly lit screen, something that would have offered a smidgen of comfort in the darkness.

She had piled mistake on top of mistake, the first of which was in opening the door to Vince's employee. How many more stupid mistakes could she survive?

Her mother's words again rang in her head:

Those women had to be strong. Their survival depended on it.

Thoughtfully, Robin took a deep breath. With a surge of energy, she rolled to one side and pressed her body against the metal trunk wall. After a brief struggle, she managed to pull up a portion of the carpeting, shreds of which came off in her hands and sent billows of cough-causing dust into her lungs.

Finding the tight space difficult to navigate, she finally managed to move the spare tire covering to one side and shove her hand into the opening. If she were lucky, either a jack, a tire iron, or some other implement had been left inside. Anything of metal would allow her to either pry open the trunk's lid or widen one of the tiny, rusted-out holes she had discovered.

As Robin raked her fingers through dust, dried

leaves, and stiff straw, something squeaked and scampered across the back of her hand. Tiny claws pricked the backs of her hands and she gasped. She recoiled as the creature shot up her arm then scampered away to either hunker down in an unreachable trunk nook or escape through an undiscovered hole.

Once her heart rate returned to near-normal, she again reached inside the spare tire well. After finding it empty of anything useful, she hurriedly replaced the cover.

Had the furry beast been a relatively benign field mouse, or had it been a small rat? The local news recently did a story about a construction worker who was bitten by a rat and had to undergo treatment for rabies. Four injections later, he was okay, but it had been a terrifying ordeal for his family, and painful for him.

On the other hand, Robin thought grimly, if rabid rats got to her before she could escape, she would not have to deal with all those injections. While needles were often necessary, they were not her friends.

"There has to be a way out of here," she whispered.

Didn't some car models have back seats that could either fold down or be otherwise dislodged? Unless the seat was secured by a heavy metal clip, she might be able to push it forward far enough to climb over. Depending on how isolated the car was, she could walk for help. Even if it were standing in someone's field, forcing her to walk miles through life threatening snow and ice, she would rather die out in the open than locked inside a metal coffin.

Robin rolled onto her back, aimed her feet toward the back seat and kicked with all her strength. The soft seat backing bowed inward, but nothing gave way. She kicked long after her thighs began to ache, her breaths coming in gasps, and her head feeling ready to explode. But like a trampoline, the seat cover always bounced back.

Her memory turned to a safety video she and her colleagues had been required to watch during her time of employment at a local credit union. Part of the video was taken up with suggestions of what to do in the event of a robbery, while another segment offered tips for escaping from a locked trunk if taken hostage. The narrator said a kidnap victim should kick out the taillights, stick an arm through the resulting opening, and wave.

That would work if the car were moving through traffic or parked in an otherwise public place and visible to passersby. But if Robin had been dumped in an old beater in someone's pasture, all the noise or hand-flapping in the world would not help. In that event, she would only be discovered when someone, maybe years in the future, found the skeletal remains of her shriveled hand and wrist dangling from a taillight opening where she had flapped until the end.

Fighting the desire to give up, Robin refused to miss out on even the tiniest opportunity for rescue. She would try everything she could think of no matter how far-fetched.

She turned on her right side. Knees bent, and her back to the trunk's opening, she aimed the heel of her left foot toward the area where she figured the taillight would be located and kicked backward with all her strength.

When several heel-bruising kicks failed to produce

the crunch of breaking plastic or glass, she moved her fingers over the taillight enclosures.

"Perfect, just perfect," she muttered.

Instead of a breakable, plastic taillight housing, she had been slamming her heel against a rounded, concave steel orb.

Her dad's patient, teaching-mode voice floated into her mind:

Car bodies built before the seventies were made of solid steel, not plastic like modern vehicles. The enclosures for head- and taillights were molded into the steel body.

"Now you tell me, o brain of mine," Robin said, likening her belated memory to a teammate who just sunk a basketball in the opposing team's net. "You're supposed to be on my side. If you and I don't figure something out soon, we're both doomed."

Suddenly, like molten rock exploding from a volcano, anger-fueled heat coursed through Robin's body. Unable to hold onto self-control for another second, she pounded her fists against the trunk lid, heedless of the pain that radiated up her arms with every blow. She kicked off the comforter and slammed her feet into the back seat, her legs moving like pistons. She screamed until her throat ached and her voice grew hoarse. The level of pain in her head ratcheted up as the wails echoed inside the metal enclosure.

The continuous roar of an airplane interrupted Robin's rant, and she stilled herself. Judging by the unusually loud sound of the engine, the plane was either landing or taking off from someplace nearby. Perhaps her prison was located near an airport.

Of the two local airports, there were no junkyards

near the small Double Eagle II. However, at least six were located within spitting distance of the Albuquerque International Sunport, each with an inventory of as many as a thousand old cars.

Robin chewed the inside of her lip. Christmas was two days away, and her piano students were on break. No one would know she was missing until she failed to show up for a recital two weeks in the future.

Without food, she could live four or five weeks. Without water, however, she would be dead within three or four days. If, however, the weather forecast proved unexpectedly correct, she could freeze to death.

On the brighter side, if what she saw in a recent survival episode on the weather channel was accurate, dying from dehydration was not so horrible once the initial thirst subsided. She would stop sweating, and her body temperature would rise. Her blood would thicken, making her heart rate increase. Her kidneys would stop sending water to her bladder, first making her urine dark then stopping it altogether. At some point, her internal organs would shut down, and she would pass out. Death would soon follow.

We begin dying from the moment of birth, you know. It's what we do with the time we're given that counts.

Teardrops fell from Robin's eyes at the memory of her mother's voice, and she stared into the darkness.

What had she accomplished with her life? Other than her brother Chris, his sons, and Petra, no one would mourn her. Her piano students might give her a passing thought for a couple of days before moving on with their own lives, but Robin's life would have counted for almost nothing. It would soon be like she never existed.

Of course, Chris would hold a memorial service at some point in the future—sans body, unless someone stumbled on her prison before the seven-year legal declaration of death was finalized. He would eulogize her with comments such as: *Robin loved television documentaries, something for which I used to tease her mercilessly. A lifelong learner, she was on a quest to understand everything about the world around her.*

In other words, Robin thought, she was born; she lived; she died. Amen. Please join the family for a small reception in the church annex.

Blustery wind sent gusts of cold air through tiny, rusted-out pinholes. Teeth chattering, Robin reached for her comforter, squared her jaw, and pulled her bedcover to her chin.

Chapter Five

A little after ten o'clock Friday night, house painter Ronnie Deetz sat at a bar sipping beer with acquaintance Lou Bradley.

Lou's belly strained at the buttons on his blue workman's shirt, and his nearly bald head reflected what light was allowed into the darkened barroom. A perpetual look of disappointment on his face, he blathered away about the load of manure that was his life, most of his words drowned out by a locally popular country western band.

Deetz tuned out Lou's standard whining rant and studied the band members.

What was it about country western songs that set his teeth on edge? Maybe it was the way the singer bleated on and on about how hard life was, about his cheating lover, and his lousy job. He would bet money that not one of the guys on stage had ever struggled for anything, never had to worry about where his next meal was coming from. The fact that people could make a living out of having fun seemed unfair.

Deetz eyed the gaggle of young women gathered in front of the band. Eyes filled with awe, they swayed to the beat as their faces broadcasted their availability.

"You lissnin' to me?" Lou tapped Deetz's shoulder.

"Yeah, sure." Deetz stared at the effervescent

bubbles in his mug. Unable to shake the feeling that he had forgotten something important, he mentally reviewed the events of the past several hours.

His throat had tightened that morning when he saw the nosey neighbor watching him tinker with the air compressor. At the time, he tried to shrug it off. What could a woman know about air compressors?

But then Banda became one of most unlucky people in the world by standing in exactly the wrong place at exactly the wrong time, and got his neck sliced open by a piece of exploding air compressor shrapnel. Splattered with amber-yellow paint, blood pumping from his neck, Vince took a few steps, then collapsed.

Deetz hadn't intended to kill the old man. He had been completely taken by surprise when the planned inconvenience turned into Banda's going away party.

His initial surprise, however, had quickly worn off. Although unforeseen, the outcome had been perfect. Dead, Banda couldn't run whining to the police with suspicions that his employee was burgling wealthy customers.

Of course, Deetz was out of a job now, but no matter. The boom in construction meant painters were in high demand. Besides, he had plans that didn't involve doing grunt work for the rest of his life.

Deetz smiled and mentally patted himself on the back at his efficiency in handling the tense situation with the Marcato woman. He made a plan and then carried it out almost perfectly.

First thing he did after entering the woman's house was to turn off that blazing porch light, a caution that later proved unnecessary since he wound up hauling Marcato's body out the back door. The work gloves he was smart to wear ensured he left no fingerprints. Even so, he had been careful of what he touched.

Unfortunately, in setting up his timetable, he had not allowed for cleaning blood from the nosebleed. That little exercise had taken at least fifteen minutes after tracking down the bimbo's gallon of Clorox.

The memory of that witch unexpectedly poking him in the chest then kneeing him in the face made him wish he had taken time to bash her head into mush instead of just whacking her once. But the wind was high and knocking trash cans around outside, and Deetz feared the noise might attract the attention of yet another nosey neighbor.

As Banda's employee, he was often in Marcato's neighborhood. But if anyone had come outside to secure a noisy trashcan and noticed his pickup parked behind her house late in the evening, suspicions could arise.

What he had miscalculated, though, was the amount of time it would take to haul the bimbo's dead weight to the junkyard, drag her to the farthest corner, dump her, then hustle to the bar to set up his alibi with Lou. That bit of oversight had been plain sloppy.

Deetz took an uneasy sip of beer. Maybe what was making his insides jittery was the realization that he had not immediately gotten rid of the lead pipe, bloody rags, and blood-spattered gloves. But the *time's a-wasting* feeling had gripped his guts, and he hurriedly tossed everything into the back of his pickup for later disposal.

First thing in the morning, he would build a fire in his charcoal grill and deal with the rags and gloves. Then he would throw the pipe into the Rio Grande. All flapping loose ends would be nicely snipped, and he could get on with his business.

"Hey, Deetz." Lou took a deep pull on his beer then wiped the back of his hand across his mouth. "Earth to Deetz. Come in Deetz."

"I heard you, Lou. Your life is one screwed up piece of work. Your boss is a jerk, your ex-wives are taking you to court for more money, you're in hock up to your eyeballs, and your knees are acting up."

"Thass the reason I like you, buddy, you're so unnershtanding." Lou slapped Deetz's back, burped, and took another swig of beer. He licked his lips, glanced heavenward, and again embarked on his tale of woe. With only an occasional variation in wording, it would be the same sob story repeated a million times over the two years Deetz had known him.

Although Deetz considered Lou more useful connection than friend, he never corrected the man's insistence on referring to him as his *best buddy*. A loner by nature, Deetz only allowed Lou to hang around because the guy worked at one of the junkyards in the Albuquerque area, thereby offering unlimited access to auto parts Deetz could either use for repairs to his pickup or sell for spare cash. There was, however, no getting around the fact that Lou was a loser with a capital *L*.

Deetz glanced at the other man then wiped the sneer off his face when he saw the bartender studying him. Other than acting as a conduit for limitless spare parts, the only upside to the relationship was that Lou was so predictable.

Where some guys were mean when they got drunk, Lou was what Deetz's dad referred to as a *whining meat sack*. Apparently blessed with intelligence hovering around the average range, Lou habitually yammered on and on about how life had taken a dump on his poor innocent head. Then once he reached a certain level of drunkenness, he would start blubbing. His mouth gaping wide, he would send out the most godawful sounds, lay his head on top of the bar, and whimper. Then, with a mournful, much-maligned expression on his face, he would lift his head and peer at the bar's other patrons, careful to make eye contact with each one.

It never ceased to amaze Deetz how often that *poor pitiful me* stuff got results. Within minutes someone would inevitably buy Lou a drink. They would give him a pat on the back, murmur something supposed to be comforting, then shoot either an apologetic or accusatory look at Deetz before returning to their friends.

During a typical night, after Lou had used up his own money, he could pull one or two drinks before he got so hammered the bartender stopped serving him. Deetz had a feeling the bartender felt sorry for the bum, otherwise he would have barred him long ago.

"Why're you sho quiet tonight?" Lou said. "Firsht, you're late, and now you're just sitting there like a shtump." Squinting, Lou peered at Deetz's face then pointed his index finger at Deetz's nose. "What happened to your schnozzola, you run into a door?"

Deetz smacked the hand away but remained silent.

"I shed—"

"Yeah, yeah, I heard what you *shed*." Gingerly, Deetz touched the tender bridge of his nose, then ran his index finger up and down the outside of his cold mug, describing lines in the condensation on the glass. "Got a lot on my mind, that's all."

"You get that pick-em-up truck of yours fixed?" Lou burped and smacked his lips.

"Yep."

"Good," Lou said. "There ain't no parts ever been made that you can't find at the yard." He weaved sideways and Deetz put a restraining hand on his shoulder to keep him upright. "They're a lot cheaper than the new ones from an auto parts shtore. You could even re-build one of them junks from the yard if you wanted. You could customize it and make it special. By the way, the bossh shed he's been getting calls about three or four of the older models. Looks like shumbody's goin to be busy." Lou cocked his head at his friend. "You ever been to one of them customized car shows?"

Deetz's pulse ticked up a couple of notches. "Which older models?" he said.

"Whazzat?"

"Which older models is your boss trying to sell?"

What were the chances anyone would suddenly be interested in the old Caddy that had been sitting in the junkyard for decades?

"Dunno." Lou shrugged and righted himself. "Anyways, as I was shaying…"

While offering random head-nods at Lou's unheard monologue, Deetz stuck his left hand into his pocket and fingered copies of the keys to the junkyard's front gate. He congratulated himself on the flash of inspiration that had led him to take Lou's originals when they fell from his pocket as he fumbled to get into his apartment a few months earlier.

Casually, as Lou stumbled into his apartment, Deetz had picked up the keys then pocketed them. He took them to an all-night Walmart for copying, his initial thought to have unrestricted access to the junkyard to harvest free parts for his pickup. He quickly realized he had scored the keys to a kingdom.

Deetz shot a sideways glance at Lou weaving back and forth on the barstool, and the sight reminded him of his old man. His upper lip curled at the memory of his dad sitting in the living room watching television and drinking beer.

"Boy," his old man had yelled at the ten-year-old Deetz. "Get in here. I got something to tell you."

Afraid to go, yet more afraid not to, Deetz left his toys on the floor and hurried into the living room.

"Come here," the old man said. "Stand in front of me so's I can see who I'm talking to."

Deetz had done as commanded.

The old man slid forward. He leaned forward and without warning, shot his fist into Deetz's crotch.

The boy screamed and doubled over while the old man laughed and laughed.

"Today's lesson," his old man said. "Never trust nobody."

Lesson learned.

Over the couple of months after copying Lou's keys, Deetz made several midnight forays to the junkyard where he took the opportunity to load up a couple of hundred or so pounds of copper and other metal to sell at a local recycling company. The unforeseen bonus, however, made itself known when Deetz needed to find a place to hide the Marcato woman's body.

"Maybe I will stop by your workplace sometime this weekend," Deetz said in response to Lou's repeated badgering. "Now that I'm out of a job, it might be a good idea for me to stock up on used parts."

"Can't do it this weekend." Lou shook his head. "Monday's Chrishmuss. Ain't nobody goin' to be in the yard 'til after that."

Maybe no live body would be in the yard until after Christmas, but some dead body would.

Deetz sniggered at his word play. He nodded at whatever the hell Lou was saying and stared at the ring of moisture his mug left on the bar.

What would Lou-the-meat-sack do if he suspected Deetz had been pilfering from the yard for months? How would he react to learn that the copper, iron, chrome, and even aluminum junk Deetz had ripped off then sold had netted him several hundred dollars in untraceable, untaxable cash?

Deetz wiped a sneer from his face before it could blossom into full-blown disgust. The doofus would probably take full responsibility and offer to reimburse his boss for all losses.

He mentally shook his head at the memory of a letter he'd spotted in Lou's apartment from some rehabilitation group home expressing gratitude for five years of monetary support. The loser could seemingly barely afford to buy his own beer, yet he sent fifty bucks a month to some local flop house. Who did that?

"Sho, you goin' to buy me a beer, or what?" Lou burped, wiped the back of his hand across his mouth and swayed on his barstool.

"Your buddy is over the limit," the bartender said. "I can't keep serving him."

"What?" Deetz shot a stink-eyed glare at the man.

"I said, he's had enough." The bartender squared his jaw, daring Deetz to argue.

"All right, all right," Deetz said. "I'll settle up now." He extracted a twenty-dollar bill from his wallet and laid it on the bar.

"We don't do cash. Just cards." The bartender motioned to an electronic table-top tablet.

Deetz held his breath and jammed his credit card into the gizmo, relieved when the tiny screen indicated the plastic had been accepted. He replaced the card in his wallet then pushed the twenty-dollar bill toward the bartender.

The bartender offhandedly dropped the cash into a tip jar then started to move away.

"Excuse me." Deetz looked pointedly at the clock behind the bar. "Is that the right time?"

The bartender glanced up at the clock then down at his wristwatch. "Yep," he said.

"Okie-dokie, Lou," Deetz said loud enough for anyone near to hear. "It's nearly Saturday morning, time for Cinderella to leave the ball."

A self-satisfied smile crept across Deetz's face at the certainty that the day and time had been firmly established in the bartender's mind. That and the twenty-dollar tip should grease the skids of the guy's memory if the police ever questioned him.

"Let's go." Deetz tugged Lou's arm. "Time for you to get yourself home."

"Huh?" Lou grunted.

"He shouldn't drive." The bartender glared at Deetz.

"Yeah, okay, I'll drive him." Deetz smiled

reassuringly. It would have been satisfying to pound the nosey guy into the floor, but Deetz could not afford to lose control. Instead, he hooked a hand under Lou's arm and tugged him toward the door.

The bartender nodded. A relieved look on his face, he turned his attention to another customer.

With Lou docilely stumbling beside him, Deetz walked to his pickup.

The more he thought about it, the more he figured everything was okay. Not only did the rusted-out, thirty-five-year-old Cadillac Cimarron where he dumped the Marcato woman register low on the desirability scale for most collectors, it was located at the very back of a ten-acre junkyard. Based on Lou's drunken ramblings, not a single part had been pulled from the Caddy during all the years he had worked there. On top of that, Lou said the keys to incoming wrecks were tossed into five-gallon buckets, making it impossible to find the key to a specific junker, and rendering any closed trunk basically inaccessible.

During an earlier midnight reconnaissance trip to the yard, Deetz noted that some trunks had inexplicably been propped slightly open with bits of wood, brick, or even a crowbar. The Cadillac's trunk had been propped open with, of all things, one of those mini baseball bats some people bought their kids in hopes they would grow up to be high-dollar pro baseball players.

As a result, all Deetz had to do was remove the bat, plop the woman into the Caddy's trunk, and close the lid. Unless there was a trunk-popping mechanism on the driver's side, no one was going to get into or out of that trunk.

The average person had no idea how tough it was

to get rid of a body. That kind of thing needed careful planning. But when Deetz saw Marcato watching him fiddle with the air compressor, he was forced to consider a pile of possibilities, and he had to do it on the fly.

The first complication he *had* foreseen was the possibility of simple bad luck. It seemed murdered folks tended to get found. Luckily, Deetz had remembered hearing about a murder brought to light when a dog brought a severed finger to his master after a run in the countryside. No foraging animal could get at Marcato inside that closed steel trunk, and carnivorous insects couldn't drag off even the smallest body parts.

How to deal with the odor of decomposition had been worrisome. Sooner or later, the smell would attract unwanted attention. However, even the weather had worked to Deetz's advantage. If Marcato *did* partially thaw during the daylight hours, she would re-freeze every night through the winter months. She would not begin to smell until the spring thaw. Even then, the car's location at the very rear of the yard made it unlikely that anyone would notice unless standing downwind.

By the time her body was found, if it ever *was* found, Deetz's business dealings with a man known as *Mister Z* would be finalized, and he would be living *la vida loca* somewhere in Mexico.

"Wha'd you say?" Lou said as he flopped onto the passenger's seat in Deetz's pickup.

"Nothing, Lou-Lou. Nothing at all."

Deetz pulled a small plastic dispenser containing squares of chewing gum from his shirt pocket. He flipped the lid open with his thumb and, holding the steering wheel steady with his knee, shook two pellets into his palm then popped them into his mouth.

It was then that he realized what he had left at Marcato's house.

Chapter Six

Quil O'Farrell dreamed he was in his kitchen working on a new recipe for the perfect fruit tart. It would be the best, most sought-after, most delicious fruit tart the world had ever known. People would stand in line to eat in his coffee shop and bakery. He would be a regular guest on televised cooking programs, and his name would become synonymous with the world's top bakers.

Just as his dream was set to disclose the ultimate, secret ingredient, a *ping,* followed by a glow of light, tugged Quil awake. A light sleeper, he opened his eyes in time to see the screen of his cell phone dim then darken.

Fear for his aging parents' wellbeing jerked him fully awake and pumped adrenaline into his system. In his thirty years of life, late-night calls usually meant a family emergency.

He reached for his cell phone on the bedside table and glanced at the lighted clock beside it. Ten o'clock in central New Mexico would be the same time in Saskatchewan, Canada, where his parents lived.

While ten o'clock was not considered late to anyone over the age of twelve, Quil's mornings began at three thirty. If he didn't manage to get to bed by eight the night before, his day would be spent yawning and fighting sleep. By the time the average citizen was rising, he had already baked dozens of yeast-raised pastries in preparation for opening at six.

Bleary-eyed, he tapped the phone's tiny screen until the text came into view. He read the message, checked the sender's name, then glared at the phone.

"What in the flipping..." he muttered.

On one hand, he was grateful the message was not the feared emergency. On the other, robo and prank calls and texts were high on his list of peeves, especially at night.

The worst offense, however, was that his dream had been interrupted before unveiling the secret ingredient to the world's tastiest fruit tart. It would be an hour or more before he could fall back to sleep, and his interrupted dreams were never in re-run mode.

Quil's face grew hot and a muscle in his temple pulsed. Instead of shooting off a blistering response as was his first impulse, he tempered his reply to the person he figured to be one of Robin Marcato's teenaged nephews.

Within a couple of minutes after sending his reply, his phone pinged again. As he read the second text, he grew uneasy.

While he could dismiss the first message as a prank, the sense of pure desperation in the second was not so easily ignored. Besides, Robin's nephews only knew him as Mister O'Farrell, yet the sender had used the short form of his first name, something only his friends and close associates did.

"Let's try something," he murmured.

Within the next few minutes, he sent off several texts.

Where are you? Are you hurt? Who took you? Who

was murdered and when?

When none of his texts drew a response, Quil drew a deep breath and blew it out through pursed lips. Questions shaped themselves in his mind like bubbles on the bottom of a saucepan.

Why would Robin Marcato, a woman with whom he had no contact in years, text him for help? Why not text her police officer friend directly instead of pleading with him to do it? Better still, why not call nine-one-one to begin with? And why did she not respond to Quil's follow-up texts?

Although Robin was a nice person, she and Quil were not what he would call *friends*, at least not according to his definition of friendship. Once their responsibilities on the church finance committee were done, they maintained no contact beyond the occasional wave across the church auditorium after services.

Quil read the texts again, and his uneasiness grew with each passing second. An internal battle reached fever pitch.

What if he called the police only to learn there was no one in the Albuquerque Police Department named Petra Rooney? He would look foolish.

Eventually, unable to quieten down, Quil sat up in bed. He turned on his bedside lamp, propped his back against the bedstead, and punched numbers into his phone.

If the texts were nothing more than a prank, all he stood to lose was sleep and a bit of credibility with local law enforcement. If the texts were real, however, every minute was crucial. He would not want to live with the kind of guilt that came with the *If only someone had called the police* plaint.

"What is the nature of your emergency?" the dispatch operator said.

"I know it's late and this is kind of weird," Quil said, "but is there any chance I could speak to a detective named Petra Rooney?"

Chapter Seven

Detective Petra Rooney's eyes flew open when her phone rang. Never able to fall into a deep sleep when on call, she squinted at the clock on her nightstand, surprised to see that the time was only a few minutes past 10:00 p.m. After her twenty-four-hour shift investigating a child abduction the day before, her burning eyes felt like someone had thrown sand into them, and her head throbbed like it was sandwiched between the tightening jaws of a vise.

She took a deep breath and reached for her cell phone. Unable to answer her phone without a sense of apprehension since arriving in Albuquerque two years earlier, she glanced at the lighted screen, noted with relief the name that popped up on the caller ID, then touched the answer icon.

"What's up, Beckie," she said.

"I just got a strange call," the dispatch operator said. "I'd have left it until morning, but the guy specifically asked for you."

"Did he leave a name?"

"Yes. Do you know someone named Quillan O'Farrell?"

"It doesn't ring a bell," Petra said. "What did he say?"

"He said he's supposed to give you a message from someone named Robin Marcato."

Petra sat up straight. "Sorry. My brain's mush. Give me a sec." She turned on her bedside lamp then reached for a pen and paper on the lampstand. "Okay, I'm ready."

She jotted down the gist of what the operator said, thanked her, then broke the connection. Uneasiness flapped its wings of dread in her mind as she dialed O'Farrell's number.

"Quillan O'Farrell," a sleepy masculine voice answered.

"This is Detective Petra Rooney. I understand you have a message for me."

"Do you know a woman named Robin Marcato?"

"I do, yes."

"At least that's something," O'Farrell said. "I got a couple of really bizarre texts from someone claiming to be her a little while ago."

"From someone claiming to be her?" Petra's pulse picked up speed.

"Yeah, her name and number came up as the one sending the texts. I thought at first it was a prank, but I couldn't get back to sleep after the second one."

"What was the message?" Petra interrupted, struggling to keep her voice level.

"She said she's locked inside a car trunk, that she witnessed a murder, and for me to call you." O'Farrell's voice sounded apologetic. "I didn't know what else to do. I had a feeling I shouldn't wait until morning."

"What's your relationship to Robin Marcato, Mister O'Farrell?"

"That's just it; there isn't one, at least, not anymore. I worked on a church committee with her a few years back, but we didn't stay in touch." O'Farrell released a long breath.

"Can you forward the texts?" Petra said.

"Be glad to. Shall I send them to this number?"

"Yes, please. I'll call you back once I've looked them over."

"Okay."

Petra broke the connection. Biting her lower lip, she stared at the phone's screen, praying the texts would turn out to be either a hoax or a mistake.

Why had Robin not contacted her directly instead of texting a casual acquaintance? Or why had she not called the emergency hotline or the police for immediate help?

Earlier that evening Petra had heard about the weird accidental death of a man who lived across the street from Robin. Although it struck her at the time as interesting, the death was considered an apparent accident, so she relegated it to the back of her mind. If the texts were indeed from Robin, however, the man's death had moved beyond coincidental and into the realm of special interest.

Petra's phone lit up and *ting*-ed. Her throat tight, she read the forwarded texts.

...kidnapped. trapped in old car trunk. low batt. Then the second text: *Quil, it's me. please call Petra Rooney in APD. no gag. witnessed a murder.*

While Friday morning's briefing had included reports of a couple of shootings downtown, there was nothing about a recent murder anywhere near Robin's house. If Robin had witnessed such a thing within the past four or five hours, the police knew nothing of it.

It was possible that Robin had misinterpreted something she saw or heard, and there had been no actual murder. But if that were the case, why would someone abduct her?

Petra called O'Farrell. "I got the texts, thanks."

"Is that it? I mean, is there anything else I can do?"

"I'll need to take your statement. I'll also need your cell phone, at least for a while."

"Shall I bring it by the police station?" O'Farrell said.

"That's not necessary. I'll drop by within a couple of hours to pick it up, but I'd appreciate it if you could meet me at the police main station first thing tomorrow so we can take your full statement."

"No problem." O'Farrell gave Petra his address. "Give me a heads up when you're on the way over, and I'll have a pot of coffee on by the time you get here."

"Thank you for the thought," Petra said, "but time is tight. I should be there within half an hour." She broke the connection, jumped from her bed, and headed to the closet.

Her stomach shoved acid up her throat as she put on a pair of jeans, tennis shoes, and a polo T-shirt with an Albuquerque Police Department patch on it. She strapped on her handgun, grabbed her handcuffs and laptop, and headed for the connecting door between the kitchen and garage. Since APD detectives used their own vehicles on and off duty, her bulletproof vest was in the car, along with a roll of crime scene tape and official hard copy statement and release forms.

With the feeling that time was shooting by at record speed, Petra hurried to her car. She placed her laptop on the passenger seat, then called Robin's phone.

"Hey," she said after Robin's voice mail prompt. "It's Petra. I hope the reason you aren't answering is because you're asleep, but I got a troubling call from a man named Quillan O'Farrell. I'm on my way to your place. If you hear this before I get there, call me, okay?"

Petra broke the connection, scrolled down her list of contacts, then tapped the screen. A masculine voice answered on the third ring.

"What's up, Rocky?" Cody Rankin said, using the nickname Petra's fellow officers coined after one of them spotted her working out with a punching bag in the police gym.

"Sorry for the late hour, Cody, but I just got a call-out about the possible abduction of a friend of mine," Petra said. "Can you come with me to check her house?"

"What's the address?"

Petra gave Cody Robin's address then added, "Did you hear about the weird air compressor death that happened this afternoon?"

"Yeah."

"My friend's house is across the street from where the dead guy lived," Petra said. "You want to meet me there, or shall I pick you up?"

"It'd be quicker for me to meet you," Cody said. "I'm on my way."

As Petra's teammate in the Violent Crimes Unit for the past two years, forty-four-year-old Cody Rankin had repeatedly proven himself a superior officer. He was capable, dependable, trustworthy, and hard-working. There was no one Petra would rather have cover her back, and no one she trusted more to help her find out what was going on.

Lips compressed, Petra started her car and headed

for Robin's house.

****

Fighting the urge to charge into her friend's home guns-a-blazing, Petra parked half a block up the street in case someone was either still inside the house or might return. Her neck ached from grinding her teeth during the drive, and she rotated her head to loosen the iron-taut neck muscles.

While waiting for Cody, she exited her vehicle and surveyed the neighborhood. Adrenaline pumped like a fire hose into her system, sharpening her senses and enhancing her ability to absorb every detail of the scene.

No movement was visible either in Robin's yard or on the street. Light shone through the windows of a few neighboring houses, but Robin's house was dark except for light sifting through venetian blinds on the lower level.

The crisp, gusty wind smelled faintly fragrant with remnants of smoke from someone's wood-burning fireplace. The only sounds were of dogs barking in the distance.

Cody arrived within minutes. He parked his vehicle behind Petra's, stepped out, and strode toward her.

"Have you seen anything?" Cody said as he neared Petra.

"No movement." Petra motioned toward Robin's dark porch. "But Robin religiously leaves her porch light on all night as a safety precaution. The fact that it's off raises a flag."

Body cams turned on and handguns drawn, the two detectives walked almost back-to-back to provide cover for each other. Scanning the yard for movement, they approached Robin's front door.

Pounding on the door with her closed fist, Petra shouted, "Albuquerque Police Department. If anyone is in there, come out with your hands raised above your head." When there was neither sound nor visible movement after a few seconds, she repeated the command two more times, waiting three or four seconds between commands. Nothing stirred.

Petra tried the front door, not entirely surprised to find it unlocked.

"Albuquerque Police," Petra yelled. "Is anyone here?"

After seconds of continued silence, she and Cody exchanged glances, stepped through the door, and entered Robin's silent house.

Chapter Eight

The corners of Deetz's lips pulled into a frown. He powered down the driver's side window of his pickup and glanced at the sleeping Lou who half-sat, half-lay propped against the passenger door. Snorts, growls, and snoring hoots testified that the doofus had passed out.

"You stink, Lou-Lou, you know that?" Deetz turned his head toward his open window and took a deep breath of cold, fresh air. "No wonder you can't hold onto a woman. You got no pride. You need to work on your image." He sniffed. "Aftershave would help. Even the cheap stuff."

Lou chuckled in his sleep, repositioned his head against the closed passenger window, and resumed snoring.

Just a few more days, that was all Deetz needed. Ripping off cars for Mister Z's local chop shops had barely paid enough to keep him in cigarettes, especially when his cut was so little. Then there was his run of bad luck at the casinos. He had been forced to work for Banda to cover expenses, but not before borrowing several thousand dollars from some bimbo who thought he loved her.

Any day now, Deetz would hire on as one of Mister Z's truck drivers, transporting high-dollar illegals into the country. He would have to relocate to Mexico, but that was fine with him. The cost of living was a lot less, and he had heard that the place was swarming with beautiful women.

Deetz's mouth stretched into a grin. Two thousand dollars per load was a ton of money just to drive a truck. A couple of years spent raking in that kind of income, and he could retire with enough cash to live like a king. What some people called *human trafficking* Deetz called *helping the less fortunate find a better way of life*. It was win-win in his books.

His decision to use Banda's laptop to contact Mister Z when his own computer died had been an unfortunate misstep. How could Deetz have known Banda would be tech savvy enough to figure out someone else had used the thing? The old geezer hadn't even secured it with a password.

When Banda confronted him that morning about the laptop, every nerve in Deetz's body ignited. With the realization he had only minutes to generate a plan of action, he decided to set up a distraction in the form of an equipment failure. He figured that when the compressor shut down, Banda would have to secure a replacement, giving Deetz a chance to grab the laptop and hide it for later retrieval. He had, it seemed, over-tightened the pressure release valve.

Deetz smiled at the thought that Banda's expensive laptop was now his to do with as he pleased. He had considered selling or pawning it but discarded that idea. Not only did the device contain all of Banda's business information, thereby proving it to be his property, but its undeletable hard drive contained enough of Deetz's communications with Mister Z to paint a bullseye on them both. A techie pawn shop employee could take it on himself to hack into the laptop then either take his findings to the cops or decide to try his hand at blackmail.

Although the idea pained him, early the next morning, he would take the laptop apart, pull out the mother board, and take a hammer to it. After that, his burner phone would be his sole connection to Mister Z.

One by one, he would erase everything that connected him with Banda and his nosey neighbor. Then he would leave the country.

Lou mumbled in his sleep. His breaths came fast and noisy. His hands and legs twitched and jerked.

"Yo, Lou-Lou." Deetz tapped Lou's shoulder. "Wake up, man. You're having a bad dream."

Lou jerked upright. Eyes remaining closed, he murmured something then plopped his head back against the window and resumed snoring.

Deetz glanced at his passenger then resumed mulling over his options.

He would have to take precautions regarding *how* he made his escape out of the country. If true crime stories on television were accurate, in the U.S. there were cameras on virtually every building, at every intersection, on phone towers, on houses, in parking lots, and in stores. Not to mention the camera apps on every cell phone on earth. Some people said nowadays it was impossible for anyone to completely disappear.

The good news was that while all those *Big Brother's Watching* stories might be true in the good old U.S. of A., there were places in Mexico that were completely off the grid. Ronnie Deetz would be as hard to trace as a puff of smoke in a high wind.

Lou snorted then sat up. "You're a good pershon, you know that Ron, *urp*, Ron?" He cocked his head.

"Hey, wasn't there a shong on that radio shtation you listen to, you know the one that plays shongs from the fifties? Some shong that says *duh-DOO-ron-ron*?" Lou chuckled. "Shho, what're you goin duh-DOO-Ron-Ron, now that you're out of work?"

"I have a job interview tomorrow afternoon," Deetz lied. "If everything goes well, by the end of next week, I'll have a job that pays twice what Banda was paying."

"Ooh. You're hittin' the big time." Struggling to keep his head upright, Lou continued, "You'll 'member your frens, won't you?"

"Sure, Lou-Lou. We're almost at your apartment. Can you manage?"

"Shh'okay," Lou said. "I'm a big boy." He straightened one leg for easier access to his pants pocket. "Juss need to find my keys."

After a monumental struggle, during which Lou flopped around in the seat like a beached whale, he finally fished his keys from his pocket. He managed to drop them onto the floor, then spent what felt like fifteen minutes trying to find them in the dark cab. Deetz ground his teeth, turned on the overhead light, then reached across the hump on the floor, snagged the keys, and dangled them toward Lou.

"Yo, Doofus."

Lou grinned, burped, and palmed the keys. He sent a mock salute in Deetz's general direction then stumbled out of the pickup's cab. Barely remaining upright, he schlumped to his apartment.

Once Lou finally managed to unlock his front door and stagger inside, Deetz backed out of the drive and started toward Marcato's house.

While he understood that returning to the scene might ordinarily have been a bad idea, he had to find the wad of chewing gum that had flown from his mouth when the woman kneed him. When the cops finally discovered Marcato was missing, they would go over her house with a microscope. They would find the gum then break out the champagne at the DNA it would offer up. Deetz might as well have left a note telling them to come get him.

On top of that, the evening news had been full of Banda's death. Although the report inferred the police considered it an accident, if the cops found anything that could tie Deetz to both Banda *and* the nosey neighbor, it might light a fire in their suspicious minds. As he knew all too well, once the cops sunk their teeth into something, they would never let go.

Deetz glanced at the clock in his dashboard. Midnight, four hours since he had taken care of Marcato. The broad had lived alone, and Christmas was coming. No one would miss her for several days.

Smiling, Deetz turned on the radio. He turned up the volume and bopped his head in sync with music that was loud enough to vibrate his bones.

He could clean out everything in Marcato's house if he wanted, but he told himself he would stick with jewelry and other small, easy-to-pawn stuff. Never let it be said that Ronnie Deetz was greedy.

Chapter Nine

Detectives Petra Rooney and Cody Rankin slowly and methodically made their way through Robin's house, careful to disturb nothing, alert to any movement or sound. Knowing the floor at a crime scene is the most common place to find evidence as well as the most easily contaminated, they stepped cautiously.

Her investigative antennae twitching and every sense on high alert, Petra murmured visual, auditory, and olfactory impressions into her recorder, a habit she had cultivated from her days at the Ohio Police Academy.

"The front door is unlocked and slightly ajar. No sign of forced entry, suggesting Robin either opened the door to her abductor, or he had a key," Petra said. "The windows downstairs are closed and locked. Living room and kitchen lights are on. A small television on the dining table is on and tuned to channel two. Dishes of partially eaten food are on the table. I don't detect any unusual odors or signs of unusual activity in the rooms on the lower level."

"Rocky," Cody called from upstairs. "You need to see this."

Petra hustled up the stairs. She strode toward Cody, who stood next to the open bathroom door, a bleak expression on his face.

At the sight of a few barely detectible blood drops

on the white bathroom rug and strong smell of bleach, Petra took a deep breath. "I'll call it in."

Within minutes the detectives had secured the house with crime scene tape. They stood on the front porch and waited for the major crime scene's mobile lab to arrive, knowing that with every passing second their chances of finding Robin alive grew slimmer.

Petra repeatedly glanced at her watch, rocked back and forth on the balls of her feet, and raked her teeth across her lower lip. The early hour notwithstanding, she and Cody would question any of Robin's neighbors they could rouse. Those who did not answer their door would be interviewed later in the day.

When the mobile crime lab arrived and began processing the scene, Petra glanced at her wristwatch. "Not quite midnight." She gestured toward the house south of Robin's. "Let's start the door-to-door there then work our way around the block."

For the next hour, Petra and Cody knocked on doors. Of the initial homeowners who responded, none reported hearing or seeing anything out of the ordinary during the night. However, when the officers got to the house next to Banda's, their luck changed.

"Good morning," Petra said to the tiny elderly woman who answered the door. "I'm Detective Rooney and this is Detective Rankin with the Albuquerque Police Department." She and Cody simultaneously flashed their credentials.

"Oh, good," the woman said. "You're here about Mister Banda's suspicious death?" She stuck her head out the door and peered across the street. "You need to tell the crime scene people they're at the wrong house. That's Robin Marcato's place, not Vince Banda's."

Petra and Cody exchanged looks.

"What makes you say Banda's death was suspicious?" Petra said.

"Instinct," the woman said. "Pure instinct. You'd best come in." The woman pointed to a lighted room just inside the front door. "Follow me."

She closed the door behind the detectives then led them to a small room, the furnishings of which appeared to have air-dropped into place directly from the nineties. Pillows of zebra and leopard-patterned faux fur populated a sofa positioned beneath an unlit neon sign, the bent glass tubing of which pronounced its owner *Born to be wild*. A lava lamp atop a glass-topped metal table completed the time-out-of-whack ambiance.

"Please have a seat." The woman motioned toward two green-plastic lounge chairs. After pushing a couple of pillows aside, she sat on the sofa, positioned her fluffy emerald-green slippers squarely on the floor, clasped her hands in her lap, and nodded in Petra's direction. "Fire away," she said.

"Have you been home all night?" Petra said.

"Oh yes, as per usual." Although the woman energetically bobbed her head up and down, not one strand of her thin, purple-from-a-bottle hair so much as twitched. "I know all about door-to-door canvassing, so before you ask, my full name is Reena-Belle Bibble. That's Reena hyphen Belle Bibble—like Bible, but with two *b*'s. I'm seventy years old; I live alone; I've never been married; and yes, I recently saw something unusual in the neighborhood." She squinted and pointed an index finger at Petra. "Is your body cam on?"

"Yes, ma'am." Petra smiled.

"Good. I hate to repeat myself." Miss Bibble adjusted the folds of her silky, geometric-patterned, neon green robe over her knees, cleared her throat, then continued. "Just before Mister Banda was blown up yesterday, he had a loud argument in his front yard with one of his employees. At least, I assume the man was an employee; he has been in and out of the neighborhood quite a bit over the past month or so. He's maybe twenty-five years old, stands about six-foot-one or two, weighs maybe one eighty and has thick dark hair long enough to brush the top of his collar. He drives a rusty Chevrolet pickup, the color we used to call *powder blue*. I happened to be mulching my cacti and noticed him arguing with Vince. I couldn't make out the words, you understand, but there was no doubt in my mind Mister Banda was reaming the guy a new, um, well, you know. Robin was pruning her roses, so she might have heard more. I don't enjoy other peoples' drama, so I came inside while they were still yelling at each other."

"How about before that, during the last couple of weeks?" Petra said, "Have you seen any vehicles or other people in the area who don't live here, or anything that felt out of the ordinary?"

"I can't say as I've noticed anything out of place before yesterday," Reena-Belle said. "I'm not nosey, you understand, just observant."

"How well do you know Robin Marcato?" Cody said.

"I know she lost her husband some time ago and that she teaches piano." Reena-Belle shook her head and made a *tsk* noise through her teeth. "It's such a . shame. She's a sweet person and a good neighbor. She brings me cookies every Christmas." She cocked her head. "Has something happened to her? Is that why the mobile crime lab is at her house? Is she okay?"

"That's what we're trying to find out." Petra stood, removed a business card from her pocket and handed it to the old woman. "If you see anything suspicious, or if you remember anything else, please call me at that number."

"I will, of course." Reena-Belle accepted the card, stuffed it into the sleeve of her housecoat next to what appeared to be either a wadded Kleenex or old-fashioned cloth handkerchief, and squinted at Petra. "You're going to investigate what the news called Mister Banda's *accident* as well, aren't you? He argued with someone then was blown up, and now something is going on with Robin, who just happens to live across the street. I've seen a few verifiable coincidences in my lifetime, but not many."

"We'll be looking at every possible angle," Petra said. "Thank you for your time, Miss Bibble."

"It's Reena-Belle, please."

Petra and Cody exchanged looks then both smiled at the crusty old woman.

"Thank you, Reena-Belle," Petra said. "You've been a great help."

Petra and Cody moved toward the front door with Reena-Belle following close behind.

"If you need any help with your investigation, you know, eyes in the neighborhood, that kind of thing, I'm up for it. My undercover days are over, but I still notice things."

"Undercover?" Petra said.

"Didn't I tell you? I spent thirty-five years with the

Roswell Police Department. I made rank, got shot, then retired."

"Thanks for the offer," Petra said. "We'll keep that in mind. And thank you for your service."

With Reena-Belle standing on her front porch staring after them, Petra and Cody headed toward their vehicles.

Once out of the old woman's earshot, Cody said, "What's your take on Miss Bibble?"

"I think she's given us our first legitimate lead. We need to talk to Banda's employee."

"You want me to check him out in the local employment records?" Cody said.

"Yeah," Petra said. "I want to know how long he worked for Banda and what he did before. Then we need to talk to O'Farrell. But first, I need to tell Robin's brother Chris what's going on. I'll give you a call when I'm done, then meet you at O'Farrell's."

After Petra gave Cody the man's address, Cody nodded once, and the detectives hurried to their respective cars.

Petra buckled up then turned off her body cam. She relied heavily on the recording device, but it had limitations. None of her visceral reactions to the uneaten dinner on Robin's table, to the blood on the bathroom rug, or to the strong smell of bleach in the same bathroom would register on the digitized recording. No sense of what must have been the absolute terror still hanging in the air would find its way onto the machine. It would offer only a cold, soulless record of the visible.

Petra briefly considered the possibility that Robin's intruder let himself into her house with a key. But

Robin would never have given someone her house key unless they were either a relative or a close friend. Her only relative was a brother living nearby, and her texts did not point to him. Her heart was still a gaping wound from the loss of her husband, but if she had started dating again, she would have told Petra. So, she must have opened the door to the person who intended to hurt or kill her.

What had she seen, known, or stumbled upon that made her someone's target? Who stood to gain by removing her from the picture?

Could her abduction have been a case of mistaken identity? Perhaps it was a random act of violence perpetrated by a stranger. *People take notions*, as one of Petra's psychology professors was fond of saying a lifetime ago. But as Petra well knew, it wasn't generally a stranger of whom one had to beware.

Cold tendrils meandered up Petra's spine as images and sounds from her own past life flashed into the present: memories she had tried to cauterize, feelings she had spent the past two years trying to eradicate.

She took a deep breath and repeated the self-talk learned from a departmental therapist who specialized in PTSD. Within a few minutes, her breathing and pulse rate calmed, and she resumed mulling over what she knew of Robin's abduction.

Since Robin's car was still in her garage, whoever took her must have used his own vehicle, or perhaps a borrowed or stolen one. Another possibility was that more than one person was involved, and an accomplice had provided a vehicle.

Robin's status as an endangered missing person would immediately be sent, along with her physical description and other personal information, to the National Crime Information Center. As a result, every law enforcement agency in the United States would know to be on the lookout for her.

That fact would have offered Petra more hope if her friend were being transported over a public road. But based on Robin's texts, she was trapped inside an *old* car trunk. While that single word implied *abandoned* or *junked*, at least the detectives knew to look for a car, not a moving truck, not a van, and not an SUV.

Petra pounded the palm of her hand on the steering wheel. She hoped the reason Robin had not answered calls or texts was due to her phone's weak battery. It was possible, however, that the kidnapper discovered her using the phone and destroyed it.

Witnessed a murder.

Refusing to allow her mind to imagine what could be happening to her friend, Petra drove to Robin's brother's house. Along the way, she tried to prepare herself for the family's agonized responses as she told them of the abduction.

The task of informing the families of victims of violence always distressed Petra. No matter how she tried to steel herself beforehand, the raw anguish, fear, and anger of those left behind overwhelmed her emotional defenses.

Petra pulled into Chris's driveway, walked to his front door, and rang the bell. After the second ring, the porch light came on. A few seconds elapsed during which Petra held her face to the peephole.

A look of confused concern on his face, Chris opened the door and stood running a hand through his tousled hair. "Petra? What's going on?"

As Petra offered carefully sifted details of the abduction, the expression on Chris's face ran the gamut of emotions. "Is there something I can do?" he finally said.

"Not at this point," Petra said. "If she gets in touch, if you see anything suspicious, or if someone you don't know contacts you, call me immediately." She pulled a card from her vest pocket and handed it to Chris. "We have every available officer working on this around the clock."

"Thanks, Petra." Chris accepted the card, his hands trembling. He cleared his throat. "Was she hurt?"

"We don't know much yet," Petra said, unwilling to tell Robin's brother about the drops of blood found on the bathroom rug. "But I'll update you as we learn more."

His face grim, Chris nodded then slowly closed the door.

Within twenty minutes, Petra had parked her vehicle behind Cody's in O'Farrell's driveway.

She pulled a bottle of antacid from her glove compartment, shook out two tablets, and popped them into her mouth. Grateful for the instant cooling to her acid-pumping stomach, she stepped from her car and hurried toward O'Farrell's front door.

Chapter Ten

On the way to Marcato's house, Deetz bobbed his
head in time with the radio music pounding its rhythm
in the cab of his pickup. He gently touched his sore
nose and chuckled at the thought of revisiting the place
where he had proven himself physically and mentally
superior to Banda's nosey neighbor.

He glanced at the box of purple latex gloves on the
passenger's seat, a purchase made weeks earlier in
anticipation of knocking over a few of Banda's
wealthier customers.

If there were such a thing as a burglars' union, they
should award a medal to whoever invented the skin-like
coverings. Light-weight and tight-fitting, yet thin
enough to grip even the smallest treasures, they were
the perfect accessory.

The more Deetz thought about the nice things he
had seen in Marcato's house, the more convinced he
was that he could take some of the larger stuff. He had
a freaking pickup truck, and it was not one of those
wimpy short beds. He could even take furniture if he
wanted, anything he was strong enough to carry.

For sure, he would take the two Native American
sand paintings on Marcato's living room wall directly
across from the front door. Native American art was in
high demand, especially originals signed by the
artisans. He could pawn them for a nice chunk of

walking-around money.

Gleefully, he lip-synced the lyrics to the radio music. Yessir, life was going to be good.

As he rounded the corner two blocks from Marcato's house, however, his eyes flew wide open, and he slammed on the brakes. He gulped, nearly choking on his chewing gum.

A huge motor home with *Crime Scene Investigation* printed on the side was parked in front of Marcato's house. Official-looking people in special garb moved in and out of the front door. Some carried what Deetz recognized as plastic evidence bags, filled with whatever they deemed worthy of further investigation.

How did the cops find out about Marcato so quickly? Banda had said she lived alone, but just to be on the safe side, Deetz made sure there was no one else in the house when he came calling.

Maybe Banda lied, or maybe he didn't know as much about his neighbor as he thought. Maybe someone moved in with Marcato when Vince wasn't looking, someone who worked nights, someone she kept secret, who came home and found her gone then called the cops.

What if he was seen standing in the spotlight of that damned thousand-watt overhead porch light before he turned it off? What if someone saw him force his way into the house? What if the police had his detailed description? What if his photo was even now turning up on the national watch-list?

It had taken about forty-five minutes from the time he entered the house to chase Marcato down, wrap her up, clean up all the blood he could see, pull his truck around to the back of her house, then load her up. Surely if someone told the cops about him, they would have tracked him down by now. He would be sitting in an interview room waiting for a court-appointed lawyer instead of parked up the block watching the crime scene crew move around Marcato's house like a bunch of ants.

Deetz thoughtfully rapped curled knuckles against his chin. Cops did not park their mobile crime lab in front of random houses.

Maybe a neighbor got up in the middle of the night for a drink of water, randomly looked through a window, and noticed Marcato's kitchen light was still on. Knowing Marcato lived alone, maybe the neighbor got suspicious and called the cops to do a wellness check on her.

The whole mess was shaping itself into a line of dominoes just waiting to tip over. The first domino toppled when Banda lost his fight with the air compressor, forcing Deetz to deal with Marcato. And now what his old man had called *the flying fickle finger of fate* was moving toward a second domino -- his freaking chewing gum.

Forensic people got their kicks from scraping dandruff and eyelashes off carpets and stuffing them into tiny plastic bags. They would wet themselves when they found his wad of chewing gum.

Slowly, in order not to attract attention, Deetz pulled his pickup into the driveway next to Banda's house. As he did, his headlights panned across the yard and front of the house. The light shone on a wrinkled face peering from a picture window, one of the few lighted windows in the neighborhood.

Fighting to stay calm, he stared into the eyes squinting at him from under purple hair. Grateful that his headlights in the old woman's face made him invisible to her, he pushed his gearshift into reverse, turned the vehicle around, and headed back the way he had come.

Careful to drive under the speed limit, Deetz pounded the palm of one hand against the side of his head. His brain roiling, he tried to come up with a plan.

He had to get rid of the incriminating evidence in the back of his pickup. Then, he had to find a new set of wheels and a place to hide until he could disappear. Fortunately, he basically lived out of a suitcase. Like that old song said, a rolling stone gathered no moss.

The fifteen-minute drive to Deetz's apartment felt interminable. His eyes darted around like a ping pong ball in an international competition, and his ears strained for the sound of approaching sirens.

He drove into his numbered parking slot outside his apartment and shoved the pickup gearshift into park. He jumped from the still-shuddering vehicle and hustled to his front door.

When several fumble-fingered attempts to unlock his door proved unsuccessful, Deetz nearly puked. Precious minutes were wasted before he discovered that he had been trying to use the copies of Lou's keys. By the time he managed to open his door, he was shaking so badly he could barely stand.

After giving himself a couple of minutes to calm down, he hurried around collecting only the things he needed. He closed and locked his front door then hauled two suitcases to his pickup.

Unable to shake the feeling that his world was

about to blow up, Deetz drove to the Rio Grande. He pulled onto the ditch bank and scanned the area for movement. Grateful for the lateness of the hour and the cover of darkness, he retrieved the lead pipe, bloody rags, empty bleach bottle, and towel from the pickup bed and threw them into the river.

Careful to observe the speed limit, he pulled onto the road toward Lou's apartment. He cringed at the thought of stepping into the guy's living space but figured the doofus would twist himself into knots to help someone he considered a friend.

And right then, the one-sided friendship was exactly what Deetz needed.

Chapter Eleven

When Robin awakened again, the air inside the trunk had grown colder. Gusts of wind moaned and shoved the car, gently shaking it.

"Rock-a-bye baby," she whispered.

The pain in Robin's head had subsided to a dull throb, but her thirst had ratcheted up several notches. She licked her dry lips and moved her sticky tongue around her mouth to start the saliva flowing. Her eyes burned, and nausea trailed fingers along her insides. Waves of hunger ebbed and flowed. Her toes were numb, but whether it was due to the cold or the inability to completely straighten her legs in the confined space, she did not know.

She pulled her arm from inside the moderately warm cocoon of her comforter and squinted at the dimming phosphorescent face of her wristwatch, a birthday gift from her husband two weeks before he died.

"Three o'clock Saturday morning," she muttered.

She had been imprisoned for about seven hours. How long would the watch's dimming glow hold up in the trunk's darkness?

The next day would be Christmas Eve. For lots of people, Christmas and Hanukkah were times of rejoicing, a time for dinner parties, the season for gift-giving, for donating food and money to local charities.

But for Robin, it would mean two more days without food and water, unless she could escape.

She licked her lips at the memory of the unfinished grilled cheese sandwich and tomato soup sitting on her kitchen table. Had she known what lay in store for her, she would have made dinner earlier and put away the week's music books later.

Robin's thoughts flew to the spicy, shortbread *biscochitos* she and Petra had baked only days before, and her mouth watered. For the past two Decembers, just before Christmas, they spent a Saturday making the crisp lard-based cookies flavored with cinnamon and anise. The recipe, which countless New Mexicans had tweaked since the Spanish colonists brought it centuries earlier, had been passed down from Robin's great grandmother.

As usual, the two women had sipped homemade lattes and sampled the still-warm cookies as they came from the oven. They regaled each other with life experiences and laughed at funny stories gleaned along their lives' pathways. While Robin got the feeling Petra had a history she was unwilling to completely share, her friendship had been like a life raft in a hurricane after John's death.

A muscle in Robin's left thigh twisted itself into a cramp, dragging her back to the present. Grimacing, she tried to straighten her body, but the trunk's interior proved neither deep nor wide enough.

Finally, flexing her toes and bending her body at the waist, she pressed the back of her neck and shoulders against the trunk's lid and straightened her legs until her feet abutted the car's back seat. She massaged the now-twitching thigh muscle until it calmed.

Robin's comforter suddenly moved of its own volition, and something scampered up her left leg. Frantically, she kicked her feet and flapped the comforter.

A squeak followed by a *thump* offered testimony that she'd basket-tossed something living against the metal trunk wall. The instant receding *tick-tick* of toenails against metal suggested the visitor had opted to leave rather than stand its ground.

"Run, you little bugger," Robin shouted. "If you come back before I'm dead, I'll eat you raw, toenails, fur, and all. Yeah, you heard me."

A cold knot pushed Robin's bravado aside at the memory of a documentary about rats that made their homes in tenements in some large cities. Some of them grew to the size of cats and were completely without fear of humans. Reportedly, they had been known to gnaw toes and fingers off sick or otherwise vulnerable babies as they lay in their cribs.

On the brighter side, Robin strongly suspected that the creature she had just encountered was a mouse rather than a rat. While a mouse might have the same basic diet as a rat, at least mice were smaller and, hopefully, easier to intimidate.

The bottom line, however, was that once Robin became incapacitated or lost consciousness, it would be only a matter of time before platoons of small neighborhood carrion-eaters found her. She would be a veritable smorgasbord, not only for mice, ants, and roaches, but for blowflies and anything else small enough and hungry enough to finagle its way into the trunk.

Ashes to ashes and dust to dust. Or, in her case, recycle and re-use.

Images from the rat documentary segued into a story about a prisoner of war who was captured, bound, and put inside a stockade to await execution. Unwilling to be tortured before dying at the whim of his captors, he stripped flesh from his hands with his teeth until he died from the resulting blood loss, thereby choosing both the time and manner of his death.

Although that level of determination and courage was beyond anything Robin could imagine, she found the story strangely heartening. She was unwilling to give up just yet, but if she were unable to escape within the next three days, and her vital organs began to shut down, she could hopefully choose her own way out.

Her abductor may have temporarily taken her freedom, but he had destroyed neither her brain nor her will.

Chapter Twelve

Quillan O'Farrell peered at the man and woman standing on his front porch at three o'clock Saturday morning. The only items of clothing identifying them as officers of the law were the Albuquerque Police Department insignias on the fronts of their shirts and the body cams clipped to their APD jackets.

"Mister O'Farrell?" the woman said. "I'm Detective Rooney. This is Detective Rankin. Sorry for the lateness of the hour."

Where Rankin was stout with thick silver hair, Detective Rooney was willowy with short, light-brown hair in a pixie-like cut. Large brown eyes gave her an almost ethereal, wraith-like appearance, but the bulletproof vest and holstered sidearm announced she was all business. Quil was taken by surprise at his visceral response to the woman's combination of loveliness and strength.

"May we come in?" Detective Rooney said.

"Of course." Quil opened the door and stood to one side.

Was Detective Rooney single, or not wearing a ring for some other reason? Were she and Rankin just partners, or could they be more? While Rankin was obviously several years older, Quil had seen enough odd couples not to be surprised at the thought.

"There's fresh-brewed coffee and homemade

cherry tarts, if you guys haven't eaten," Quil said.

"Thanks for the offer," Detective Rooney said, "but we need to get moving."

"I'll get my phone." Quil started toward the kitchen. "I'd be happy to wrap up the pastries and put the coffee in insulated cups. It'll only take a second," he said over his shoulder. "I just opened a coffee shop and bakery, so I'd appreciate your feedback on the pastry."

As Quil filled two insulated mugs with fresh coffee, he staunched the internal flow of questions about detective Petra Rooney. He had to focus all his energy on building his new business, and that left no time for emotional entanglements, no matter how attractive.

He selected two of the best-looking leftover pastries, wrapped them in waxed paper, then put them into a small, brown paper bag. After dropping his phone into a breast pocket, he slipped the paper bag under one arm, picked up the coffees, and returned to the detectives.

"For the road." Quil placed the coffees and pastries on the entry table. "Here's my phone. It's all charged up." He pulled the instrument from his pocket and held it out.

"Thanks," Detective Rooney said. "We'll need to take your statement, so we can either drive you to the main station now, or you could meet us there. Whichever is more convenient."

Quil glanced at his wristwatch. "If it's okay, I need to open my shop first. But I can come in after everything's up and going. I have a helper who can hold the fort while I'm gone."

"That would be great," Detective Rooney said.

"How about nine this morning?"

"No problem." Quil pulled a business card from his breast pocket. "Here's my work number. My coffee shop is on Central Avenue, just east of Montgomery. It's called *Higher Grounds*. I open at six and close at three in the afternoon, but if you need to reach me, you can call that number until around four or five any evening."

"Thanks." Petra dropped the phone and card into her jacket pocket then handed Quil one of her own business cards. "That's my direct line. We'll return your phone as soon as our tech guys are finished with it."

"Can you let me know when you find Robin?" Quil cleared his throat. "I know you can't tell me much since it's an ongoing investigation, but I somehow feel responsible."

"We'll let you know," Detective Rooney said.

Each of the detectives took a mug of coffee, then Detective Rankin hefted the paper bag. Both officers expressed gratitude and prepared to leave.

At the front door, Detective Rooney hesitated and turned back toward Quil. "Thanks for calling as soon as you got Robin's texts. The first few hours after an abduction are the most critical. A lot of folks would discount the whole thing as a prank, but you showed good instincts by not taking the chance."

After the detectives left, Quil showered and dressed. He would have to hustle to get the pastries done for the morning rush, but at least he was already wide awake.

As he headed for his car, thoughts of detective Rooney leap-frogged through his mind. The detective had struck him as intelligent and fiercely focused on doing her job. If anyone *had Robin's six*, as Quil learned during his years in the military, he had a feeling it would be detective Rooney.

Didn't the word *Petra* mean *rock* in Greek?

"Better watch yourself, Boy-o," Quil told himself. As he had learned the hard way, if something looked too good to be true, it probably was.

He scrubbed the detective's image from his mind, backed out of his drive, and headed to his bakery-cum-coffee shop.

Chapter Thirteen

Robin's thoughts wandered as she kicked against the still-unyielding back seat. Would Quil call Petra, or had he blown her texts off and gone back to sleep?

What had she done to piss off the Universe enough to make her the focus of its ire? She had always tried to do the right thing. She played the piano at her church. She donated time and money to a local homeless shelter. She even fed stray animals.

Heat roiled up from her insides into her throat.

"Why are you doing this to me?" she screamed at the Cosmos, half fearful a bolt of lightning would be sent in response to her spiritual rebellion.

A lump rose in her throat, and she angrily chided herself. Her situation was not the Creator's doing, it was the unexpected consequence of her own actions.

She should never have poked her nose into her neighbor's business. The police would have investigated Vince's death without Robin's input. But no, she had to go and eavesdrop.

Get off your pity-pot, Robbie. Your great, great, grandmother delivered her own baby in the back of a covered wagon. You have the same DNA. Use it.

"It may have escaped your notice, Mom," Robin said, her voice reduced to a whisper by her earlier screaming rant. "But I'm locked inside a trunk located who-knows-where. Options are limited."

Take stock of what you have; don't leave anything out. Then generate a plan.

"That shouldn't take long," Robin murmured.

Other than the clothes and leather moccasins she was wearing, a down-filled comforter, and a dead cell phone, she had nothing that could even remotely be considered useful.

Robin stiffened and jerked her head up, bumping it painfully against the trunk lid. Based on a recent episode of a popular survival series, she could remove the cell's battery and locate its positive and negative markings. Then, she could form foil or some other metal into a U and touch the ends to the markings while holding the battery over something combustible. Even if her phone battery's charge was too low to register, it might still have enough power to generate a spark. All she needed was one or two little fire-starters.

While she had no aluminum foil, she did have a metal underwire in her bra. Would that work? And she could pull a handful of stuffing from her comforter for tender, set it afire then use the second underwire to poke the flaming bits through the largest rusty hole she could find.

Contrary to Robin's earlier thinking, the foraging critter she'd heard outside testified that her prison was indeed surrounded by dry grass, leaves, or undergrowth. If not yet snow-covered, any nearby detritus should quickly catch fire. Someone would surely see the resulting smoke and come running.

Robin's initial excitement at the notion, however, abruptly died. In the event she was unable to get the flaming chunk far enough away from the car, the trunk-cum-oven could effectively roast her like a Christmas turkey in a fire that would rage through any surrounding dead flora. It would not be a pretty, easy, or quick way to go.

Her phone's only other value was that if worse came to worst, she could break the screen and use a shard of broken glass like a razor blade. At least her death would be quicker and a lot less dramatic than using her teeth to tear flesh from her wrists.

Robin pulled the comforter up to her chin and curled herself into a ball. Despite her determined effort not to do so, she sobbed.

The sound of a low-flying airplane again caught her attention. Unlike the deep-throated roar of a passenger jet, however, the sound was higher in pitch, like a small private aircraft.

What if she was in a pasture located along the flight path of a rancher's personal plane? Robin had seen a local news article highlighting small hangars and landing strips on surrounding ranches. If so, maybe a small plane would come within hearing-range, if she could only raise enough ruckus.

What she needed was a schedule. No more random chaos.

Every half-hour, she would yell at the top of her lungs and beat against the trunk's roof with her shoe. Then for at least ten minutes of every hour, she would flex her muscles to keep them from turning into over-cooked noodles. She would point her toes, rotate her feet at the ankles, then move up to her calves.

Hunger interrupted Robin's litany of body parts. Visions of her well-stocked pantry danced in her head.

If she were home, she could soon be having a breakfast of oatmeal with raisins, cinnamon, and brown sugar. Or she could opt for bacon, eggs, and buttered toast with raspberry jam, followed by about a gallon or two of freshly brewed coffee -- the full-strength stuff, none of that namby-pamby decaffeinated swill she reluctantly drank in the evenings.

Scenes from a documentary about a shipwreck bubbled up from her memory. Sometime in the1800s, a storm sent a ship crashing into a shoal surrounding a small island. One young sailor harvested seaweed and ate it. Eventually rescued, the seaweed-eater was thin but rosy-cheeked and healthy. When asked how he had managed to do so well, he reported that as he ate the slimy, salty leaves, he imagined he was eating steak and potatoes.

Robin snorted at the memory. She doubted the dried grass and leaves inside the spare tire well would provide the same health benefits as vitamin-and-mineral-packed seaweed, even if she *could* envision it as barbecued ribs and potato salad. Besides, with the pressure in her bladder becoming nearly unbearable, she had other plans for the tire well.

The alarm on Robin's watch announced it was time to raise the scheduled ruckus. She reached for her shoe, but instead of immediately going into screaming and shoe-pounding, mode, she lay unmoving.

Who was she kidding? She was good as dead. It was a waste of time to do anything more than accept her fate.

It's not over until it's over, Robbie Girl.

"Says you," Robin murmured.

If a task is once begun, never leave it 'til it's done.

If for no other reason than to stop the flow of remembered parental scolding, Robin gripped her shoe by the toe. She pounded the heels of her feet against the trunk floor at the same time she beat the trunk lid with her shoe until a cramp in her arm forced her to stop.

Her ears ringing, she glanced at the barely visible face of her wristwatch. The exhausting spurt of activity had lasted exactly two and one-half minutes.

Robin's shoulders drooped. She curled into a tight ball and closed her eyes.

Chapter Fourteen

At half-past three o'clock Saturday morning, the atmosphere inside the briefing room at the main office of the Albuquerque Police Department was somber. Of the ten detectives in attendance, some sipped coffee while others drank from cans of energy drinks. Conversation was at a minimum.

"We've called the whole team in on this," the duty sergeant said. "We have to assume the air compressor death yesterday afternoon is in some way connected to the subsequent abduction of a woman who lives across the street from the dead man." He glanced around the room. "Detective Rooney will be Lead Officer on the case." The sergeant nodded once in Petra's direction and stepped aside. "Detective."

Every eye focused on Petra as she strode to the front of the briefing room. No one spoke. No one coughed. No one yawned.

"The missing and endangered person is Robin Marcato, a personal friend of mine." Petra held up the photo of Robin she took during their recent cookie-baking day and gestured toward a stack of copies on the table in front of her. "National Crime Information Center has been alerted, and we've contacted the department of public safety and issued *be-on-the-lookout* and *endangered person* advisories." For the next several minutes Petra filled her Violent Crime

Team members in on what was known about Robin's abduction.

"Although someone did a fairly good job of cleaning blood from the bathroom floor, we found a couple of drops on the rug. Forensics is working on that. Also, a wad of freshly chewed gum was found behind the toilet."

"Could the gum be your friend's?" one officer said.

"Robin could not chew gum," Petra said. "She was under a dentist's care for jaw problems. The gum's been sent for rush DNA analysis, so we could have results within twenty-four hours or so."

Officers murmured and nodded their heads appreciatively.

"Robin managed to send two texts asking for help but has not responded to subsequent calls or texts. The preliminary canvass of her neighborhood scored a lead which Cody and I will check out. Toto." Petra nodded at a young Kansan who recently moved to Albuquerque. "You and your partner do a follow-up canvass to make sure all the neighbors have been interviewed." She gestured toward the young man's laptop. "The names of the people Cody and I interviewed are listed on the lead sheet but question them again in case they've remembered something."

"Cracker," Petra said to a young officer named Graham. "How's your work on Mister O'Farrell's phone coming?"

"The phone dump is complete," he said. "Soon as we're done here, I'll begin pinging."

"Excellent," Petra said. "Check with nine-one-one. Robin might have tried to make more than one call. If so, find out if any other cell phone towers pinged. That could narrow down her location a bit."

"Do we know whether or not she *did* call anyone else?" one of the team members said.

"No," Petra said. "We're assuming, hoping, the reason there's been no further message is that Robin's phone is dead." She slowly moved her gaze around the assembled team. "We don't want word of her final texts to get out in case the perpetrator or perpetrators hear about it, realize she's alive, and decide to finish the job. Robin's car is still in her garage, so she was transported by some other means."

A young female officer raised her hand. "I can go over traffic cams, private home security cameras, and any local business' closed-circuit cameras, starting with the area around her address and moving outward."

"Excellent." Petra nodded.

"Any idea what kind of vehicle we're looking for?" the young woman added.

"I'm not certain. But make a note if you spot a rusty, powder blue Chevy pickup."

Another officer raised his hand. "Miss Marcato's text said she witnessed a murder; do we know what that's about?"

"We don't yet know of any direct connection between Vince Banda's death and Robin's abduction," Petra said. "His death was initially assumed to be accidental, but it's too much of a coincidence to ignore. I have already contacted Robin's closest living relative, a brother. He will let us know if anyone gets in touch with him. Cody and I will interview Banda's heirs and the employee to find out if anyone had issues with him as well as who benefited from his death." Petra moved her gaze around the room. "Any other ideas or suggestions?"

"Her text said she was inside an old car trunk?" Cracker said. "There must be thousands of abandoned cars in and around the Albuquerque area, and that's not allowing for parking lots, personal garages, and the like."

Subsequent grim expressions on every officer's face testified that they were all remembering the recent discovery of four bodies in various stages of decomposition inside a van parked in long term parking at the local airport. Although no one was willing to give voice to the thought, they all knew Robin could be the latest addition to a serial killer's improvised body dump.

Petra took a deep breath then turned toward another officer and said, "Tex, didn't you just qualify for a Certificate of Authorization to fly the department's new drone?"

"Yessum." A man wearing cowboy boots nodded. "Thirty-minutes of flight time between charges, and a five-mile range. Just so you know, FAA regulations allow daytime flight only."

"Dawn's not for another five hours," Petra said.

"I'll have Nellie charged and ready to go as soon as the sun's up," Tex said.

Petra looked around the briefing room. "Anyone else got anything?" After several seconds of silence, she added, "Thank you all for your help. Now let's go find Robin Marcato."

While the other detectives paired up in keeping with protocol then filed out of the briefing room, Petra collected her personal effects.

Every person on her team was seasoned and

dedicated. This group of detectives would do everything in their power to find Robin. They would put all their active cases on temporary hold and focus on her case day and night, stopping only to take the occasional catnap at the main police station in a room fitted out with twin beds and a couple of recliners. They would not return to their own caseloads until all leads had been exhausted.

The weather forecast for the coming days made Petra uneasy. Overnight temperatures had dipped into the single digits, and the forecast was for heavy snow followed by a hard freeze on Saturday. If Robin survived the next forty-eight hours, it would be a miracle. However, if she were not found within the next three to four days, the trunk -- wherever it was located --would become her coffin.

Petra pulled the phone from her belt and checked for messages. She frowned at the blank screen, tapped it a few times, then began typing.

I'm going to find you. Don't give up.

She sent the text then glanced at Cody, who stood silently waiting.

"We have the employee's name and address," Cody said. "Ronnie Deetz. He has a history of assault and breaking and entering. Seems he broke his girlfriend's jaw when he lived in Denver, then beat up a co-worker in El Paso." Cody raised his eyebrows. "The co-worker wound up in intensive care; Deetz did a couple of years for that. I Googled him but didn't learn anything beyond what we already know. He isn't on Facebook, Twitter, or any of the other social media platforms."

"So, a history of physical violence," Petra said. "I

want to be back here by nine to take O'Farrell's statement, but I think we have time to track this Deetz character down.

"Any suspicions about Robin's brother being involved?" Cody said. "You know as well as I do that most abductions are not done by strangers."

"Normally, I'd suggest we look at him first. But not only is Chris a doting brother, I obviously pulled him from a deep sleep to inform him of Robin's disappearance. Besides, the wording in Robin's texts doesn't fit with his being involved."

"Okay," Cody nodded. "Did he have anything useful to add?"

"Nothing we don't already know," Petra said. "They were close. If Robin was worried or had recent trouble with anyone, I feel certain she would have confided either in Chris or me." She sighed then added, "No, this smells like an act of pure desperation, not a carefully or well-planned attack. Robin saw something and it made her a target." Petra glanced at her watch. "Let's find Deetz. We can take my car."

As the detectives were buckling their seatbelts, Petra's phone rang. She glanced at the caller ID then looked at Cody and mouthed *Reena-Belle*.

"Detective Rooney," Petra said into the phone.

"That powder blue pickup I told you about, the one that belongs to Vince's employee?" Reena-Belle said. "It just pulled into my driveway, idled for a couple of seconds then backed up and took off like his butt was on fire. It seemed to me the guy spotted the forensic folks at Robin's house and got the wind up."

Petra's pulse quickened. "Was anyone with him?"

"No idea. I couldn't see much because of his

headlights, but I figured you ought to know." Reena-Belle cleared her throat then added, "I couldn't get a good look at his tags, so no help there. But it's the same pickup, all right."

"Thank you," Petra said. "Much appreciated."

"I'll call if I spot anything else." Reena-Belle broke the connection.

"What's up?" Cody said.

"Reena-Belle just spotted Deetz's pickup in her driveway."

"Whoa." Cody whistled. "That guy is turning up all over the place."

"Yeah," Petra said. "Like a regular Jack-in-the-box."

"What are the chances he is our guy?"

"Too soon to tell," Petra said, refusing to allow herself to give energy to the budding hope that Robin's disappearance might be quickly cleared.

She had learned some hard lessons during her years as an investigator, many of which came at a high emotional cost to her. While some cases could be solved within hours, most of them could only be cleared through dogged persistence over time. Whoever said time was the enemy must have been a detective.

The unspoken recognition of her friend's dire situation hanging in the air, Petra punched Deetz's address into her GPS and fired up her engine.

Chapter Fifteen

Deetz pulled his pickup into the tenants' parking lot of Lou's apartment complex. He drove to the rear of the lot and into a space as far from the street as possible. He peered through the darkness at the other vehicles and the surrounding area. Once convinced he was unobserved, he pulled his phone from its cradle, punched a number into the screen then held it to his ear.

Lou's recorded voice mail prompt immediately kicked in, "Leave a number, and I might call you back. If this is Janelle, Loren, or Tammy, call my attorney."

"Lou-Lou, it's me," Deetz said after the ensuing *beep*. "I gotta talk to you, man."

When three more calls went to voice mail, he angrily tossed the phone onto the passenger seat next to Banda's laptop, then bounced his leg up and down on the ball of his right foot.

He was running out of time. He desperately needed to get some sleep but couldn't take the chance of going back to his own apartment because the cops could be watching. His best option was to get into Lou's.

The thought of that chunk of chewing gum was galling. He had been so proud of himself for cleaning up the blood, then went and left the freaking gum for the cops to find.

Deetz rapidly ran his fingers through his hair several times. If Lou's track record held true to form, once passed out from a night of drinking, he would wake up sometime around noon the next day, and that was still hours away.

When Deetz saw the crime scene mobile lab parked outside Marcato's house, he had nearly passed out. Then, when his pickup lights panned across the squinty, old eyes peering out at him from beyond the driveway in which he stupidly made a U-turn, his head nearly exploded.

Sooner or later, the nosey old bat would tell the cops about seeing him. While unable to see him clearly enough to offer a description, she would certainly describe his pickup.

Another thought set him chewing his thumbnail. Maybe it was that same old woman who called the cops about Marcato in the first place. Every old person Deetz knew went to bed by seven o'clock then complained about insomnia. Maybe she was doing whatever old people do when they couldn't sleep and saw him at Marcato's house. Maybe she even watched him load the body into his pickup. Since the old woman was a neighbor to both Banda *and* Marcato, the cops would sift through her words like they were panning for gold.

Maybe he should have taken the time to deal with the old woman instead of driving off in such a hurry. The idea of squeezing that wrinkled old throat until the nosey old bag's eyes bugged out was tempting. But three deaths in the same neighborhood within the space of a few hours would grab the attention of every cop in the Midwestern United States, and then some.

According to the news, Banda's death was considered accidental. There was a chance, although slight, that the cops wouldn't connect Vince's worldly exit with the nosey neighbor's disappearance.

"Keep telling yourself that kind of fairy tale crap, and you'll find yourself back inside in no time," Deetz muttered.

He ran his index finger along the inside of his collar and blew out a series of short breaths. Regardless of how hard he tried to convince himself otherwise, he had to admit that evidence against him was piling up.

Factoid number one: he had been dead-man Banda's employee. Number two: Banda lived across the street from the now missing Marcato woman. Three: He was spotted in the neighborhood in the middle of the night, within hours of both occurrences, and with no apparent reason to be there. Four: There was the little matter of his police record, not to mention the problem of the chewing gum.

Deetz stared at the clock on his dashboard. Maybe he should pound on Lou's door. The bum might regain consciousness long enough to let him in.

But once Lou passed out, he could sleep through an earthquake. Deetz's door-beating exercise would, however, wake everyone else who lived in the complex. Not only did people frown on middle-of-the-night disturbances, but their reactions tended to result in negative consequences for the person responsible.

A better idea would be to sneak around to the rear of Lou's apartment and climb in through one of the guy's windows.

Deetz shut off the pickup's interior light to prevent it coming on when he opened the door. He stepped out, slowly allowed the door to close until it clicked, then hurried toward the back of the complex.

When he rounded the building's corner, he stopped

in his tracks and murmured a series of invectives. A row of eight, small, nearly identical ground floor windows stared back at him. Most likely bathroom windows and situated at a height of seven or more feet off the ground, they would require some tricky gymnastics to reach.

He studied the building's rear layout. Since Lou lived in apartment two-zero-five, his bathroom window should be the third from the left. No, make that the fourth from the right.

Deetz cracked his knuckles. The trip from the front of the complex around to the rear must have disoriented him, because the fourth window from the right was covered by a frilly yellow curtain. Lou-the-slob slept on a mattress on the floor. The guy didn't even own a sofa, not to mention window coverings.

The next few minutes could be life-changing, especially if he climbed through the wrong window. The residents were within their legal rights to blow his ass to kingdom come.

He envisioned the self-righteous apartment dwellers calling the cops and staring down at his bullet-riddled body, explaining how they had feared for their lives. The cops would understandingly nod their heads. Hell, they might even give the shooter an award for saving them the work of bringing Deetz in for questioning.

Thoughtfully chewing the inside of his lower lip, Deetz stared at the dark windows.

Lou didn't live in a corner apartment, so that eliminated the two outside windows. After discounting the ones sporting either curtains or venetian blinds, that left the two in the center of the complex.

Careful not to step into any of the roughly six-inch diameter prairie dog holes dotting the open lot behind the complex, Deetz silently approached the windows.

While one window appeared to be tightly closed, the other sported a vertical, two-inch band of darkness along one side.

Deetz smiled. His window selection could not have been made easier had a note drifted down from the heavens with the words *This is the one* inscribed on it. He confidently tip-toed toward the partially open window.

Chapter Sixteen

Robin sucked at the drop of blood oozing from under the nail of her index finger, surprised that injuries resulting from prying up flakes of rusty metal were more painful than those from a paper cut. She would need to get a tetanus shot within the next forty-eight hours.

Snippets from an article on the deadly disease known as *lockjaw,* popped into her head. Without access to the appropriate vaccination, the infected victim's muscles would spasm, making it impossible to breathe. Death by tetanus would not be gentle.

Robin tightened her lips. Unless she found a way out of her prison, she would either be dead from dehydration or frozen stiff long before tetanus's seven- to ten-day incubation period was up. Problem solved.

Based on her barely readable watch, it was four o'clock Saturday morning. It had taken her the better part of an hour to enlarge a hole in the trunk large enough to poke her pinkie finger through. Even if the trunk were a soft mass of flaking rust, it would take a year to make an opening large enough to squeeze her body through. On top of that, underneath the rust lay razor-sharp steel. She was doing more damage to her fingers than to the trunk.

"Okay, Mom, words of wisdom would be much appreciated about now."

When no comforting or helpful memories of her mother's voice were forthcoming, Robin fumbled in the darkness for her phone. She grasped the rectangular scrap of technological hope and repeatedly jabbed her finger around the screen in hopes of hitting the power button. Maybe the head trauma had affected her eyesight, and she had mistakenly thought the phone was dead when it still held a tiny charge. She didn't need much, just enough to send a word or two.

"Please, please, please," she whispered.

But the tiny screen remained devoid of even the dimmest glow.

Sobbing, Robin hugged the useless thing to her chest.

Never in her wildest imaginings had she foreseen herself dying in such circumstances. Since heart attacks, strokes, and cancer ran in her family, she assumed one of those would escort her into the next realm. Even her doctor had intimated her demise would most likely be from natural causes.

Robin sniffed. Was death at the hands of Mother Nature considered a natural cause?

Why hadn't she taken the time to charge her phone when she first noticed the low battery? Sometime in the distant future, someone would find her with the phone clutched in her skeletal right hand. Once the shock of finding her body wore off, they would wonder why she chose to die inside a trunk rather than use the phone to call for help. Or maybe they would view her death as a harsh reminder to keep their own phones fully charged.

"She could have lived a full life," the newscaster would say as listeners sagely nodded their heads and made mental notes. "But for some sad, unfathomable reason, she didn't charge her phone."

Gusts of cold air sifted through tiny sieve-like holes along one side of the trunk, and Robin reached for the comforter. As she pulled the fabric up to her chin, her hands ran across several small, wet patches on the cloth covering, and her throat constricted.

Dampness could prove deadly. If too much of the cotton fabric got wet, she would be unable to stay warm and dry. The human body could become hypothermic in weather as mild as forty degrees, and the forecast for that day was snow followed by temperatures in the low teens.

Robin ran trembling fingers along the trunk's walls. As she feared, moisture from melting snow was seeping through the three largest rust holes at which she had been working.

Not only was her warm breath heating the metal trunk lid enough to melt the snow surrounding the holes, but by widening said holes she may have sealed her fate. A solid, block-of-ice comforter could become her shroud.

In a frenzy, she pulled at the tattered edges of the rotted carpet underneath her until she managed to tear up a few small pieces. Her icy fingers trembled so badly she repeatedly dropped the fragments, but she finally managed to stuff them into the holes.

During the next several minutes, she ran her fingers over the grafted plugs in search of new wetness. She allowed herself a breath of relief when the areas around the holes remained dry.

"Water, water everywhere," Robin murmured. "And not a drop to drink."

What are you waiting for, Robbie Girl?

"What?

The longer you lie there feeling sorry for yourself, the weaker you grow.

"I love you, Mom, but you're telling me something I already know."

You are learning what doesn't work. Figure out what does.

"Everything I do makes my situation worse. Even my warm breath is a threat."

So? You're not dead yet.

"I'm cold, I'm hungry enough to eat this rotten carpet, and I'm considering drinking my own urine from a moccasin." Robin paused then added, "All that melting snow out there, and I'm in here dying of thirst."

Calm yourself. Terrified people make bad decisions.

Thoughtfully, Robin ran her fingers along the damp spots on her comforter. The cotton fabric had acted as a wick, pulling the moisture into its fibers from the melting snow outside.

Like a thunderbolt, an idea skittered across her brain's synapses. She removed the moccasin she was still wearing and moved her hands along the comforter until she found its edge. She gnawed at the fabric until she managed to tear off two short, thin strips.

Her heart pounding, she dislodged the tattered bits of carpet from the two largest holes and replaced them with strips of comforter. She removed the absorbent foam insoles from her leather moccasins then wiped the shoes' insides with a corner of the comforter. Carefully, she placed one shoe under each of the two strips of fabric.

Barely allowing herself to breathe, she waited.

Chapter Seventeen

Deetz studied the partially opened window at the rear of Lou's apartment complex. Unhappy to discover that the window's ledge was a good two feet higher off the ground than it appeared from a distance, he sucked air through his teeth and considered the best plan of attack.

Now, if he could find something to stand on.

He scanned his surroundings hoping to score a discarded wooden box or anything else strong enough to hold his weight. Even something only a few inches tall would help.

When nothing presented itself, he groaned inwardly. He would have to somehow hoist his body high enough to hook his arms over the windowsill and then pull himself through the opening, hopefully with as little noise as possible and without leaving swaths of skin on the rough brick facing.

A nervous tic in Deetz's right eye pulsed, and the flesh on his forearms rucked up. Time was flying. Daylight was approaching. Cops were hustling.

Sleep deprived, that's what he was. He had made some of the worst decisions of his life when running low on sleep.

Deetz shook his head to clear the fuzzy gray cloud clogging his brain. He had to get hold of a set of wheels that couldn't be traced to him, because, as certain as it rained in Seattle, there would be a BOLO out on his pickup.

He had to assume the cops found his chewing gum. If the process had not changed since his last brush with the law, the DNA test would take at least a day or two. Deetz had every intention of being gone long before the cops got their hands on the results.

At some point, the cops would seek out all his *known associates*. Hopefully, it would take them a few hours to learn about his connection to Lou, allowing Deetz time to grab a few ZZs, get hold of Lou's truck keys, and haul ass to Mexico.

Maybe somewhere along the way he would find a car or truck where some forgetful owner had left the keys. The more often he could change vehicles, the tougher he would be to track. It never ceased to amuse him how many cars were stolen because the owners left them warming up in the driveway during cold weather.

Deetz cursed himself for not making copies of Lou's front door and pickup keys when he had the chance. He had been in possession of every key the guy owned but had duplicated only the ones labeled *Work*.

Short sighted, as usual. He could hear his old man growling out the words. *Dumbo, that's what you are.*

As it turned out, the old bum had been every bit as short sighted as his son. A body couldn't get much more short-sighted than to carry a loaded pistol into a bank and threaten to shoot a teller unless she loaded a pillowcase with the cash from her drawer, all while a plain clothes cop stood not ten feet away.

Deetz scouted the area behind the apartment complex. He approached a stand of cottonwood trees and sifted through several fallen branches until he found one about three feet long and an inch in diameter. He picked up the branch and returned to the window.

Standing on his tiptoes, he worked the branch into the opening along one side of the aluminum window frame. He held the limb with both hands for leverage and pushed it against the window's edge.

Accumulated grit blown into the runner by high New Mexico winds hissed as metal scraped sandy granules against metal. Deetz froze and slowly counted to ten. When no one raised an alarm, he continued pushing until the window was open as wide as it would go, then tossed the branch aside.

Unsure if he could squeeze through such a small opening but determined to try, he bent his knees then catapulted himself upward, arms stretched high, and fingers set to curl over the windowsill.

His reach just short of the ledge, he landed on the hard-packed ground with a *whump*, jarring an old injury to his back. A bolt of pain shot up his spine. His knees turned to water, and he plopped onto the ground, biting his tongue to keep from yelping.

Part of his brain whispered that his current avenue of attack was a dead end and suggested he change tactics. However, another part bellowed in his dad's voice that only a wuss would quit.

Once the pain in his hip subsided, Deetz retrieved the branch he had used to push the window open then gathered several more fallen limbs and arranged them in a pile beneath the opening. Mentally giving his old man the finger, he gingerly stepped onto the pile of wood. Although the branches drooped under his weight, they added several inches to his reach. Deetz squelched a gleeful *whoop*.

He pressed his hands against the brick wall for support, then hooked his fingers over the windowsill, jammed the toes of his boots against the bricks and climbed up the wall. After several seconds of circus-quality contortion, he draped half of his torso over the window's ledge.

Caught high center with his upper body inside the window and his legs and butt dangling outside, he scrambled for handholds to pull himself all the way into what had proven to be a bathroom.

Reaching for the faucet to help pull himself the rest of the way inside, Deetz's groping fingers brushed against a plastic bottle. In less time than it took for him to tell himself he was screwed, the bottle tipped over. It fell into the round-bottomed sink and rocked back and forth several times, the resulting sound muffled, yet distinct.

A tickle at the base of his skull grew in strength. Something was off.

No bathroom owned and frequented by Lou-the-doofus would have a bottle of anything remotely hygienic on its counter. And it certainly would not smell like flowers.

"Did you hear something," a woman's sleep-fuzzy voice said from beyond the closed door.

The tiny hairs at the base of Deetz's skull stood straight out. Unable to move, he held his breath.

"I didn't hear nothing," a muffled masculine voice said after a short pause. "Go back to sleep. I got to get up early."

"I keep hearing noise coming from the bathroom," the woman said. "I'm pretty sure I just heard something plop into the sink."

"You're dreaming. You couldn't hear a bomb explode in the next room once you're asleep," the man said.

"Something woke me up." The woman's voice rose in pitch and intensity.

"The window must be over eight feet off the ground. Nobody's tall enough to climb through that."

"Are you going to just lay there while someone breaks in?" the woman whined. "If you don't do something, I will."

"Okay, okay." The man added something unintelligible. Bedsprings squeaked and groaned. "If I check the bathroom, will you shut your yap and let me get some sleep?"

"Where are you going?" the woman stage whispered. "The sound came from the bathroom, not the closet."

"I'm getting my baseball bat. If someone's there, I'm going to make mush out of his skull."

Adrenaline jetted into Deetz's vital organs, and he shoved himself back through the window, ignoring the burning scrapes the metal frame dealt to the sides of his ribcage. As he fell backward, he ineffectually scrabbled to grip the window frame, the ledge, anything he could use to control his descent.

Arms flailing, he landed flat on his back among the piled-up branches beneath the window. The air whooshed from his lungs, and he gasped for breath.

Light poured through the open window, describing a patch on the branches beneath it and highlighting Deetz. His survival instinct fully operational, he rolled off the pile of branches until well out of the patch of light, then lay still.

"Nothing here." The man's voice was crystal clear in the frigid air, as he looked out the window.

Deetz held his breath.

The woman said something, relief in her voice.

"It's like an icebox in here," the man shouted. "No wonder our electric bill is so high. I keep telling you to keep the window closed in the winter."

The windowsill's resident grit ground out its complaint as the man slammed the window shut.

Deetz lay unmoving until he could breathe. When he finally managed to stand, it was on rubbery legs. His insides jittered from the rush of adrenaline, and a buzzing sound filled his ears.

He glanced back toward the row of windows and considered trying the one he now knew belonged to Lou. However, not only was the bum's window tightly closed, but that mouthy bimbo next door would most likely be lying awake, staring at the ceiling, her ears like radars.

As he knew all too well, it took a person a while to come down off a fear-induced adrenaline high.

Deetz's brain felt like a useless glob of wood putty. Struggling to focus, he tapped the fingertips of both hands against his temples.

While the idea of giving up on getting hold of Lou's pickup keys rankled, driving his own vehicle back to the bar to retrieve the other man's wheels seemed risky. He couldn't shake the image of Albuquerque's streets crawling with cops, all intent on finding him.

Deetz considered calling a taxi, or maybe an Uber. However, the probability of a cab or Uber driver remembering him was high, especially since it was nearly four o'clock in the morning.

"Yes, Officer," the driver would say, "I was suspicious about the guy."

"Would you know him if you saw him again?" the cop would say.

"Oh yeah, I'd recognize him." He would chuckle and add, "He walked with a limp and sat on the edge of the seat like his ass was on fire."

Deetz figured a better idea would be to walk to the bar, hijack Lou's pickup, then drive it back to his own pickup for his luggage. The morning sky was still dark as tarpaper, and he would keep to side streets.

His eyebrows rose, and a smile tickled the corners of his mouth at another thought. Lou never locked his pickup, so no key would be needed, and it was old enough to hotwire.

As a bonus, the hunk-of-junk had been built before auto makers started putting GPS systems into their over-priced products, and that meant no auto dealership could help the cops track the pickup's movements.

Satisfied with his decision, Deetz took a tentative step forward but froze when pain shot up the backs of his legs along his spine. He cursed under his breath. He could not walk a block, let alone the mile or so to the bar. Against his better judgement, he limped to the parking lot.

Hopefully, he could make it to the bar without being spotted. It would take longer to use side streets but would be a lot smarter. Never let it be said that Ronnie Deetz was stupid.

Maybe he would crash at Dierdre's place. While the thought of having to explain himself to his cash-cow lover left a bad taste in his mouth, he could conjure up a suitable lie to keep her from asking too many questions. Then, after a few hours of sleep, he would be pleased to put Albuquerque permanently in his rearview mirror.

By the time Deetz reached his pickup, his hips felt like they were on fire. Slowly, he climbed into his pickup and sat unmoving until the pain subsided.

He retrieved his phone from the passenger's seat, then punched a speed-dial number and held the device to his ear.

"Hey, baby," he said when Dierdre answered. "You miss me?"

"Pollock," the bimbo burbled. "Where are you?"

"It's a long story." Deetz tightened his lips at the nickname the broad insisted on using after learning he was a house painter.

"I love long stories," Dierdre said.

"You want some company?"

"Sure," Dierdre said. "I'll keep the porch light on."

"I'll be there in ten."

Deetz shut down the call. He sighed and questioned the wisdom of contacting the woman. But what choice did he have? Lou was comatose. The cops were on Deetz's tail, and he was exhausted and broke. Dierdre could be the solution to all those problems.

Of course, she would ask questions, questions Deetz would refuse to answer. Knowing her, she would not let it go, but would harangue him until he lost his temper. Resignedly, Deetz sighed and cracked his knuckles.

He hated being harangued.

Chapter Eighteen

Petra pulled her vehicle next to the curb in front of the apartment complex listed as Ronnie Deetz's address. She put the gearshift in park then she and Cody studied the building.

Surrounded by what appeared to be a horseshoe-shaped parking lot with numbered slots for residents, the complex faced the street. Determined weeds poked their winter-dried, dead heads through potholes in the parking lot's asphalt and along the cracked, uneven sidewalk skirting it. A cluster of mailboxes, some with doors hanging uselessly by one rivet, stood dejectedly against one end of the building. Faded plaques bearing barely discernible apartment numbers canted at various angles above some of the front doors. A couple of apartments had numbers inscribed in what appeared to be magic marker above the doors. Cars, SUVs, and vans in a wide range of vintages, colors, and decrepitude dotted the lot.

"I only see one old pickup in the vicinity," Petra said. "But it's the wrong make and color." She nodded her head toward a barely visible vehicle parked in a weed-strewn patch at the back of the complex.

"No lights on in Deetz's apartment," Cody said. "If he's home, he's not up and moving around."

"How current is your information on his address?"

"He was living here about a month ago, give or

take a couple of days." Cody looked sideways at his partner. "You think this might be an old address?"

"Could be. Based on his record, he's never stayed anywhere long."

"It would be a lot easier to call him," Cody said, "but there's no record of him having a phone."

Petra drove into the parking lot and pulled into a visitor's slot, then the detectives exited the car and silently approached Deetz's apartment.

Petra knocked on the front door. "Ronnie Deetz," she shouted. "Albuquerque Police."

After allowing a few seconds for a response, Petra again knocked on his door.

This time, the door next to Deetz's opened a slit, spilling a vertical bar of light across the small, square concrete stoop at its front. The sign above the apartment's door announced it belonged to the Manager.

"He cleared out," a feminine voice said through the crack. "You really with the police?"

Petra and Cody held out their IDs.

The woman opened the door a bit farther and peered first at the identifications then at the detectives. Black, heavily penciled eyebrows formed chevrons over false eyelashes caked with mascara. Faded, red-hennaed hair waged a losing battle with salt and pepper brown roots. The woman's face was coated with a thick layer of what appeared to be theatrical pancake makeup, but the back of the hand holding the door open was crisscrossed with the beginnings of bluish veins. She could have been anywhere from forty to sixty years of age.

"And you are?" Cody said.

"Dierdre Mozul." The woman glanced upward at the sign above her door. "I'm the owner and manager of these lovely apartment dwellings." She waved her right arm in an arc. "What you see here is the sum-total of my most recent divorce settlement." She looked speculatively at each detective in turn, then added, "Either of you looking for a fine investment opportunity? I'll make you a good deal."

"What can you tell us about Ronnie Deetz?" Petra said.

"Not much." The woman's eyebrows rose. "He came back an hour or two ago. Made enough noise to raise the dead then left." She shrugged. "I thought about trying to stop him; he owes me three months' past-due rent. But I decided it would be smarter to put his bill in for collection."

"Did he say anything to you when he left?" Petra said.

"No." Mozul shook her head unconvincingly, her large brown eyes pools of innocence. "I usually don't get to bed until around midnight, so it's a bit early for me to be up and about." She glanced pointedly at her wristwatch.

"Did you see which direction he went when he left?" Cody said.

"No," Dierdre said. "But I'd be obliged if you let me know when you find him so I can tell the collection agency where to look."

"If he comes back or contacts you for any reason, please give me a call." Petra held out a business card.

"Sure thing." Mozul palmed the card then stepped backward through her door and closed it behind her. The metallic *click* as she engaged the deadbolt sounded loud in the frigid, early morning air.

The two detectives exchanged looks then headed back to Petra's vehicle.

"Anything strike you as odd about Miss Mozul's reaction to our visit?" Petra asked.

"For one thing, she never looked directly into our eyes." Cody buckled his seatbelt then turned toward Petra. "She was awfully anxious to get rid of us. And she's an awful liar."

"Yep." Petra nodded. "Just in case you wondered, no woman sleeps in that much makeup. And don't think I didn't see the way you were looking at her." Petra smiled at her partner's obvious discomfort.

"She said she's divorced," Cody said, his face red enough to raise blisters. "Besides, I may be pushing forty-five, but I'm not dead."

"Her being divorced doesn't mean she was alone," Petra said. "All that makeup, and a black lace teddy under that satin bathrobe. No divorcee is going to wear one of those scratchy, butt-flossing things unless she's trying to impress someone."

"Maybe she's been to a Christmas party and hasn't had time to wash her face," Cody said. "It *is* Friday night, and tomorrow's Christmas Eve."

"Maybe," Petra said. "What struck me was that she did not ask a single question about Deetz, not *is he dead*; *is he in trouble*; *what's he done now*? People always want to know what's going on when the law shows up, even if only out of curiosity." She glanced sideways at her partner. "Have you ever seen *anyone* drive by a vehicle the police have pulled over without slowing to see what's happening?"

"Maybe she didn't want to get involved, or just

didn't care enough to ask questions."

"She said he owes her money," Petra said. "Unless she lied about that, she cares." She reached for her phone. "I want surveillance on Deetz's and Mozul's apartments. Something about her felt off." She dialed dispatch and put in a request for two plainclothes beat cops in unmarked vehicles to go to the apartment complex. "I need one to cover the front and one in the alley. I want to know everyone who goes in or out of either apartment."

"Got it," the dispatch operator said. "Jay and Stubbs are available. I'll have one of them call you once they are in place."

"Thanks." Petra disconnected the call a nano-second before her phone rang. She glanced at the caller ID then pushed the speaker phone icon to avoid having to repeat the conversation to Cody. "Hello, Cracker," she said to the officer charged with pinging Robin's phone. "What do you have for me?"

"You were right," Cracker said. "Mizz Marcato did call nine-one-one. The call only lasted a couple of seconds, but one of the two towers in the vicinity is equipped with directional antennae, and we were able to identify the direction of the phone's signal."

"How big an area are we looking at?" Petra said.

"Unless she has been moved, she's somewhere inside a four-mile radius at the western edge of town. I've drawn up a schematic." Cracker paused then added, "You want me to text it to you?"

"Not necessary. We're on our way in. I'll drop by your office when I get there, and you can go over the details."

"I'll be here," Cracker said as Petra broke the

connection.

"That's good news, right?" Cody said. "At least we'll have an idea where *not* to look,"

Petra twisted one side of her mouth into a demi-smile in recognition of her partner's obvious effort at encouragement, but her insides felt like she had just swallowed fifty pounds of wet cement. The city's industrial area located inside the four-mile radius at the western edge of town was home to at least a dozen junkyards, each one with an inventory of vehicles numbering in the hundreds, some, in the thousands. She and her team members would have to search countless trunks, and they had to do it within the next forty-eight to seventy-two hours. After that, the search would no longer be a rescue effort; it would become a recovery. The investigation would slim down to only a couple of detectives as the rest of the team returned to their own cases. By then, whatever had happened to Robin would be known to God alone.

Petra interrupted the downward-spiraling thoughts. Every ounce of her energy had to be laser-focused on the investigation.

"How're you on sleep?" Petra glanced sideways at her partner.

"I'm pretty wired," Cody said. "You know me, a slave to my coffee addiction. What do you need me to do?"

"Make a list of the rest of Deetz's known associates. If he is hiding out somewhere, he'll need help."

"Will do," Cody said.

"Good." Petra shook her head. "I'm surprised he wasn't on Google."

"He's living life on the down-low," Cody said. "Hate to say it, but that raises a red flag for me. Nobody escapes Google."

"Sad, but true," Petra said. "I'm amazed at the personal information people post on social media sites."

"A boon to investigators the world over." Cody cracked his knuckles. "I'll check out Mozul and Bradley as well, but I'll start with this Deetz character. His actions so far make him look guilty as sin. I mean, why would he show up in Robin's neighborhood in the middle of the night then take off when he saw the police?"

"It's possible he was in the neighborhood in hopes of getting into Banda's house, not Robin's." Petra glanced at Cody. "Deetz has done time for breaking and entering, and Banda owned a lot of expensive tools and equipment."

"Yeah, that's right," Cody said. "He could use all that to set up his own paint business, or hock it and pocket the cash."

"On the other hand," Petra said, "What's roiling my insides is Deetz's history of violence. Somewhere along the line, he learned that the way to gain or keep control of other people is through aggression. That moves him several ticks up on my person-of-interest meter."

Her lips compressed, Petra gripped the steering wheel and sped toward the main police station. Once she had studied Cracker's pinged grid, she would grab a three-hour catnap then meet the team for briefing before interviewing Quillan O'Farrell.

Although the chance of the coffee shop owner's having any helpful information was remote, Petra would carefully review his statement.

She was grasping at straws and knew it. But time was the enemy, and she could not afford to ignore even the tiniest possible clue.

Chapter Nineteen

After Dierdre engaged the deadbolt behind the departing cops, Deetz stepped around the heavy drapery next to her front door where he had been crouching. He smiled and patted her arm.

"You shoulda been in the movies, baby. That was some acting."

"Who says I was acting?" Dierdre said.

"Aww, come on now, you know you love me." Deetz puckered his lips and playfully kissed the air near the woman's face.

"Why are the cops looking for you?" Dierdre said. "What kind of trouble are you in?"

"It's just a minor misunderstanding." Deetz cut his eyes sideways at the woman who had proven so useful over his time in Albuquerque. "You know how cops are. Probably a parking ticket I forgot to pay."

"The cops don't send two detectives out in the middle of the night for parking tickets."

"I promise it's nothing," Deetz said.

His glance slid to the dozens of framed photographs and posters on Dierdre's walls. Arranged from the earliest to the latest, each echoed memories of her years in Vegas as *Garnette Redd*. A glossy print in which she stood center stage wearing a scarlet-sequined, tuxedo hung next to a nearly life-sized poster of her in front of a sixteen-foot metal sphere while wearing deep red motorcycle leathers and sitting astride a bright red Harley Davidson with silver flames painted along its side. The shiny scarlet helmet tucked under her arms matched her outfit. The look in her eyes was pure seduction.

Deetz found it hard to believe that the frowsy-haired woman standing in front of him and the one in the pictures were the same person. His upper lip curled as his gaze moved from the glamorous past to the present Dierdre. What was it that made some women think they could hide their age forever?

"You promised to take me away from here." Dierdre's eyelids lowered to half-mast, giving Deetz the uncomfortable feeling she had read his mind. "You said we'd move to Vegas once you got a house painting business up and running to the point you could sell out for a nice profit."

"Yeah, yeah." Deetz made a shushing motion with his hand. "Keep it down. The cops could still be outside." He turned toward the front door, half expecting the police to come busting in. "It's just a temporary change of plans, that's all."

"You wouldn't try to con me, would you?" Dierdre lightly stroked Deetz's cheek with her right hand. "I have been conned by some of the best and developed an allergy." With every stroke, the fingers pressed harder and harder into the flesh. "You said you needed money for a start-up, but that was months ago, and I don't see anything starting up."

"It takes time to build a new business." Deetz tried to pull his features into what he hoped was a reassuring smile. "Nothing has worked for me here. It's time to move on."

Especially since the local casinos are so tight-fisted. Four thousand dollars down, and the only thing to show for it was a made-in-China coffee cup with a casino logo on it.

"I'll get something solid going in Vegas then send for you. There's always construction going on in Sin City. A good painter can name his price."

"Sounds promising." Dierdre nodded once. "Vegas is a booming place, always has been."

Deetz fought back the smirk creeping across his face at what he considered the woman's determined gullibility. Why would he want to start a business? Why work when the world was full of women just waiting to give him their money in exchange for a little attention?

"If you're lying to me---" Dierdre was saying.

"Why would I lie to you?" Deetz reached up and pulled the woman's now claw-like fingers from his face. "You're the only woman I've ever really loved."

...and the money you keep throwing at me.

"You mean that?" Dierdre placed both arms around Deetz's neck and drew his head down for a kiss. "The difference in our ages doesn't matter to you?"

"Like I've said a hundred times," Deetz said, "I prefer a mature woman." He plastered what he hoped to be a reassuring smile on his face. "Besides, fifteen or twenty years isn't all that much difference where love is involved."

Dierdre grinned and moved closer, determined to kiss him.

"I got to get some sleep." Deetz wound his fingers in his lover's spiderweb hair, absently returned the kiss, then drew back. He fumbled in his pants pocket for his pickup keys then tossed them onto the coffee table. "I left my truck at the Cacahuate Bar. Do me a favor and wait until I'm gone, then go get it and park it at the rear of your lot, somewhere it can't be seen from the street." He looked intently at Dierdre. "But not until late tonight, after it's dark. You understand?"

"You left your truck at the bar? How did you get here?" Dierdre cocked her head and peered at Deetz. "Did another woman drive you?" Her face twisted into a mask of suspicion. "Is that where you were last night, with some other woman?"

"How many times do I have to tell you, there's no other woman." Deetz said. *Not yet.*

"If you want to play the field," Dierdre interrupted, "just let me know, and I'll bow out. There are some things I'm no good at sharing."

Deetz's face grew hot. Like a month-long monsoon that finally set off a village-covering mud slide, the events of the past twenty-four hours pulsed through him.

He had killed two people in the space of a few hours. He had been forced to scrap an attempt to get inside the Marcato woman's house to find his chewing gum, after which some old biddy had watched him haul ass out of her driveway. He had re-bruised his tailbone during the balled-up effort to break into Lou's apartment, and now here was this used-up old bimbo putting him on the spot, pumping him for answers, quizzing him.

Ignoring the tiny portion of his brain that warned him to keep his cool, Deetz snarled. He grabbed Dierdre's shoulders and dug his fingers into the flesh.

"Stop haranguing me. How many times do I have to tell you I hate being harangued?"

Dierdre's lips twisted into a grimace and her eyes narrowed. "You're hurting me," she said.

"You're hurting me," Deetz mimicked in a whiney voice. "You think that hurts?"

"It'd be in your best interests to let go of my arm," Dierdre said, her voice soft.

A warning light finally went off in Deetz's head, and he loosened his grip. He could not afford to alienate his cash cow lover, not when he had less than fifty dollars to his name. He held his open hands up as though warding off a charging rhinoceros.

Dierdre massaged her shoulders and shot a hard look in his direction.

"I'm sorry, baby." Deetz shook his head and tried to assume a contrite look. "All the stress is getting to me. I watched my boss die in a terrible accident yesterday, a guy I really looked up to. He was like a father figure to me, took me under his wing. Seeing his neck sliced open and then all that red blood mixing with the yellow paint really messed with my head."

Dierdre studied his face for several seconds. "Yeah," she finally said. "Life can have some sharp edges, that's for sure."

"I'll find a good job in Vegas and set us up in a nice apartment then call you. You can sell my pickup and this property then come to Vegas."

"You want me to sell your truck?" Dierdre said. "How will you get to Vegas?"

"I'll take the bus," Deetz said, searching for rational explanation. "The summer in Vegas can get to over one hundred twenty degrees. The leaking radiator in that old pickup wouldn't last a week."

"How am I going to sell it when the title is in your

name?"

"The title is in the glove compartment," Deetz interrupted. "I'll sign it over to you before I leave." He smiled at the ease with which the lies had come and arranged his face into a mischievous look. "Considering the way Albuquerque is growing, you should get a nice price for both the pickup and your place."

"Better not wait too long to call," Dierdre said. "I might just sell your pickup and keep the money."

"Kelly Blue Book says it's worth about three thousand." Deetz laughed, hoping to lighten the mood.

"That would cover three out of the four you owe me."

Deetz grinned outwardly, but inwardly he sneered.

The old bimbo was welcome to the hunk of junk. Once Deetz got going with Mister Z, he would buy himself a metallic orange, late model Corvette, just like he had always dreamed. Women would flock to him. He would exude success.

"I'll make it up to you, baby." Deetz twisted his mouth into the grin that someone once told him made women melt.

Instead of melting, however, Dierdre squared her jaw. Deetz's earlier lapse in impulse control clearly still uppermost in her mind, she said, "I *will* find you if you try to stiff me. I still have contacts in Vegas, powerful contacts."

Deetz assumed a hurt expression. "Come on, now. I have never even looked at another woman since I met you. You're the one I love."

All you gotta do is tell 'em you love 'em, Boy. They'll put up with anything you dish out as long as you tell 'em you love 'em. The only words Deetz's old man ever said that had proven over and over to be true.

"You do know I love you, don't you?" Deetz said.

The look on Dierdre's face softened, and her body language relaxed. She stepped to a fake electrical outlet in the living room, slid the cover to one side, extracted a wad of hundred-dollar bills from inside the hidden compartment then handed the stash to Deetz.

"Thanks, baby." He stuffed the money into his pants pocket, turned and started down a short hallway. "Wake me up at seven."

Chapter Twenty

For the hundredth time in a space of a couple of minutes, Robin ran her index finger along the insides of the barely damp moccasins. She tentatively touched the cloth strips, and although the fabric was moist, she could not tell how much melting snow was making its way down the strips toward the shoes.

"Aargh," Robin bellowed. Heat rising from her ribcage into her neck and face, she pounded her fists against the trunk's roof and kicked the back seat.

While she had not expected rivulets of water to course down the strips, she had hoped for more than a few drops.

Take a deep breath, Robbie Girl. Think.

"I love you, Mom, but that's easy for you to say."

What do you know about your surroundings?

"I'm locked inside a freezing trunk; the weather forecast is bad; I'm hungry and thirsty; my head feels like it's about to explode; mice have discovered me; I may have tetanus, and I'm pissed as hell."

What did you hate about the snow when you were growing up?

"Whatever in the world are you talking about?"

I said---

"Okay, okay. I hated that in our part of New Mexico, we hardly ever got much snow. If it *did* snow, the sun came out and melted it within a few hours. I

123

would spend half a day scraping up enough muddy, twig- and leaf-filled slush to make a scrappy, skinny little snowman."

And? Her mother's memory interrupted.

Robin stared at the tiny rays of light filtering in through the pinholes then mentally snapped her fingers.

Once the sun rose, the trunk's metal top and the rear window would grow warm enough to melt their snowy covering. When the sun went down, the liquid would freeze into a solid sheet of ice, but for a few hours, she should be able to harvest some of the dripping water.

"Two moccasins and strips of cloth," she muttered. "Look, Mom, I've invented a water catchment system. Maybe I'll get a patent when I get out of here."

Robin carefully positioned the shoes. She would set her alarm for thirty minutes; that should be long enough to test her *system*.

She peered at her timepiece and groaned. The watch face had gone completely dark.

"Great," Robin said. "I can't set the alarm in this darkness."

Mississippi.

"I'm fighting for my life, and you want to play a state name game?" Robin said. "I'll see your Mississippi and raise you a New Mexico."

How long does it take to say Mississippi?

"About one second. Your point?"

Your internal counter still works. How many seconds in thirty minutes?

"Two thousand, give or take," Robin said.

Then what's the holdup?

"One Mississippi, two Mississippi, three

124

Mississippi," Robin began. As soon as she uttered the words, "two thousand Mississippi," she stuck the tip of her right index finger inside one shoe.

An electrical charge shot through her mid-section as her finger swished through between an eighth to a quarter of an inch of icy water. While the other shoe proved to hold a smaller amount, the cloth leading to it was wet. It was just a matter of time.

Careful not to spill a single precious drop, Robin lifted the shoes one at a time, placed the heels against her lower lip, and allowed the cold liquid to pour over her dry tongue. The water tasted like the rubber insole smelled, but Robin didn't mind.

She tugged the two strips of cloth from the holes, sucked the moisture from the fabric, then carefully returned them to their respective places.

Not enough water to keep her alive, but it would buy her a few hours.

Now you're cooking, Robbie Girl.

"Oh, really?"

Snottiness is unbecoming, young lady. Where there's life, there's possibility.

Robin sniffed and opened her mouth to offer a searing retort just as her watch alarm called her to stretch her legs.

Mechanically, she pointed her toes and counted to fifteen then worked her way upward, tightening each muscle group as she went. By the time she got to her neck muscles, her body had warmed noticeably.

She interrupted the recurring thought that her behavior was equivalent to whistling past the cemetery at midnight, an exercise in futility, a way to pass the time that neither affected her survival nor offered a means of escape. The bottom line was no matter how long she worked at keeping her strength up, she would never kick her way out of the trunk.

Keep on the sunny side, always on the sunny side, keep on the sunny side of life.

The words and melody of the song Robin's mom used to sing while doing the dishes floated into her memory, and she sighed.

"Tell me, oh mother of mine, just exactly what is the sunny side of being coldcocked and left for dead in an abandoned trunk?"

Sarcasm is also unbecoming.

Robin harrumphed then returned to her muscle stretches. At least having a schedule gave her something to do.

If nothing else, she would be the most limber cadaver-in-a-trunk in history.

Chapter Twenty-One

Petra's wristwatch alarm pulled her from sleep in the main police station's rest area. Scrubbing at her burning eyes with the palms of her hands, she sat on the edge of the cot hastily set up only three hours earlier. More sleep would have been nice, but she could not allow herself the luxury of one minute more. She would rest after Robin was found.

She hurried to her personal locker in the gym and restroom area where she kept workout clothes, tennis shoes, bath items, and a towel. After she showered and dressed, she blew her hair dry and put on lip gloss. She stepped into the briefing room just as her team members were taking their seats, weariness, concern, and determination etched every face.

Petra looked around the room as she brought her teammates up to speed on what she and Cody had learned. Then she opened the floor to feedback.

One young officer raised his hand. "Forensics has finished inspection of Banda's air compressor and determined someone tampered with it recently, based on the freshness of the tool markings. Consensus is that whoever did it couldn't know *when* the thing would blow, but it was just a matter of time before it *would* blow."

"Okay," Petra said. "That means we're investigating a suspicious death as well as an abduction and possible attempted murder. We need to find out who tampered with the compressor."

"Who had access to the equipment?" the officer asked.

"Banda and his employee, certainly," Petra said. "The compressor was too heavy to remove from the truck's bed, so any passerby could get to it once the pickup was parked at a job site. All anyone would have to do was wait for Banda and his employee to go inside the customer's house."

"Do we know if anyone held a grudge against Banda?" another officer said.

"At this point, we don't know much about him or his business," Petra said. "But we will interview his grown kids when they get into town. And we'll be interviewing his customers." She looked at an officer. "Do we have DNA results from the chewing gum found in Robin's house?"

"Not yet," the officer said. "I was told it could be within the next few hours."

An officer nicknamed Toto raised his hand. "We've finished canvassing the rest of Robin Marcato's neighborhood. Other than Mizz Bibble, no one saw or heard anything out of the ordinary."

"Do we have anything on the traffic cams?" Petra said.

"The Automated License Readers on Central Avenue caught the pickup you described as it travelled east just before ten o'clock last night," the detective checking area cameras said. "The same vehicle returned around twelve. The driver, a Ronnie Deetz according to Department of Motor Vehicle records, was alone during the first sighting, but he had a passenger coming back.

We lost him once he got into a residential area, but I'll check surrounding businesses for closed circuit TV."

"Could you see the passenger well enough to describe him?" Petra said.

"Oh yeah." The officer nodded. "He was a balding, heavy-set male of about the same age as the driver. He was wearing a blue work shirt with what appeared to be a company patch on the front pocket. I'm working on identifying the logo."

"Good work," Petra said. "Text me the location where the pickup was last seen. Maybe we'll get lucky and track down the passenger. We could be looking at two perpetrators rather than one."

"I sent Tex the schematic generated from pinging Robin's call," Cracker said. "He marked the area off into quadrants and has Nellie up and recording. He'll call if he spots anything."

"Cody's making a list of Deetz's known associates. He and I will pursue that after I take O'Farrell's statement this morning. Anyone else?" After a short silence, and when no one added anything more, Petra said, "Thank you all for your hard work."

The detectives murmured among themselves as they filed from the briefing room. Each of them nodded toward Petra in unspoken support as they exited.

Cody stepped away from the wall against which he had been leaning and walked toward Petra. "I found a couple of interesting things online, Rocky." He held up his phone so Petra could see the screen. "First, the apartment manager's social media accounts indicate she's got the hots for one of her residents, someone she calls *Pollock*. She spends a lot of time gushing about him. He makes her feel sixteen again, yadda, yadda."

"Pollock?" Petra said. "I don't remember seeing that name on her lodger's list."

"It's not."

"The only person I've ever heard of with that name was an American painter named Jackson Pollock."

"Yeah," Cody bobbed his head, "and our friend Deetz makes his living as a house painter."

"That would put a new spin on things."

"So, are we looking at three perpetrators?" Cody said. "Deetz, Bradley, and Mozul?"

"Anything's possible."

"Maybe Deetz left his pickup somewhere and walked back to his apartment," Cody said. "Maybe he knows we are looking for him and is hiding out."

"That's also possible, especially in light of how Reena-Belle said he reacted to seeing the crime scene lab."

"Curiouser and curiouser." Cody looked at Petra. "Any word from Jay yet?"

"He called just after I got back to the station. He spotted Mozul getting into a taxi and asked if I wanted him to follow her or stay put. I told him to follow and let me know where she gets off. Stubbs is sitting tight in the alley behind Deetz's apartment in case anyone tries to go in or leave the back way."

"Why would Mozul take a taxi?" Cody said. "This is Albuquerque, not New York or D.C. She must own a car, why not just drive herself?"

"Exactly."

"Maybe she had to catch a flight," Cody said.

"Jay said she didn't have any luggage with her," Petra said. "We'll need to talk to her again." She pointed at Cody's phone. "You said you found a *couple* of things?"

"Yeah, look at this," Cody scrolled through several screens on his phone then held it toward Petra.

"You wanted me to see a blurry selfie of Mozul with two men?" Petra said.

"I think the guy on her left is Deetz, but look at the guy on her right," Cody said. "Doesn't he match the description the street cams caught of Deetz's passenger? He's a bald guy wearing a blue workman's uniform."

"Good catch." Petra smiled at her partner. "The background looks like a bar. Get that photo enhanced. Maybe we can figure out where this was taken. Then get a blow-up of that logo."

"I'm on it." Cody slipped his phone into his shirt pocket and left.

Petra pulled her phone from its pouch, opened the screen, and touched the message icon next to Robin's name. Although she knew in her head that the message would be unread, her heart demanded she send it.

I'm making progress. Hang tough.

Petra glanced at her watch. Fifteen minutes before O'Farrell was due to arrive, just enough time to chugalug a gallon of much-needed coffee.

She strode toward the staff kitchen.

Chapter Twenty-Two

Lou dreamed he was trying to fly, but every time he got a few feet off the ground, no matter how hard he flapped his arms, he lost altitude. The sky filled with telephone poles strung with thousands of wires. He frantically tried to steer clear of the lines and opened his mouth to scream for help as he plummeted toward earth, but no sound came. As usual, he jerked awake just before hitting the ground.

Breaths coming in gasps and heart pounding, Lou raised a trembling hand to wipe sweat from his face, grateful to be awake.

With little variation over the years, the nightmare was what psychologists call a *repeating dream.* Lou's therapist said the dreams were the subconscious mind's way of telling him his life was out of control then suggested Alcoholics Anonymous meetings might help. Lou had attended a few, but the twelve steps had proven too painful to pursue. A binge-drinker, he had tried going cold turkey but never managed to stay sober for longer than a work week. Even three marriages had not dispelled the hole in his soul that no amount of booze could fill -- the feeling that he could never measure up.

From atop the cardboard box doubling as a nightstand beside the mattress on which Lou slept, the insistent ringing of his phone kept him from falling back to sleep. More to stop the noise than out of a desire to talk to anyone, he grabbed the infernal machine he had forgotten to turn off the night before. He peered at the screen then punched the green answer icon when his boss's name showed.

"Hello, Mister Haynie," Lou mumbled.

"It's about time." His boss's voice sliced through the ether and caromed around inside Lou's pounding head like a ball bearing shot from its stainless-steel housing. "I need you to get to the yard and pull three cars for transport sometime between now and Monday afternoon."

Background noise competed with Haynie's voice, transforming his sentences into barely decipherable gibberish. People laughed and talked; their voices punctuated by recorded Christmas carols some joyful nincompoop had set at a decibel level high enough to start a snow avalanche.

"I said, would you like some coffee cake?" A woman said, her voice, high pitched and strident.

Good King Wenceslas looked out on the Feast of Stephen...

"Sorry, Mister Haynie, what did you say?" Lou blinked several times to kickstart his tear ducts.

"Turn off that infernal noise," Haynie bellowed at someone. "It's enough to drive a wooden man around the bend."

After several seconds, the music was turned off, and Haynie continued. "You've been begging for overtime, so now's your chance to get double time for half a day's work. You remember my telling you a couple of collectors have been looking at some of our inventory?"

"Yessir," Lou said.

"One of them just called. He's willing to pay us to haul three old junks to Ruidoso."

"Which ones?" Lou said.

"I'll text you the details."

Lou yawned noisily.

"For the love of Mike, it's the middle of the morning. Are you just waking up?"

"I've been fighting a cold." Lou cleared his throat. "I just need a little bed rest."

Someone turned the music back on in evident defiance of Haynie's command.

Bring me mead and bring me wine. Bring me pine logs hither.

Lou's mind conjured up images of his boss's bustling holiday household: kids running amok, smells of food cooking, family, laughter.

"*Give it back*," some kid screamed. "*Mommy, he won't give me my...*"

Lou moved the phone a few inches from his ear and glanced through the open kitchen door at the half-empty bottle of cheap booze on the counter.

He sighed. For him, Christmas would be just another day.

"The guy customizes old cars," Lou's boss was saying. "I'm selling three complete junks in one fell swoop. Merry Christmas to me."

"*Can't I open just one, please, please, please,*" a little girl whined.

"*I said no,*" a woman said. "*If you're good, you can open one gift on Christmas Eve.*"

"When does he want them?" Lou rubbed crusty flakes of sleep from his eyes with the fingertips of his free hand.

"What?"

"I said when does he want them?"

"Turn that infernal noise off or no one gets dessert," Haynie yelled, his voice somewhat muffled as he evidently placed a hand over the phone's microphone. He repositioned the phone then added, "Tuesday afternoon, but it's a four-hour drive one way, so you'll need to load them on the hauler sometime between now and Tuesday morning."

"Monday's Christmas." Lou coughed. He gritted his teeth against the subsequent surge of pain in his head then dragged the back of his hand across his mouth and licked his dry lips.

"That is correct, Sherlock. By the same token, tomorrow is Christmas Eve. Do you want the job, or not? I can always get one of the other guys."

"No, no," Lou said. "I can use the overtime."

"Good." The boss paused then added, "Like I said, it should only take three or four hours to load the hauler and get it ready to go. If you start the drive early Tuesday morning, you can make it to Ruidoso, make the drop-off, and then get back to the shop before closing time. I don't care which day you load up; that's your call. But I'm only paying overtime for half a day."

God rest ye merry gentlemen…

"You got a delivery address?" Lou said.

"I'll text everything as soon as I hang up." A *click* followed by the sudden cessation of sound announced the call had been terminated.

Lou turned his phone off to prevent further disturbances and tossed it onto the ratty bed cover. He would check his boss's text later, after he'd sobered up a bit.

Careful not to jar his pounding head, he lowered himself onto his mattress then stared at the ceiling. He closed his eyes but was unable to fall asleep as the echoes of Christmas carols played on a loop in his head.

Maybe he would call his best buddy later. Deetz hadn't said anything about having plans for the holidays, so maybe he would welcome the company. He might even be willing to stand a few rounds of Christmas cheer for a buddy.

Lou wrapped the pillow around his head and closed his eyes. Monday would be soon enough to load the hauler.

Chapter Twenty-Three

At five minutes before nine Saturday morning, Quillan O'Farrell stepped through the front door of the main police station and glanced around the small waiting area. Two chairs sat against the wall just inside the door, while a waist-level counter topped with thick, clear plexiglass prevented further entry into the building beyond. Behind the partition, a young female gatekeeper sat at a desk and studied three large monitors that Quil suspected were for surveilling the building's periphery. Two cameras affixed to opposite corners of the ceiling pointed at the front entrance, a sad testament to public service in the twenty-first century.

The young woman looked up from the monitors and smiled. She asked to see some identification then patiently waited while Quil fished his driver's license out of his wallet and passed it through a circular hole in the plexiglass.

"I'm here to see Detective Rooney," Quil said.

"I'll let her know you're here. You can sit over there." The woman nodded toward the chairs then returned her attention to her desk. She lifted the handset of a desktop telephone, punched the keypad, spoke briefly into the phone then replaced it in its cradle. "She'll be right down."

Within a couple of minutes, Detective Rooney

opened the steel door located next to the gatekeeper's domain. Sad, tired eyes and tight lips telegraphed her exhaustion, and worry for Robin.

"Thank you for being on time." Rooney held the door open and motioned for Quil to follow her. "We'll be in the second room on the right." She escorted him down a hall and into the indicated interview room then motioned toward one of two chairs facing each other across a small rectangular wooden table.

Quil took a seat and looked around the room. A couple of high-tech-looking electronic gizmos sat on a small table next to the wall, while a camera hanging from the ceiling aimed its cyclops-eye toward the chair in which he sat.

"This interview will be recorded," the detective said. "Both audio and video are voice activated, so if you're ready."

"I'm ready," Quil said.

For the next few minutes, Detective Rooney asked, among other things, where Quil was and what he was doing when he got Robin's texts and how long he had known her. She ended the interview by asking if Robin had ever mentioned anyone who might be angry with or hold a grudge against her.

"I've been racking my mind for any detail that might help," Quil said. "But we weren't really close. We probably never said more than two or three words to each other outside of our church work. The only thing I can figure is that she texted me by accident."

Once the short session was terminated, the detective stood and motioned toward the door.

"Thank you for the cherry tart and coffee," Petra said as she and Quil exited the interview room. "They were delicious."

"You're most welcome, Detective."

Rooney stopped walking and turned toward him. "Did I detect just a bit of almond flavoring in the cherry filling and butter in the coffee?"

"Yes to both," Quil said. "My mom used to add almond extract to her cherry pies, much requested at family get-togethers. The butter in the coffee was an experiment."

"The tart crust was perfect, flakey. It reminded me of my grandma's." Detective Rooney nodded and added, "And I really liked the coffee."

"The secret to the crust is cold butter and ice water," Quil said as he exited through the steel door the detective was holding open. "Any time you or your partner stop by Higher Grounds, there'll be a cup of coffee and pastry for you."

"I'll remember that." Detective Rooney smiled. "Thanks." She stepped back through the door and allowed it to close behind her.

As Quil walked across the parking lot toward his car, he tried to remember details from the interview. But all he could think about was the way the harsh light in the interview room flashed off the tall, slender detective's pixie-ish, light-brown hair, and the way her huge brown eyes studied his face as he answered her questions. Mostly, though, he remembered her smile.

Maybe after his bakery business grew enough to hire more help, and he had more time, he could ask her to dinner.

Quil snorted. How could he even consider starting a relationship?

Love was a crapshoot; one at which his track record had proven him woefully inept.

Chapter Twenty-Four

Robin tilted her head back and poured water from her shoe into her mouth. This time, she had counted to three thousand before allowing herself to drink. Nearly an hour, yet she had only managed to collect a mouthful of water. Either the sky was growing overcast, and any melting snow was in the process of re-freezing, or she had already harvested all the snow immediately surrounding the holes.

Struggling to ignore the voice of despair running in a loop through her mind, she kept telling herself someone would find her. Or she would find a way to MacGyver herself out of the steel prison if she could hang on long enough.

Did I ever tell you that your grandfather knew when he was going to die, Robbie Girl? Almost like he was prescient.

"Yes, Mom, you did, several times."

During one Thanksgiving visit, after my siblings and I were grown and had left home, he called us together and told us it would be the last time we saw him alive. We grew concerned about his mental condition and spent a lot of phone time trying to figure out what to do, but within a month he was gone, just as he predicted. A drunk driver plowed into him.

"Are you saying I'll have some kind of precognitive twinge when my time is up?"

I'm just telling you how it was with your grandfather.

Robin chewed her thumbnail and inventoried her senses. Was that feeling at the base of her skull an after-effect of her concussion, or was it a forewarning of her impending death? Was it time to make peace with her Creator?

Maybe her life *was* all over but the crying. Maybe her short-lived joy at discovering how to syphon a few teaspoons of melting snow had merely been a refusal to look at reality.

Instead of prolonging her life, maybe she was prolonging her death.

Robin shuddered as horrific images pulsed through her mind, images from a documentary of the locations in the United States called *body farms* where donated human cadavers were subjected to all sorts of environments in pursuit of forensic knowledge. She wondered if the research scientists at any of those locations had put a corpse into a car's trunk, then checked the progression of decomposition as the seasons changed.

Robin's imagination turned to visions of a future in which some poor, unlucky soul opened the trunk in which she was imprisoned. Would the discovery traumatize her finder, forever altering his life?

Would she be found early on, her body freshly curled into a fetal position, and her filmed-over dead eyes staring into eternity? Or would no one discover her until the insects and carnivorous animals had completed their recycling efforts and only a waxy skeleton remained?

With shaking fingers, Robin wiped tears from her

cheeks.

Memories of finding her husband's body flooded her with compassion for whoever was fated to find hers, and she sent up a quick prayer for that person. As if it were five minutes ago instead of over a year, the memory of John's precious, still form lying peacefully in their bed caught at Robin's throat and she whimpered.

There had been no warning, no clue to his impending death. Assuming him to be asleep, Robin had gone for her habitual early morning walk. When she returned, she was surprised that he was not in the kitchen preparing breakfast as usual, surprised not to smell the aromas of brewing coffee and toasting bread.

A perpetual optimist, John had been robust and overflowing with *joie de vivre*. But his traitorous brain had harbored an undetected aneurysm that simply, and without preamble, blew out his life's candle.

It's not over until it's over, Robbie Girl.

"I may not make it out of here, you know," Robin said to her mother's memory.

Never give up. Don't you ever give up. I didn't raise you to just lie down and quit.

"But you gave up, Mom," Robin whispered. "You stopped fighting, and then you left me, just like Dad and John."

I didn't give up until I had done everything I could, not before trying every medicine and procedure available. Don't you dare…

"Okay, Mom," Robin said. She took a deep breath and noisily blew it out through her nose. "Message received."

She repositioned her moccasins under the cloth strips and began to count.

That's more like it.

Chapter Twenty-Five

At nine o'clock Saturday morning, Dierdre Mozul retrieved the keys to Deetz's pickup from the coffee table where he had thrown them. Careful to make no sound, she tip-toed from her apartment, locked the door behind her, and hurried through the deepening snow drifts to a waiting taxi that would take her to the Cacahuate Bar.

Although her lover had asked her to waken him at seven, he had looked so peaceful in his sleep, she could not bring herself to disturb him. Besides, she would only be gone a few minutes. By the time he woke up, she would have made a nice breakfast for them to share. Then they would sip coffee in front of her fireplace and make plans.

Dierdre smiled to herself in anticipation of her future with Deetz. She wasn't overly concerned about the money he owed her. Having someone in her life was worth ten times the amount she'd given him.

She had, in fact, suspected it was her generosity that kept him linked to her. As a result, she would be the first person to admit that Deetz was less than perfect. But neither was she.

Perfect was a myth, something only found in fairy tales. While some people might suggest Deetz was more of a gigolo than a true love, Dierdre told herself his motivation for staying with her did not matter.

Every human on the face of the earth had glitches. Part of building a relationship included sifting through a prospective lover's quirks then deciding whether to settle in for the long haul or ditch that person and move on to the next prospect. Dierdre had long ago learned to pick and choose the hills upon which she was willing to die emotionally and romantically. While her depth of feeling for Deetz ran shallower than she had initially hoped, having an imperfect someone was better than having no one. She had long ago stopped looking for mister right and learned to be content with the occasional mister right-here-right-now. People died of loneliness.

"Whatever gets you through," she murmured.

"What's that?" the cab driver said, his gaze shifting to the rearview mirror.

"Nothing. Just talking to myself."

"I do that all the time," the driver said. "They say it's only a problem when you start answering yourself." He emitted a hearty belly-jiggling laugh and made eye contact with Dierdre in the rearview mirror.

Dierdre offered the requisite chuckle at the guy's attempt to establish a connection with his paying fare.

"Are you sure you want me to leave you here?" The cab driver's voice broke into Dierdre's thoughts. "This is a rough neighborhood."

"That's my boyfriend's truck." Dierdre pointed toward the vehicle parked at the rear of the otherwise empty parking lot. "I'll only be here long enough to get it."

"I'll wait until you start the engine," the cab driver said. "A lovely lady such as yourself shouldn't be on her own out here."

Dierdre thanked the driver. She paid the fare, including a nice tip in recognition of the man's blatant flattery, then hurried to the pickup.

Humming the melody to a golden oldie, she drove to her apartment and parked next to Lou's pickup at the rear of the lot, exactly as her lover had commanded.

She would kiss Deetz awake and tell him she had already taken care of his pickup. He would be grateful.

Smiling in anticipation, Dierdre unlocked her front door.

Chapter Twenty-Six

After Petra completed her conversation with Quillan O'Farrell, she uploaded the videoed interview into an evidence locker where it would be saved in the event Robin's or Banda's cases came to trial. While O'Farrell had been unable to shed any light on Robin's abduction, he was her last known contact, and that made him important to the investigation.

Petra had been struck by O'Farrell's concern for Robin, especially since the two could not be described as close friends. She would share as much of the investigation with him as she could. Perhaps she would drop by his shop and give him the occasional update. Maybe after Robin was found, she would stop in under the guise of asking him for a recipe or two.

Petra shook herself and interrupted the chain of thought. O'Farrell was probably married or in a committed relationship. While he seemed like one of the good guys, she knew all too well that most people carry a virtual knapsack of masks for strategic use as dictated by perceived need.

Taking a trip to visit wealthy, ailing Auntie Grace? The mask of *Kind Concern* should impress the old biddy. Attending a promotion party for a despised co-worker? The no bridge-burning, *Good Luck* mask would be appropriate. Then there was the *Defer to me for I Know all Things* mask useful with underlings, and the *You are Amazing* mask for face-to-face meetings with an arrogant, ego-centric boss.

However, in Petra's experience, it was not the masks themselves that posed the major problem. It was the inability to know what lay concealed beneath them until it was too late.

"Focus," Petra muttered as she pulled her phone from its holder. She was in the process of punching in Cody's number when it vibrated.

"Rooney," she said.

"It's Jay here. The Mozul woman took the taxi to a bar on Central. She got into a pickup that matched the description of Deetz's vehicle then drove it back to her apartment."

"Was anyone with her?"

"Nope, just her," Jay said. "No stops along the way."

"Good work," Petra said. "Where are you now?"

"Back at the apartments. Stubbs said no one has gone into or come out the back of either Deetz's or Mozul's as far as he can tell."

"Okay." Petra glanced at her watch. "You guys sit tight for the time being."

"Will do."

Petra broke the connection then keyed Cody's number into her phone.

"Hey, Rocky," Cody answered. "I was just about to call you. Lou Bradley still doesn't answer his door, so he's either not home or he's hiding out. I got a description of his pickup from the department of motor vehicles." He muffled a cough then added, "You remember the one we saw behind Deetz's apartment complex? I'd lay odds that's Bradley's."

"Sounds like a Nascar version of musical chairs," Petra said. "Mozul knows both Ronnie Deetz and Lou Bradley, and now she's driven Deetz's pickup to her apartment and parked it next to Bradley's."

Cody whistled through his teeth. "So, where are Deetz and Bradley, and why are their vehicles stashed at Mozul's place?"

"Those are good questions."

"You figure all three of them might be connected to Banda's death and your friend's abduction?" Cody paused then did a noisy intake of air. "Hey, maybe for some reason Mozul did away with both men and is in the process of cleaning up any loose ends. I mean, think about it, neither Deetz nor Bradley can be located."

"We have to consider that possibility," Petra said. "But we haven't found anything that connects either Mozul or Bradly to Robin and her dead neighbor. Besides, it seems likely that Deetz has gone into hiding, based on Reena-Belle's call."

"The only person linking all three of our suspects is Deetz," Cody said. "And he definitely had access to Banda's air compressor."

"Deetz is not the only person of interest on my list," Petra said. "But right now, he is leading the pack."

"We know Mozul is hooked on Deetz, but is she the type to get tangled up in a kidnapping or murder?" Cody yawned then noisily took a couple of swallows of something.

"I think we have to consider her and Bradley as possible accomplices," Petra said. "Did you see the look on Bradley's face in Mozul's selfie? His eyes were riveted on her like a kid looking through the window of a candy store."

"People do strange and sometimes horrific things in the name of love," Cody said before loudly sipping then swallowing.

"True," Petra said. *As she knew too well, frustrated love could erupt into something vile and terrifying.*

"But," Cody said, interrupting Petra's train of thought, "none of Mozul's online posts indicate that Bradley is anything more than an acquaintance. It's Deetz she's into. And Deetz was not only Banda's employee, but he showed up in the neighborhood in the middle of the night then took off like a bat out of hell when he spotted the crime lab, according to Reena-Belle."

"Still circumstantial," Petra said. "But I'll call for someone to sit on Bradley's apartment. Meanwhile, I've called Dispatch to start background checks into Mozul and Bradley. We should have something within the next couple of hours."

"What do you want to do while that's percolating?"

"We need to talk to Mozul again," Petra said. "Although she did not outright lie to us, she failed to mention her relationship with Deetz." She glanced at her watch. "Meet me at her apartment."

"I'm on my way," Cody said.

Petra shut down the call, slipped on her down-filled jacket, and hurried to the parking garage. As she opened her car door, movement from her periphery caught her attention. She took in a quick breath as a blur of black shot across the garage floor within a few feet of her.

"Just a cat in search of someplace warm to roost," she muttered.

Just a cat, this time.

After commanding herself to stop jumping at shadows, Petra stepped into her car, put the key into the ignition, and drove toward Mozul's apartment.

Chapter Twenty-Seven

Deetz drifted awake to the sound of keys turning in a lock. A door opened then closed, *shush*-ing as it raked across thick pile carpet. He yawned, stretched, and rubbed the sleep from his eyes. Bright daylight filtered through sheer fabric panels covering Dierdre's bedroom window, too bright for seven o'clock on a winter morning.

He peered at his wristwatch. The air whooshed out of his lungs, and he jumped out of bed.

"Dierdre," Deetz yelled. "I told you to wake me up at seven." He pulled his trousers from the chair onto which he had tossed them a few hours earlier. "Dierdre," he hollered as he strode across the bedroom and into the living room.

"Not so loud." Dierdre turned from the door she'd just latched and held an index finger against her lips. "Someone will hear you yelling and call the cops." A playful smile lit her face.

"Where the hell have you been?" Deetz said through tight lips. "It's almost nine-thirty."

"You told me to go get your pickup, so I did." The happy expression on Dierdre's face melted, and she threw Deetz's pickup keys onto the coffee table. "What are you so pissed about?"

"Did the cops see you?" Deetz said.

"Cops?" Dierdre furrowed her brow. "What are

you fired up about?"

"I'll tell you what I'm fired up about, you dumb bimbo. I told you to wait until after dark to get the pickup. What if you were followed?" Deetz hurried to the front window and pulled back the curtains. He peered down the street, relieved at the absence of sirens or flashing cop car lights.

His attention was drawn to a black SUV parked on the street across from the apartment complex's circular drive. Its driver, a youngish male, periodically glanced toward the apartments then lowered his gaze, studying something either in his lap or in his hand.

A chill crackled up Deetz's spine. One of many by-products of his past brushes with the law was the ability to spot a plainclothes cop on a stakeout.

The question was who was the cop watching?

While it was possible that he was tracking one of Dierdre's low-life tenants to execute an arrest warrant, Deetz had a sinking feeling some cop had spotted Dierdre driving his pickup, followed her, and called it in. The guy was probably waiting for Deetz to show up and bring him in for questioning. One question would lead to another, and the next thing he knew, he'd be hauled off to jail.

"Dumb bimbo?" Dierdre's frown deepened.

Deetz jerked away from the window and turned toward the woman who suddenly looked the same age as her birth certificate. "Excuse me," he sneered. "Did I say that out loud?"

"I'm a lot of things," Dierdre said, "but dumb isn't one." Her upper lip curled, and she added, "Besides, look who's talking. You are the one hiding from the police. What I want to know is why?"

The needle on Deetz's impulse control governor shot into the red zone, but he didn't care. Hands clenching and unclenching, he strode toward Dierdre, gripped the woman's shoulders, and shook her. "What did you say?" he said through gritted teeth, a shake punctuating each word. "Did you just call me dumb?"

Dierdre's eyes opened wide enough for the whites to show all around as her head flopped back and forth like a bobble-head toy.

The sight stirred memories buried deep in Deetz's psyche, images of his old man smacking his mother around, flashes of his mother cringing as the old man took control, the look on his dad's face announcing he was the boss.

At the time, Deetz had hated his old man for what some would call abuse. But over the succeeding years, he chose to think of it as a sign of strength. Nobody messed with his old man and got away with it.

"You're pathetic, you know that?" Deetz said. "Pathetic and used up. Did you honestly think that inch-thick pancake makeup would make you look twenty again? Huh?" He snorted, and flecks of spit flew from his mouth. "Has that pea brain of yours never wondered why I have to close my eyes every time we kiss? Here's a news flash, it's not out of passion."

Dierdre swiped Deetz's saliva from her forehead with the back of her hand and stared at him with an expression on her face like a universal truth suddenly dawned on her.

Again, something in Deetz's head yelled for him to back off, but by then he was incapable of doing anything but hammer on.

"All I asked you to do was wake me up at seven

and wait until after dark tonight to get my pickup. It was just a simple request. But you're so smart. You drove my pickup around in broad daylight, an open invitation for the cops to follow you." Deetz pulled one hand from Dierdre's shoulder and fisted it with every intention of smacking the offended look off the woman's face. "What part of *if the cops find me, I'm screwed* did you not understand?"

Dierdre looked at Deetz's raised fist and stiffened.

He felt the woman's shoulder muscles tighten. Before he had time to recognize her intentions, she raised her hands to either side of his head and slapped her palms hard against his ears.

The force of the blow compressed the air inside Deetz's ear canals, painfully concussing his eardrums. His ears ringing, his mouth flew open at the sheer unexpectedness of the attack.

Surprisingly agile for her age, Dierdre hopped back out of his reach.

"You nasty bitch," Deetz said. "That was a mistake."

Dierdre snarled and hissed like something feral. Narrowing her eyes, she clenched her fists and shifted her weight onto her left leg.

At Dierdre's change of posture, Deetz's internal warning siren sounded, but it was too late. In the next nano-second, Dierdre kneed him in the groin.

Deetz yelped, doubled over, and fell to the floor where he lay moaning and writhing.

Dierdre stooped over him. "I enjoyed loving you, Deetz, but I'm not *anyone's* punching bag."

She jammed a hand into his pants pocket, retrieved the wad of money she had given him the night before, then stepped into the kitchen. When she returned, she was clutching a butcher knife.

"I'm going to count to ten, but if you're anywhere near as smart as you seem to think, you will be out of here by the time I get to nine. *One*."

Tightening his jaws against waves of nausea, Deetz managed to stand.

The realization that he still needed Dierdre, and her money, compelled him to swallow his pride.

"Can't we just talk this through?" Deetz brought his eyebrows together over soulful eyes.

"*Two*." Dierdre said.

"I don't know what came over me." Deetz made a move toward the woman, his hand extended in supplication. But even he could hear the false remorse in his voice.

"*Three*." Dierdre lowered her eyelids and lifted the blade just enough to telegraph her determination.

"I do love you, you know. You're the only woman for me."

"*Four*."

"Okay, okay," Deetz said. "At least let me leave by the back way." He reached for the pickup keys on the coffee table but stopped when Dierdre lifted the knife slightly and took a step in his direction.

"Drop the keys," Dierdre said. "*Five*. Like I said, the pickup will cover some of what you owe me. *Six*. And I don't give a rip which door you use." She snatched up the keys and dropped them into her handbag.

By the time Dierdre counted to eight, Deetz was staggering out the back door. A blast of icy air shot its freezing breath down the neck of his light shirt, and he shivered.

The door behind him squealed as it opened again, and Deetz inwardly smirked. The old broad was going to ask him back inside. He was even more of a stud than he realized.

That thought deflated like a punctured balloon when Dierdre tossed his jacket into a pile of drifted snow next to his feet.

"I hope you have someplace to sleep tonight," she said. "Shame you didn't have the foresight to take your apartment key off your pickup fob. If I even *think* I see you around here again, I will call those cops you're so afraid of. Consider yourself evicted." She slammed the door and shot the deadbolt home, the sound final in the icy morning air.

Cursing, Deetz retrieved his jacket, shook it free of snow, and pulled it on. He shoved his hands into the pockets and glanced toward the kitchen window where Dierdre stood glowering at him. In a show of mock surrender, he raised both hands and started toward the backyard gate.

Grateful for the cover offered by a five-foot high wooden fence around Dierdre's back yard, Deetz reached for the gate's latch. But his hand froze midair.

Just visible through a small gap between the fence's wood slats was the dark SUV he'd noticed earlier. He jerked his head back from the gap and crept toward the connecting fence between Dierdre's backyard and the one next door.

Deetz glanced toward Dierdre's window. Relieved to see the bimbo no longer stood watching him, he eyed the length of the fence.

A broken, leaning fencepost caught his attention.

He slogged through deepening snow to the post then pushed it to one side. Stooping, he crept through the resulting gap and into the yard next door then moved the post back into its original position.

Grateful when no one yelled at him or otherwise raised an alarm, he crossed the yard and exited its side gate. His back flattened against the building, he peeked around the corner.

A white coupe sat where the black SUV had been only a few minutes earlier. A solitary driver, bearing the unmistakable look common to the blue brotherhood of cops, stared in the general direction of Dierdre's front door.

At least Deetz had the foresight to park Lou's vehicle out of view. He could drive down the dirt road behind the complex then connect with a frontage road that would take him to the interstate. The cops would be looking for *his* pickup, not Lou's.

His breath steaming in the frigid air, Deetz made a circuit of the apartment complex. Once he arrived at the rear of the building, he scuttled toward Lou's vehicle, climbed in, and started the engine.

Every molecule in his body screamed that he needed to get out of town. He should have left hours earlier, but how could he have known his plans would be so thoroughly sabotaged by that stupid old broad?

On top of everything else, when she pulled the money from his pocket, she also took the few dollars belonging to him. He was penniless.

Unless he was up for bumming a ride on the Union Pacific railroad, he was going nowhere without money. The rails were no longer as easy to hop as they once were. Besides, as far as he knew, there was no rail that ran directly from Albuquerque to the Mexican border.

The *major complicating factor*, as Deetz's old man used to say, was his lack of funds. He could save a few bucks by sleeping in Lou's pickup on the road to Mexico, but he would need at least three or four hundred dollars for gas and food.

Maybe he could talk Dierdre back around. Of all the women he had known over the years, she had consistently proven the most grateful for his attention.

As quickly as the thought of groveling at the woman's feet entered his head, he dismissed it. The look on her face had been stone cold. Besides, as the saying went, there were always plenty more fish.

A smile crept across Deetz's face at a new thought. There was no telling how much money Dierdre had salted away inside that fake electrical outlet in her apartment. Other than a deadbolt on the front and back doors, she had no security system. A determined toddler could break in.

He would lay low until she left at noon for her daily yoga class and get in through her back door. He would take every cent he could find then tear the place apart. Maybe he would leave a sign only she would recognize, something that proved it was he who had taken her precious stash, something proclaiming him the winner.

Deetz drove onto the frontage road to the interstate. If everything went as planned, he would be on the way to Mexico by that evening. He would start a new life; Dierdre would have been taught a lesson; and the cops could go pound sand.

Chapter Twenty-Eight

Robin threw her head back, tilted the moccasin over her outstretched tongue, and carefully poured the couple of tablespoons of melted snow into her mouth. Running her tongue over as much of the wet shoe's inside as she could reach, she sucked up the last drops then replaced the shoe under the siphoning wick and resumed counting.

Her watch alarm rang, reminding her to do her muscle-stretching exercise.

"What's the point?" she whispered. Maybe it was time to face reality; maybe she was not getting out of that trunk alive.

I do not want to hear any more negativity coming out of your face. Her mother's remembered voice was filled with disappointment.

"I can't figure out what to do."

You figured out how to get water; that bought you some time. Now figure out how to get yourself out of here.

"I'm tired."

So what?

"I can't feel my toes," Robin said. "My nose is an ice cube, and my fingers are so numb I can barely grip the shoes tightly enough to drink the water."

I repeat, so what? Get on with the muscle exercises; that will warm you up.

161

Robin opened her mouth to deliver a retort but grew silent when the high-pitched whine of a small motor caught her attention.

Unlike the deep-throated sound of a car or truck engine, and different from the frequent overhead airplane noise, the sound reminded her of the model airplanes her brother used to build from balsa wood kits when they were kids.

She smiled at the memory of her brother gluing the plane's wood skeleton together, covering it with fabric then shellacking the whole thing before adding decals to the sides. Once the plane was dry, he would connect wires from a control box, and the two of them would carry it to a nearby field where they became absorbed in the process of getting the thing off the ground. She remembered how his face lit up with that perpetually lopsided grin as he gleefully manipulated the control buttons that made the plane dip, dive, and climb high into the sky.

The sound seemed to grow louder, then nearer.

"Hey," Robin hollered. "Is someone there?" Like a woman possessed, she screamed and banged her fists on the trunk lid. She kicked against its sides.

The whining engine sounded clear and stationary, as if hovering over her trunk.

Yelling at the top of her lungs, Robin jerked the wet syphoning strip from the largest hole in the trunk lid and jammed her index finger as far through the opening as the surrounding jagged metal would allow. She wiggled her finger in a circle, moving it back and forth, and jerked it in and out of the hole even after the sharp metal bit into her finger, and her hand grew slick with blood. She yelled and kicked.

Robin told herself that surely the model airplane's owner could hear her yelling or see her fingers waving. She yelled until her throat spasmed, and her voice was reduced to a hiss.

However, the engine noise receded, then disappeared altogether.

It did not return, and no one came to help.

Maybe the whole thing had been an auditory hallucination conjured by her weakening brain. Maybe hypothermia was tricking her and distorting her reason.

If that were the case, she had less time than she had realized.

Robin pulled her finger from the hole. Her arm too heavy to hold up any longer, she let it drop to the floor beside her. Her body trembled, and she curled into a ball, staring into the darkness.

Great workout, her mother's voice interrupted. *You can skip one muscle-stretching session and go straight to finding a way out of here.*

Something in Robin's mind caved in on itself. Mindlessly, she thrashed. The comforter fell away from her, leaving room for the icy air to bite her flesh.

Heedless of pain in her arms, hands, and knees, she struck out at her surroundings until her muscles seized up. She tried to yell, but her aching throat refused to cooperate, and her voice came out in a hoarse whisper.

Finally, exhausted, she lay panting. Perspiration generated from the outburst coated her back, underarms, and inner thighs. The warm moisture quickly grew cold. She shivered, and her teeth chattered. Frigid air settled over her body, greedily lapping at even the tiniest pools of warmth.

How much longer would it be before she froze to

death? Would she be dead within the next few minutes, or would it take hours? Could there be days of torment left?

A muscle in Robin's back cramped, and she straightened her body until her feet abutted the back seat. That dang, unmovable back seat with its thick nylon upholstery that kept her prisoner. The back seat--
-

At a new thought, Robin frantically ran her hands over the floor. Once she found the phone, she placed it face-up on the floor in front of her and covered it with one corner of her comforter. Bending her right arm, she brought her elbow down onto the portion of the fabric covering the glass face. A resulting muffled *crack* sent flutters of anticipation through her mid-section.

She lifted the comforter, turned the phone face down onto the trunk floor then tapped its back to dislodge the bits of shattered glass. Gingerly, she ran her fingers over the shards until she encountered a two-inch-long piece that felt about an inch wide at one end and narrowed to a razor-sharp point at the other.

Gripping the broken glass in her right hand, she turned on her left side, tore off a square of rotten carpet, and carefully covered the remaining slivers. The last thing she needed was to grind chunks of glass into her flesh every time she moved.

She scooted across the trunk and faced the back seat. With a strength that surprised her, she jammed the piece of broken glass into the tightly woven fabric. She emitted a hoarse *whoot* when the shard buried itself deep in the upholstery.

That's more like it, Robbie Girl.

Chapter Twenty-Nine

Dierdre Mozul stood in the middle of her bedroom and stared at the photos and posters from her past. For the first time in her forty-five years of life, she allowed herself to see reality peering back at her from the youthful eyes in each picture.

As if in a dream, she ran her fingers along her not quite firm jawline then moved up her face. When had her eyelids grown puffy and the bags under her eyes become so pronounced? When had the flesh on her throat grown thin and creped? When had the once cute freckles sprinkled across her forehead and the bridge of her nose morphed into the beginnings of misshapen brown age spots?

Her shoulders sagged, and the corners of her mouth drooped. She crossed to her vanity and sat on the stool in front of its huge mirror.

Tears pooled in her eyes at the bluish veins beginning to show on the backs of her hands. She squinted at the red nail lacquer she'd thought sexy that suddenly made her over-long nails look like bloody talons on a bird of prey. Emerging knots of arthritis slightly ballooned her knuckles, making it difficult to wear the expensive rings a parade of suitors had gifted her over the years.

Dierdre pulled a tissue from a decorative holder on the vanity and dabbed at her eyes. She had once been beautiful. Men had thrown themselves at her.

But she had jealously guarded her independence. Even her two marriages had not dimmed her determination to remain self-sufficient, a result of her dad's exhortations that if she could support herself, she would neither be required to depend on anyone's largesse nor take their baloney.

She sighed long and deep then opened a vanity drawer. After retrieving a bottle of acetone and a handful of cotton balls, she removed the polish, trimmed her nails with a tiny scissor, then filed them down with an emery board. She dampened another cotton ball with makeup remover and dabbed away the dark mascara, under-eye concealer, and matte pancake makeup.

One at a time, she removed the vanity drawers and dumped the contents into a trash basket. Nail polish in every shade of red known to man plopped into the bin, followed by black and dark brown mascara, false eyelashes, and compacts filled with a dozen or more shades of eye shadow.

Squaring her shoulders, Dierdre stood and strode to her walk-in closet. She pulled outfits from hooks and hangers and tossed them into a pile on the floor.

Red sequins glinted and flashed in the sunlight pouring through her blinds. Scarlet, yellow, and orange silk floated onto a red leather pantsuit. Designer, flame-red four-inch-heels came to rest beside a gold lamé vest and scarlet, elbow length gloves.

She picked up a pair of red leather Doc Marten high-topped boots. Her heart rate spiked as she relived the feeling of freedom that came from sitting astride the red Harley for which she had become known. She felt again the rumble and vibration of the revving engine during her nightly pre-show preparation. She felt the incomparable exhilaration of a successfully completed run followed by images of the spectators' awe-filled faces and hoots of appreciation.

Fans had thrown red roses at her feet. Men proposed marriage. Women had looked at her with envy.

A sense of loss the like of which she had never experienced flooded Dierdre's spirit. Sobbing, she lovingly placed the boots on the floor beside the pile of clothes.

Once everything was folded and carefully arranged in a large box, she stepped to a rolltop desk against one wall of her bedroom. She booted up her laptop, opened a search engine, and typed in the words *jobs in the filming industry in New Mexico*. Of the nearly one hundred openings that popped up, she selected two positions for costume and makeup personnel, completed the online applications, then sent them along with photograph portfolios and resumés.

Next, she did an online search for real estate agents. If statistics on the local housing market were accurate, she could clear enough money from the sale of her apartment complex to buy a small condo in the Sandia foothills and still have a couple hundred thousand left to add to her retirement account.

She stood, took one last look at the posters papering the walls, then pulled a business card from her pocket and keyed in the number on its front.

"Detective Rooney?" Dierdre said. "Are you still looking for Ronnie Deetz?"

"Yes," the detective said. "We'd like to talk to him

as well as to Lou Bradley."

"I'm guessing Lou is passed out in his apartment. He usually is after a night of drinking. But Ronnie was here when you came by earlier. I am sorry I didn't tell you at the time, but I didn't realize, I didn't think, anyway, I felt I should let you know."

"Is he there now?" the detective said.

"No, I threw him out."

"What time was this?" Detective Rooney said, her voice rising in pitch.

"A little before ten this morning. He, um, he left without his pickup keys, so he's either found other means of transportation or is afoot."

"Did he give you any indication where he was going?"

"I don't know where he *is* going," Dierdre said, "but I can tell you where he *isn't*. I have the only keys to his apartment, so unless he breaks in, he won't be there. We used to talk about going to Vegas, but that could have been him blowing smoke." Dierdre cleared her throat. "This morning he tried to borrow a few hundred dollars from me so he could leave town. I didn't give it to him, so he's broke."

"Did he say where he wanted to go?"

"He said he was going to Vegas," Dierdre said, "but as I said, that was probably a lie."

"Did he ever mention anyone's name?" the detective said. "Maybe make a phone call that you overheard?"

"No to both questions." Dierdre sighed. "As far as I know, the only friend he has in town is Lou Bradley."

"Okay," the detective said. "Thanks for the call. Is this the best number to reach you?"

"Yes," Dierdre said.

"Do you mind telling me where you're going, so I can reach you in case I have any follow-up questions?"

"I'll be at Ojo Caliente for the next two weeks," Dierdre said. "I will have my phone with me. I'm expecting several calls, so I will keep it on."

"Thank you for letting me know," the detective said.

Dierdre took in a shaky breath and stared at the wall. What had Deetz done to make him a blip on the police radar? Whatever it was, she would be willing to bet a month's income it had something to do with his violent temper. Grateful for the lessons in self-protection a past lover had insisted she take, she shivered at the thought of what he could have done had she not known how to fight back.

Although she had grown mildly suspicious of Deetz's persistent unwillingness to talk about his past, she never pressed him. She had fallen for all that romantic claptrap about allowing your significant other to maintain their independence. Give them distance. Make no demands, ask no questions, and be content to receive whatever they were willing to give. That horse-puckey cliché about loving someone enough to set them free.

An uncomfortable thought tugged at the edges of her mind. Had her relationship with Deetz put her in the police crosshairs as an accessory to whatever the jerk had done? Was she going to be investigated?

Maybe keeping his pickup had been a mistake. Hadn't she read somewhere about a man who kept his girlfriend's Jeep locked inside his garage as payback for her leaving him? When the girlfriend called the cops and reported the vehicle stolen, the guy was charged with auto theft.

Dierdre couldn't sell Deetz's rusty, dented old piece of junk; the title was still in his name. But in the heat of the moment, keeping it had seemed to lessen the pain of the jerk's vicious comments.

"If you remember anything Deetz might have told you," Detective Rooney was saying, "any plans he might have had for the future, names he might have mentioned, places he frequents or talked about wanting to go, I'd appreciate a call back. Even the tiniest detail could be helpful. Sometimes, someone has a bit of information they don't realize is important. We would rather you give us a hundred seemingly unimportant details and have them *not* be pertinent than for you to leave out something that later turns out to be crucial."

"If I think of anything, I will let you know," Dierdre said. "I'll keep your card handy."

The detective asked a couple more questions then broke the connection.

Dierdre's hands trembled as she dropped the phone back into her smock pocket. How could she have been so off the mark with Ronnie Deetz? She had prided herself on her ability to read a man within the first ten minutes of meeting him, but this guy had slithered past her emotional barbed-wire defenses.

All she had ever wanted was someone of her own to love, someone to trust with her deepest dreams and secrets. Someone who would never use those secrets to emotionally beat her up, even during a heated argument. She needed a good man, a man who treated her as he wanted to be treated, a man like so many she realized she had met but inexplicably turned aside.

Dierdre exhaled and shook her head. Forty-four, twice divorced, and she had just realized that her happiness was up to her. She was the composer of her life-song. Anyone else's rendition would be just that-- their rendition.

In a flash of introspection, Dierdre recognized the truth of her relationship with Deetz. Transactional, that's what her first after-divorce therapist had called the kind of give and take in a relationship's early stages. While the counselor had added that nearly all blooming relationships start out as such, over time, if healthy, they evolve into a more selfless bond in which one partner considered the needs and desires of the other as important as their own.

She had tried to convince herself that the money and expensive gifts she showered on Deetz were purely out of affection, but she now recognized they were given out of desperation to make him love her the way she wanted to be loved. Everything she did for Deetz had been with an expectation of reciprocation.

Of course, the only *pro quo* bad-boy Deetz had ever offered in response to Dierdre's numerous *quid*s was the ever effective *I love you.*

Can you spare a few bucks? By the way, I love you.

After a few more minutes of mentally and emotionally beating herself up, Dierdre moved around her apartment removing posters and photos. She carefully propped them against a wall, retrieved her phone and punched in a number from the past.

"Hello, Fastball," she said when the phone at the other end was answered.

"I'd know that voice anywhere," her old friend said. "How the hell are you, Babe?"

"I'm good. Got a proposition for you."

"I'm listening," the man said.

"You want some memorabilia to add to your collection?"

"Are you kidding?" The man chuckled. "Like I said at your retirement party, I can use everything you're willing to part with. I have just the right place, a nook all to your fine self. Nobody has rocked Vegas like you did, before or since."

"Thank you," Dierdre said. "That means a lot. I'll take the costumes, photos, and posters to a packing and shipping store this morning. You want them sent to your home, or your pub?"

"Address them to Fast Charlie's Retro Vegas Pub and Eatery."

The two agreed on a price, and Dierdre gave the man her PayPal account information. After a couple of minutes spent catching up, she shut down the call.

An unexpected giggle bubbled up her throat, and she smiled in wonder. For the first time in many years, she felt unfettered: free from society's pressure to maintain a youthful façade, free from the shame that came with showing her age, and free from the guilt of daring to live beyond the age of thirty.

It was time to abandon the search for someone to *complete* her. Time to open herself up, instead, to simply sharing a life with someone decent.

Dierdre walked to the fake switch plate in the living room and slid the cover to one side. After double checking to ensure she was leaving no bills behind, she removed her stash and stuffed it into her smock pocket.

Mouthing the lyrics to a song that declared the singer's determination not to allow anything to break her stride or slow her down, Dierdre danced down the hall to her bedroom. She pulled a suitcase and overnight bag from a closet, packed them with clothes and toilet articles, then changed into a pair of jeans, a blue turtleneck shirt, and a tan leather jacket. She locked the windows, closed the drapes, and hauled everything to her car.

Standing in front of her apartment, Dierdre took one last look at what remained of her past. She sniffed, pulled a Kleenex from her tote bag, and wiped her eyes. She then retrieved her phone and punched in a number.

"Hello, Mizz Jenkins," she said to the friendly old widow who lived a few doors down. "It's Dierdre. I'm going on vacation and was just wondering if you'd keep an eye on the place for me."

"I'd be happy to. It's about time you take a break," the old woman said. "How long you going to be gone?"

"Two weeks. If you need me, though, you call, okay?"

After a few more niceties, Dierdre broke the connection and walked to her car.

As she slid behind the steering wheel, she gave herself a mental hug. A couple of weeks of pampering in the popular New Mexico hot springs and spa were in order.

If all went to plan, by the time her vacation was over, she would have a new look, a new job, a new place to live, a new wardrobe, and enough money to do whatever she wanted.

Who knew, she might even meet someone looking for a comfortably off, independent, mature woman with whom to spend some time.

"Hasta la vista, Ronnie Deetz," Dierdre murmured

as she pulled onto the road toward Ojo Caliente.

Wryly, she glanced in the rearview mirror at her receding apartment complex and added, "Rest in peace Garnette Redd."

Chapter Thirty

Petra had been a few blocks from Mozul's apartment when her dash-mounted phone rang. She noted the caller ID then pushed the blue tooth button on her steering wheel.

"Detective Rooney," she said.

"This is Dierdre Mozul, Detective. There are some things I need to tell you." For the next several minutes, she explained and apologized for the mistakes she had made regarding Deetz.

Petra had thanked her then ended the conversation and called Cody.

"Hey, Rocky," her partner answered, "I'm on my way to Dierdre Mozul's. I should be there in less than five minutes."

"Change of plans, Cody. I just got off the phone with Mozul. You were right; Deetz was in her apartment when we were there. She said she kicked him out and is in the process of leaving on vacation."

"So, she lied to us," Cody said.

"Yep," Petra said. "At least she gave me her cell number and told me where she's going. I offered to let her know the results of our investigation, but she indicated in no uncertain terms that she doesn't care what happens to Deetz."

"Ah, love's sweet song."

"She implied that he forgot to take his pickup keys,

but that sounds a bit sketchy. Regardless of what's behind that bit of drama, unless Deetz took Bradley's pickup or called a taxi or Uber, he's afoot."

"Do you believe her latest story?" Cody said.

"As you said, she lied to us once, so we cannot take her word at face value. However, nothing we've learned points to her knowing about any illegal activities Deetz may have been involved in."

"In other words, we don't have enough to keep her from leaving town." Cody *tsk*-ed then added, "What do you want me to do?"

"I just got a call from dispatch; Banda's kids are here and anxious to talk to us. Are you where you can interview them?"

"Be glad to," Cody said. "When?"

"They said they'd be at the station about eleven o'clock." Petra glanced at her wristwatch. "That's in a little over half an hour."

"Will do," Cody said.

Petra's phone started its *call waiting* beep, and she shut down the call with Cody. At the same instant, a dog ran into the street mere inches from her front wheels. Adrenaline shot into her vital organs, and she jammed on the brakes, barely missing the animal. Shaken at the close call, she pulled to the side of the road and pushed the blue tooth answer button without glancing at the caller ID.

"Rooney," she said.

"So, it really *is* you." The man named Kent Fowler chuckled. "You should have chosen a job with a lower profile, Sweetheart. It's like you wanted to be found."

Petra gasped in recognition of the voice. She jabbed her index finger onto the disconnect button.

How had Kent found her? More importantly, where was he? While her department-issued phone number would have been easy enough to find, her current name would have meant nothing to him.

Vignettes from two years earlier cartwheeled down the corridors of her memory: images of Kent driving past her house at all hours, the sound of his voice leaving dozens of increasingly threatening messages on her phone, the tiny lifeless body of her newly adopted pound puppy.

Petra's jaws tightened as she envisioned herself staring down the barrel of what her current carefully constructed life might become. Muttering, she pulled her vehicle onto the street.

Chapter Thirty-One

Reflecting ruefully on the truth of the old *you get what you pay for* adage, Lou adjusted his clearance-rack pillow for the umpteenth time. As always, however, the pillow's bits of foam filling quickly migrated outward from its center, leaving his pounding head resting on two thin layers of cheap fabric ticking. When all subsequent attempts to fall back to sleep failed, he opened his burning eyes and stared up at the water-stained ceiling. He thought about all the times he had tried and failed to get sober.

How had he managed to mess his life up so thoroughly? When had he stopped working to build himself into a better person and chosen to follow the path of least resistance? When had he tossed control of his destiny, along with his dreams, to the wind?

As a kid he loved pretending to be a fireman. He daydreamed about waking up to an alarm bell, jumping into his firefighter's gear, sliding down a steel pole, and running to the firetruck. He envisioned himself extending a ladder toward terrified people pleading for help while flames closed in on them. He even saw himself humbly receiving a medal from the city's mayor in recognition of his heroism.

"What a sorry sack of manure," Lou muttered. "Not worth the powder it would take to blow myself up."

He reached for his phone, turned it on, and punched in an infrequently used number.

"Hello, Lou," his Alcoholics Anonymous sponsor said. "I was hoping you hadn't lost my number. It's been a while."

"I wasn't sure you'd answer." Lou sighed. "I'm messed up, man."

"That's a step in the right direction. You want to go for coffee?"

"I got no wheels," Lou said. "I left my truck at a bar last night."

"I can pick you up." The AA sponsor paused. "We can talk over coffee, and then we'll get your pickup."

"I'll need a half hour or so to clean up," Lou said, his voice soft. "I'm sober, but real hungover."

"Understood. I'll be there in forty-five minutes."

After he broke the connection, Lou sat at the side of his mattress. With his legs splayed out on the floor, he waited for the pounding in his head to calm down and his eyes to focus. Then he stood and ambled to the kitchen counter and the bottle of cheap booze on it.

He stared at the inviting liquid as an internal battle raged.

"Maybe just one hair of the dog," he whispered as he reached for the bottle.

His hand froze mid-air as two warring factions inside his head squared off for battle. In the end, his better angel bound his chattering self-medicating, self-destruct demon in the coils of a thick rope and duct-taped his mouth shut.

Lou sighed. He picked up the bottle and unscrewed its cap.

Quickly, before he could change his mind, he

poured the liquid down the sink. When the alcohol hit the air, the smell wafted up Lou's nose, and he shuddered.

Barely able to resist running his fingers through the disappearing liquid then licking them, he glanced at his wristwatch. In a little over an hour, he would have someone to talk to, someone who understood what he was going through, someone who cared.

Lou walked to the bathroom. He stripped off his clothes, stepped into the shower, and turned the cold-water on full blast then lifted his face to the punishing needle-like spray.

Chapter Thirty-Two

At exactly eleven o'clock Saturday morning, Cody entered the main police station's waiting area and introduced himself to Banda's two grown kids.

The young woman sniffed and dabbed at red, puffy eyes with a Kleenex. The young man's face remained composed but intense as he looked questioningly at Cody.

"I'm sorry for the pain and hardship this is causing," Cody said. "And I appreciate your willingness to come in and answer some questions."

"Thank you," the young man said. "Are you absolutely certain the person who died is our dad? He sometimes disappears to his cabin in Mayhill for a couple of days of R and R."

"We are certain," Cody said. "The medical examiner made the identification through fingerprints from your dad's military records."

"When can we see him?" the young woman said.

"After the medical examiner has completed the autopsy," Cody said.

"Is an autopsy necessary?" Banda's daughter said. "I can hardly bear the thought of someone cutting him." She sobbed, her shoulders shaking.

"I'm afraid it's standard procedure in the event of a suspicious death," Cody said gently.

The young man's head jerked up and his piercing

gaze fixed on Cody. "What do you mean a suspicious death? We thought it was an accident."

"That was the initial thinking," Cody said. "It has since been designated as suspicious based on the Medical Examiner's report."

"Are you saying someone purposely did that to Daddy?" the young woman said.

"We are investigating that possibility," Cody said. "Meanwhile, do you have someplace to stay?"

"We were hoping to stay at Dad's house, if that's possible," the young man said. "We've taken a few days off work."

"I see no reason why you should not stay there," Cody said. "The investigation into your father's death is in the early stages. As soon as we know more, I'll let you know." He pointed to a row of chairs against one wall. "If one of you would have a seat, the other can come with me. I need to speak to you separately."

"You go first, Sis," the young man said. "I'll wait here."

Within forty minutes, Cody had completed the interviews. Once the siblings left the station, he called Petra.

"Banda's kids don't know much more than we do," he said when Petra answered. "If Banda had any enemies, they don't know it."

"He had no disgruntled employees?" Petra said.

"None known. His business was good; he had no financial difficulties." Cody took a sip of coffee then added, "Banda didn't gamble, and the closest thing to an outside relationship was as a quasi-adoptive dad to your friend."

"Did he mention any close calls recently? Had he

said anything about feeling like someone was following him? Did he feel threatened?"

"Not as far as the kids know," Cody said, "and I got the feeling they would. By all accounts, they were a close family who kept in regular touch. As a kind of pay-it-forward initiative, Banda made it a habit to employ men who had done jail time. Evidently, over the years he even helped several of them start their own businesses. However, he was growing increasingly suspicious of Deetz. He told his son he thought Deetz might be using his job to scope out homes to burgle."

"When did Banda say that?" Petra said.

"The night before his death," Cody said. "By the way, the kids said Banda's business laptop is missing. It's not in the house; they wondered if it was impounded along with his truck."

"No laptop showed up on the evidence inventory, but I'll double-check."

"Here's an interesting tidbit," Cody said. "The daughter said Banda put Deetz in charge of maintaining the paint equipment because he was exceptionally good at it. I looked up Deetz's jail record and learned that during the time he was incarcerated, he took several courses in mechanics and electronics."

"I've just spoken to the medical examiner to find out why she categorized Banda's death as suspicious," Petra said. "It was because the expert she called in to examine the air compressor reported the pressure release valve had been compromised. *Forcefully* and *recently* were the words used."

Cody snorted then said, "Is it just me, or is Deetz edging out the rest of the competition as prime suspect?"

"There is certainly a lot of circumstantial evidence piling up in his corner," Petra said. "Jay just called. A woman vaguely of Mozul's description made several trips in and out of her apartment with several pieces of luggage and big boxes, loaded them into a car, then took off."

"So Mozul has flown the coop," Cody said. "We're down to Deetz and Bradley."

"I've told Jay and Stubbs to sit on both apartments in case Mozul lied about kicking Deetz to the curb and is letting him hide out at her place. If he *is* in her apartment or hunkered down inside his own, he'll have to come out sooner or later."

"What about Lou Bradley?" Cody said. "Is someone watching his apartment?"

"Yes," Petra said. "The guy watching him just called. An unidentified man in a hatchback showed up in front of Bradley's apartment, and the two of them left together. Our guy is following them."

"So, where do you want to go from here?"

"I want to know everything I can about Bradley before we have our tete-a-tete with him," Petra said. "Call Dispatch and ask where they are on his background check."

"On it," Cody said.

After Petra disconnected, Cody placed a call to Dispatch. Seconds later, his tablet pinged, and he downloaded the background documents on Bradley.

By the time Petra called him with Bradley's location, Cody figured he knew more about the guy than his own mother did.

"And I thought *my* life sucked," Cody murmured as he hurried to his car.

Chapter Thirty-Three

Robin grimaced as she licked warm stickiness oozing from her throbbing fingers.

"And here we have the Marcato version of death by a thousand cuts," she muttered.

Although each thrust of the glass shard's point into the backseat successfully punctured the fabric, the force of the jab pushed the shard's opposite end backward and into her fingers and palms. As a result, the pain in her bleeding digits made every poke an adventure in self-torture.

For every action there is an equal and opposite reaction.

"Thanks for that belated and unhelpful scientific reference, Mom," Robin said. "At this rate, I'll lose a finger before I can make a hole large enough to crawl through."

She tried wrapping bits of carpet around the wide end of the stiletto-sharp glass. However, the rotten carpet quickly disintegrated, exposing her flesh to the equivalent of an angry razorblade.

"Think," she whispered. "Why can't I think?"

Your breathing is shallow. You are drowsy, and you keep dropping the shard. What does that tell you?

"I'm hypothermic." Robin forced herself to take a deep breath. "Once I stop shivering, I'll feel like I'm having a hot flash and be tempted to throw off the comforter. Then I'll...I'll, what happens after that?" Her chin trembling, she added, "I can't remember what happens after that, Mom."

Courage, Robbie Girl. You must push yourself like you never have.

Fumble-fingered, Robin tore a strip of cloth from her comforter. She wrapped the scrap around the wide end of the shard then pulled the comforter around her body, careful to cover every bit of exposed flesh.

After running her fingers across the seat back in search of the damaged section, she clamped her jaws and shoved the glass into the tiny opening.

Her watch beeped its reminder for exercise, but she ignored it. With the absolute certainty that this was her last chance at survival, Robin dug at the hole in the fabric.

Chapter Thirty-Four

After Deetz left Dierdre's neighborhood, he drove a mile or so to an area known as The Bosque, a cottonwood forest bordering the Rio Grande River and bisecting the western side of Albuquerque. A ribbon of green in the high desert, the woodlands would be the perfect place to hide from the cops until time to hit Dierdre's apartment.

He pulled Lou's pickup onto a dirt road that led to the riverbank and parked under a huge cottonwood tree. Even though the ground was snow covered and the temperature hovered around freezing, homeless people and itinerants were known to camp out along the sixty-miles-long Bosque, and Deetz had no desire to be spotted.

He studied his immediate surroundings. When it became apparent that he was alone, he pulled his phone from the pickup's built-in cup holder. A gift from Deirdre, the pay-as-you-go cell phone turned out to be an unexpectedly useful perk of the relationship. Since the phone was set up on an automatic re-fill schedule, he could use it until Dierdre remembered to shut it down.

"I have a present for you," she had said as she held a gift-wrapped box toward him. "It'll be our connection."

Deetz smirked at the corniness of Dierdre's

187

remembered words, then punched a number into the keypad.

Mister Z's middleman and general flunky Flash answered after three rings. "Whaddaya want?"

"I need to talk to Mister Z."

"Yeah? Well, I'm pretty sure he don't want to talk to you, dumbo." The guy laughed, the sound vaguely threatening.

Deetz hesitated. His flesh crawled like someone had hooked him up to an intravenous drip of ice water. "Come on, Flash," he said. "I need to talk to him."

"According to the boss's contacts," the middleman continued, "the cops are looking for you. That is not good for business, so as of this minute, you are no longer an auto parts supplier to Zephyr Enterprises, LLC."

"The cops just want to talk to me about that air compressor explosion that killed my boss," Deetz said. "Did you hear about that?"

"Yeah, we saw the news," Flash said. His voice dripping sarcasm, he added, "You're quite the star. In fact, the cops are now calling you a person of interest."

Deetz cleared his throat and said, "I'm leaving town tonight, heading for Mexico."

"Is that so?" Flash said.

"I figure once I get to Mexico, I could start training to drive one of the delivery trucks."

"Whoa. What part of *Mister Z don't know you anymore* are you too stupid to understand?"

A gravelly voice in the background barked orders. Judging by the muffling of sound, the middleman had covered the phone's speaker.

"Hello?" Deetz said. His voice squeaked as it

squeezed through his tight throat.

"Mister Z says for you to forget his name," Flash said. "He don't need the cops digging into his business."

"Is he there?" Deetz said. "Let me talk to him. I can explain everything."

The background voice Deetz now recognized grew louder.

"Tell that loser if he gets caught, he won't live long enough to make any deals with the cops." Mister Z paused. "He won't even last long enough to get himself arraigned."

"But once I'm in Mexico, I'll be untouchable," Deetz said.

"No *buts*," the middleman said. "Soon as I hang up, I'm feeding this phone to Nancy, and this number will no longer exist."

Deetz shivered. *Nancy,* a machine of destruction named after Mister Z's departed mother, was a huge, terrifying bit of equipment capable of pulverizing whatever was thrown into its infeed. Deetz had seen it grind up junk ranging in size from a deck of cards to a car. *Nancy* was reputed to be Mister Z's preferred means of dealing with over-zealous business rivals, as well as anyone he dubbed a *screw-up*. He often bragged that since one of his legitimate businesses was salvaging metal, depreciation on the machine was even tax deductible.

"Oh, yeah," Flash added, "texts, emails, or any other way you think of to get in touch with Mister Z will result in the immediate administration of what might best be called a sharp learning curve."

"But I…" Deetz's voice trailed off when dead-air

silence indicated Flash had disconnected the call. He blew out a series of short breaths and rubbed the back of his neck hard enough to raise a blister.

The cost of living in Mexico was a lot less than in the States, and he would have all Dierdre's cash. Maybe he would set himself up in business after all. Multiple streams of income, that is what he needed. Like Mister Z, he could open both a chop shop and an immigrant transport operation. For a few thousand dollars, he could buy a used panel truck in Mexico. He could start small, just hauling a few illegals at first then expand. It would be kind of poetic to use the bimbo's money to set something up after all the hot air he had blown up her skirt.

Then, once he got going, he might find a way to repay Flash for being such an arrogant, disrespectful jerk. There were plenty of people willing to do anything for a few bucks. It would just be a matter of finding one. Deetz didn't forgive and he didn't forget.

He glanced at his wristwatch. Time to avail himself of what Dierdre had called her *cache of cash*.

Her noon yoga class lasted an hour, then all the old biddies would head to the club's snack bar for fruit smoothies and gossip. Deetz would have at least ninety minutes from the time he broke into her apartment to clear the place out and be on his way.

By this time tomorrow, he would be sitting on a beach in Mexico, drinking something alcoholic, and sizing up the female population. His life would be one party after another, interspersed with work, of course. Never let it be said that Ronnie Deetz was lazy.

Humming the melody from an insurance advertisement, he pulled the pickup onto the road.

Careful to stay on side streets and frontage roads, he drove toward Dierdre's apartment.

Chapter Thirty-Five

As Petra left the Medical Examiner's office, she got a call informing her Lou Bradley had just returned to his apartment.

"Was there anyone in the car besides Bradley and the guy who picked him up?" Petra asked the officer.

"No, just the two of them. And there's been no other activity in or around his apartment as far as I can tell."

"Good work," Petra said. "Once I get there, go grab some lunch. I'll let you know if I need anything else." She broke the connection then called Cody. "Bradley just got home. Can you meet me at his apartment?"

"Sure thing," Cody said. "I just finished going over his and Mozul's background. You want to hear any of it now?"

"It'll wait," Petra said. "I want to get to Bradley before he can vanish again. You can tell me the most important bits when we get there."

"I'm on my way," Cody said.

During the drive to Bradley's apartment, Petra periodically glanced in the rearview mirror. Her *something-feels-off* antennae twitched at the sight of a white rental Toyota she had noticed several blocks earlier, the driver's face obscured by a heavily tinted windshield.

The blood drained from her face when the vehicle pulled around her and stopped next to her at a stoplight. She instinctively moved one hand toward her handgun as the other car's passenger window powered down.

Instead of Kent's twisted, malevolent face staring back at her, however, an elderly female driver smiled self-consciously and leaned across the seat.

"Excuse me, Miss," the old woman said. "I seem to be lost. Can you tell me how to get to the National Hispanic Cultural Center? I'm here for a conference and the GPS in this vehicle isn't working. My son tells me I should use the one on my phone, but I never got the hang of it."

Petra took in a shaky breath. Her guywire-taut muscles relaxed, and she returned the woman's smile. "You're only a couple of blocks away," she said. "Turn left at the next light and go straight. It's on your right; you can't miss it."

The woman nodded and repeated the directions, then drove away when the light turned green.

As Petra pulled into the parking lot outside Bradley's apartment, she told herself she had over-reacted to Kent's earlier call. Cincinnati was one thousand three hundred ninety point nine miles from Albuquerque, one of the reasons she had applied for the job at APD in the first place. Surely even the obsessed Kent Fowler would balk at coming all that distance just to punish her for pressing the charges against him that sent him to jail.

By the time Cody pulled his vehicle behind hers, Petra had talked herself down from an emotional precipice and moved her focus from her past to Robin's present. She texted the officer who had been following

Bradley, alerting him to her presence, then sent him back to the main office to help the officer tasked with going over closed-circuit television cameras.

"I've copied Mozul's background documents to your phone," Cody said as he slid into the passenger seat. "As for Bradley, basically, he is a moderately decent, hard-working weekend alcoholic who can't seem to get his act together. He has no police record, been married and divorced three times, and owes more alimony than he earns. Financial records show he makes regular payments to a rehab charity. He has no kids and appears to be law-abiding. Like I said, moderately decent. It makes you wonder how he got involved with someone like Deetz."

"People tend to show only carefully selected parts of themselves to their friends and family," Petra said.

"Don't I know it," Cody said. "Just another of life's inescapable but harsh lessons."

"I need to talk to you, Cody," Petra said. "There isn't going to be a great time to do it, but you need to know a couple of things before anything else happens."

"Sounds serious." Cody stared intently into Petra's eyes. "You're not going to tell me you're sick or something, are you?

"No, it's nothing like that." Petra took a deep breath. "I used to live in Cincinnati before I took the job at APD."

"I knew you were a foreigner," Cody quipped. The playful look on his face melted at Petra's continued somber expression. "What's going on?" he said.

"Petra Rooney is not my birth name." Petra paused to take a deep breath. "I legally changed it before moving to Albuquerque."

Cody's eyes widened, but he remained silent.

"During my last year in Ohio," Petra continued, "I met a man named Kent Fowler through an online dating forum. I went out with him a few times, but something about him felt off. At first, it was small things, like the way he contradicted me in public and tried to tell me what to wear. He even insisted we both order the same food when we ate out."

"He was putting you in your place," Cody said, "a controller."

"Yeah," Petra nodded. "Things got crazy once I stopped going out with him. At first, he called my cell a dozen times a day and sent me a truckload of flowers at work. Then he started sending me other gifts, even though I texted him and asked him to stop. He started calling me at all hours and drove by my apartment several times a day. He regularly followed me to work. After I got a new phone number, it dawned on him that I wasn't playing *Polo* to his *Marco*, and he escalated. He broke into my apartment and turned on all the lights so I would know he had been there. He pulled the heads off a dozen roses and left the stems with the bruised petals on my kitchen table. You know how that kind of harassment goes."

"What finally happened to make you leave town?" Cody said.

"He killed a puppy I had just adopted," Petra said. "He left it on the balcony of my condo with a computer-generated note demanding I see him again with the veiled threat that the puppy was just the beginning. I documented everything and got a restraining order, but he had already messed up badly enough to get arrested. He was charged with aggravated harassment and animal cruelty then sentenced to six months in jail, but not before he threatened payback."

Cody sucked air through his teeth and shook his head, a look of compassion on his face.

"It seems he's found me." Petra pressed her lips together then added, "I don't know if he's in town, but you need to know he might show up." She pulled a photo from her backpack and handed it to Cody. "This was taken two and a half years ago. I've already given a copy to the Sergeant, and he said he'll run it up the flagpole so everyone can be on the lookout."

"I'm sorry you're having to deal with this on top of everything else right now." Cody studied the photo. "How can I help?"

"There's not much anyone can do until and unless the jerk shows his face here." Petra said. "He has discovered my new name and where I work, so who knows?"

"I'll keep an eye out," Cody said.

"Thanks," Petra said. "Now let's go talk to Lou Bradley."

Chapter Thirty-Six

Once Lou and his AA sponsor finished their coffee, they drove to the Cacahuate Bar to retrieve Lou's pickup. When two circuits around the parking lot proved the place devoid of a four-wheeled vehicle of any kind, Lou fidgeted in his seat.

"I don't get it," Lou said, his voice wavering.

"Are you sure this is where you left it?" his sponsor said.

"Yeah." Lou scratched his head and studied the unlit neon sign bearing the name of the bar. "This is the right place. I was in no condition to drive last night, so my friend Ronnie drove me home." He shook his head. "I don't believe it. Somebody took my truck. I am so hosed."

At his sponsor's suggestion, Lou immediately called the police and reported the theft. While his sponsor drove him home, he punched another number into his phone.

"Hey, Ronnie," he said when the call went to voice mail, "I need you to take me to the yard, man. Somebody stole my pickup, and I have to do some work for old man Haynie before Monday. Call me as soon as you get this." He closed the call and turned to his sponsor. "Sometimes I think my Higher Power is playing whack-a-mole with my life."

"Your Higher Power doesn't play nasty games,"

the sponsor said as he pulled up in front of Lou's apartment. "You need me to take you somewhere else?"

"Not necessary, but thanks," Lou said as he opened the car door and stepped out. "I'll wait for my buddy."

"Call me if you need to talk, or if you need a ride to work." The man nodded once and drove off.

Once in his apartment, Lou pulled a pad of paper and a pen from inside a junk drawer. He sat at the built-in sandwich bar in the kitchen and began working on Step Four of the Twelve Step program which required making a fearless moral inventory of himself.

A loud knock on his front door sent echoes through his sparsely furnished living room and caused him to jump, reflexively tossing the pen across the kitchen.

"Thank God," he murmured. Expecting Deetz, he hurried to the front door and threw it open. "Hey, man," he began.

His mouth fell open as he stared at the two people standing on his porch. While both wore plain clothes, the unmistakable barrel-chests lent by bullet-proof vests along with holstered handguns left no doubt as to who they were.

"Whoa, that was fast," Bradley said. He moved aside and motioned the officers inside. "I'm glad to see you guys. I'm kind of surprised they would send two of you for a stolen vehicle, but thanks for coming."

The officers exchanged looks and stepped into the apartment.

Chapter Thirty-Seven

Robin's muscles burned from exertion. Her arms trembled so badly she had to periodically lower them and count to sixty. One minute of rest was all she dared allow herself before resuming her work on the back seat. All too aware that thirst, hunger, and the frigid cold were taking their toll on her body and mind, she often flexed her hands to get the blood flowing.

She squinted in her watch's direction, hoping her eyes were playing tricks on her, praying that if she stared hard enough, she could make out the numbers. But the dark watch face left her with no idea how long she had been inside the trunk. Friday night seemed two weeks ago.

"If time flies when you're having fun," she muttered, "what evil quirk in the matrix makes it grind into slow motion when you're neck deep in rotten yogurt?"

She drank the accumulated water from her shoes then replaced them under their respective strips of fabric. Within the next few hours, the melting snow would begin to re-freeze, leaving her without water until sometime the next day, and Sunday was Christmas Eve.

Her eyelids drooped, and she struggled to keep them open. If she could rest just a bit. Surely just a few minutes would be okay.

Yo, Robbie Girl. Enough rest. Time to get back to work.

"My fingers are bloody, throbbing stems of raw meat." Robin choked back a sob, "and I'm sick of this darkness. My eyes feel like they're bugging out of my head. I would trade my house for just five minutes of sunshine."

Sounds like a load of bad excuses. Rise and shine. No one's going to do this for you.

"Do I have to die to make you leave me alone?" she said through gritted teeth.

Silence.

"I'm sorry, Mom. Please don't go."

When her mother's memory remained silent, Robin took a deep breath and clamped her lips together. She picked up her shard, checked the cloth wrapping at the wide end, and shoved the point into the back seat.

The piece of glass unexpectedly passed through the slit and beyond. But a *tick,* followed by a *crunch* announced the shard had encountered what turned out to be something metal. It splintered into a hundred tiny, useless fragments.

Robin groaned. "That's it, Mom. I'm done."

There's a hole, there's a hole, there's a hole in the bottom of the---

"So now you're down to singing me a children's nursery song?" Robin interrupted.

There's a hole.

"Okay, okay." Tentatively, Robin ran her sore fingers over the back seat. She gasped to discover her repeated jabs had widened the hole enough to squeeze her hand through.

She pressed the backs of her hands together, palms

facing outward, and poked her fingers into the slit. With every ounce of strength she could gin up, she forced her hands apart.

Fabric ripped, the sound loud in her metal prison. Robin's heart rate sped up as she felt the fabric give away, opening the hole wider with each tug.

Within a few minutes, she had managed to tear the slit from only a few inches in length to what felt like about fifteen inches, nearly wide enough for her to squeeze through.

"Glory be," Robin croaked. She might be home for Christmas after all.

When she slid her hands through the gash, however, the budding cry of victory died in her throat. What felt like a vertical lattice of zigzag springs lay beyond the fabric backing. Held in place by thin metal strips, the springs were placed too closely together to allow anything but a small animal to pass through.

"Two steps forward and one step back," Robin muttered. A knot formed in her throat, and she swallowed hard to keep from vomiting. Covering her face with her hands, she slumped to the floor.

Chapter Thirty-Eight

Assuming the cops to be on the lookout for Lou's pickup as well as his own, Deetz parked on a dirt road's dead end two blocks from Dierdre's apartment. Shoving aside a budding sense of uneasiness at leaving his luggage and Banda's laptop inside Lou's truck, he told himself he would only be gone a few minutes.

Every sense alert, he retraced his earlier escape route. He hauled himself over fences and scurried across backyards. When he tried to heave himself over Dierdre's back fence, though, his pantleg caught on the pointed picket. His forward momentum caused the immobilized leg to twist while the other shot straight out, effectively making him do the splits midair.

"Gah," he yelped before he could stifle himself.

Helplessly, he flapped his arms in search of a handhold, but to no avail. He stiffened his body almost prone and tried to catapult himself away from the sharp fence tips. His pant leg tore free, and he fell to the snow-covered ground with a *whump.*

For the second time in less than twenty-four hours, he lay, gasping for air. Half expecting one of the neighbors to raise an alarm, he remained immobile until he felt enough time had passed.

Once Deetz could breathe again, he stood on shaky legs and crossed the yard. He peered through a gap between two fence slats, relieved to see Dierdre's empty reserved parking space.

He strode to a portion of fence facing the front circular drive. The plainclothes cop had not moved. Despite the pain in his back, he couldn't help but feel cocky. Here he was, moving around unimpeded right under the cop's nose. If his old man had been there to see it, he would have been impressed.

Deetz scuttled to Dierdre's back door and jiggled the handle in hopes the bimbo had forgotten to lock it, but no such luck. Mentally thanking the builder stupid enough to install a back door partially made of glass in this neighborhood, he stood with his right side next to the pane and bent his arm at the elbow.

A portion of Deetz's brain tried to convince him that he should forget breaking into Dierdre's apartment and find another way to get hold of the money he needed. He could knock over a convenience store or even grab some little old lady's purse.

But that would take time, and time was something he did not have. He needed Dierdre's money, and he needed it now.

Deetz jabbed his elbow into the pane. Shattered glass rained onto the tile just inside the door.

Gingerly, he reached through the jagged opening, pricking his finger in the process. He glanced down at the blood dripping onto the tile, discounted a whispered warning that the cops could pull DNA from even the tiniest droplet, and stepped into the apartment. By the time the cops investigated the break-in, he would be long gone.

He strode toward the living room but stopped at the sight of the bare walls that only a couple of hours earlier had sported Dierdre's photographic history.

"What the hell?" he said.

The bimbo had been so proud of her past, looking at pictures of herself day in and day out. It was like she wouldn't allow herself to acknowledge that they were history, that *she* was history. Deetz realized he had always felt a little put off by those walls covered with photos of someone who no longer existed.

He made a sound in the back of his throat. The reality was the woman in those pictures never *had* really existed. She was a fantasy, a dress-up make-believe fantasy.

How arrogant and self-centered must someone be to plaster I-love-me pictures all over the walls of their own apartment? Deetz's parents wouldn't even pay for his school photos.

He hurried to the fake electrical outlet, pulled its cover aside and shoved his hand into the recess. When his fingers encountered nothing but air, he bent at the waist and peered into the opening. A muscle in his eye began to twitch.

He ran from room to room shoving doors open so hard some of the knobs knocked holes in the drywall behind them. His insides jittery at the swift passage of time, he searched every possible hiding place. He tried every switch plate and electrical outlet. He dumped the contents of every drawer in the bedroom onto the floor. He pulled clothes from hangers, threw them onto the floor, and stomped on them with his wet boots.

A jewelry box atop the bimbo's bedroom vanity caught his attention. He rifled through the box's contents, and a smile played on his lips. While most of the jewelry was flashy costume junk, a few bits and bobs looked worthwhile.

Deetz pocketed an antique-looking cameo brooch, a diamond-encircled ruby ring, a couple of plain gold rings, and several pair of gem-bearing earrings.

His pulse kicked up a notch at the discovery of a pearl necklace in one drawer. Even if the necklace were made of cultured rather than natural pearls, it could be worth big bucks.

A lady's Rolex glinted temptingly, and he fought down the urge to take it. If the watch was authentic, it had an identification number etched inside, and that number would tell some nosy pawn broker or cop the identity of its owner. It was not worth the risk.

Deetz noticed the trashcan filled with tiny bottles of blood red fingernail polish and cardboard containers the labels of which proclaimed them to contain pancake makeup. He smirked at the flesh-colored makeup-covered gobs of tissue tossed helter-skelter onto the vanity and wondered if the bimbo would be recognizable without all that goop.

"What have you been up to?" he murmured.

He strode to Dierdre's walk-in closet and stared at the couple of dozen or so empty hangers. Of the few outfits remaining, none were the flashy costumes Dierdre had proudly shown him while boring him into a coma with tales of her time in Las Vegas.

Was the bimbo in the process of moving? Maybe she had gone into some kind of psychological meltdown after kicking him out and just started mindlessly dumping stuff. Deetz surprised himself by chuckling out loud at images of Mindless Dierdre screaming around her apartment tearing crap off the walls.

Half hoping the arrogant witch would return so he

could deal with her properly, Deetz strode to the kitchen, pulled dishes from the cupboards, and flung them onto the floor. He raked food from the refrigerator, satisfied with the resulting broken jars of pickles, mayonnaise, and salad dressings.

A coldness replaced the burning in his solar plexus as he walked toward the back door. If he had the time, it would have been his pleasure to burn the place down.

When his phone rang as he neared the kitchen door, he checked the ID then pushed the green answer icon.

"Hey, Lou-Lou," he said. "Sorry I missed your calls, but I'm in a fix. You remember offering to loan me a few hundred bucks to start up a custom paint shop?"

"Yeah, about that," Lou said. "I'm afraid I have to renege on that offer. Would you believe somebody stole my truck? I called the cops and reported it, but if they don't find it, I'll need whatever funds I can scrape together for a down payment on some new wheels. Is there any way you can come pick me up?"

Every hair on Deetz's body moved. Wordlessly, he shut down the call.

Chapter Thirty-Nine

Petra and Cody stepped inside Bradley's apartment and waited for him to close the door.

Fighting the urge to hold her nose against the nearly overpowering odor of unwashed humanity, Petra did a visual scan of the living room. One orange, molded-plastic chair sat next to a cardboard box upon which a coffee cup rested. No other furnishings were visible, no photos on the stained and faded walls, no sofa, no television.

"I really appreciate you showing up so fast," Bradley said. He handed Petra a scrap of note paper and added, "This is my license plate number, although whoever took my truck has probably put on different tags by now." He pointed toward the paper. "I've included a description of my pickup, too."

Petra's brow furrowed as she glanced first at Cody then back at Bradley. "You're saying someone has stolen your pickup?"

"Yeah," Bradley said, a look of confusion on his face. "Isn't that why you're here?

"When did you report it?" Cody said.

"Not twenty minutes ago." Bradley cleared his throat. "Like I told the police operator, I went out with a friend last night and left my truck at the bar, but when I went back this morning, it was gone."

"Mister Bradley," Petra interrupted, "who were

you with last night?"

"Ronnie Deetz. We sometimes go out when neither of us has anything else going on."

"What time did you get to the bar?" Cody said.

"A little before nine. That's when Ronnie told me we'd meet up."

"And what time did Mister Deetz arrive?" Cody said.

"I'm not sure of the exact time," Bradley said. "I just remember he was late." He grimaced. "I was pretty well hammered by the time he got there, so it had to be at least ten or later."

"Do you know where Mister Deetz is now?" Petra said.

"I have no idea," Bradly said, "but he called me just before you got here."

"Did he say anything that would indicate where he is?" Cody said.

"Only that he was needing some cash." Bradley's gaze moved back and forth between Petra and Cody. "What's going on? Is Ronnie in trouble?"

"What is your relationship with Mister Deetz?" Cody said.

"I guess we'd be called drinking buddies." Bradley lowered his gaze and studied the tops of his work boots. "I've known him a couple of years."

"Have you seen him today?" Petra said.

"Naw." Bradley shook his head. "I haven't seen him since he brought me home last night."

"Do you know any other place he might hang out," Petra said, "maybe someplace he always wanted to go?"

"Have you talked to his girlfriend Dierdre Mozul?"

Bradley said, a wistful look on his face. "She might know where he is."

After a few more questions, Petra removed a business card from her pocket and handed it to Bradley. "If he contacts you again, I'd appreciate it if you would give me a call."

"Sure." Bradley palmed the card, studied the printed front, then put it into his pocket.

"Meanwhile, we'd like to examine your phone, if that would be okay with you," Petra said.

Bradley pulled the phone from his pants pocket and held it out toward Petra. "When can I get it back? I'm supposed to work this weekend, and I need to find a ride."

"It would be better if you brought it with you to the main police station," Petra said. "We have software there to access the information on it. We'll drive you to the station and then bring you back." *...and so you will not have a chance to delete any texts, photos, contacts, or messages.*

"Sure, okay," Bradley said. "But what about my truck?"

"If you haven't done so yet, you should probably contact the New Mexico Motor Vehicle Department to cancel the registration," Petra said. "Otherwise, the thief may re-register it, using falsified documents."

"Great, just great," Bradley said. His shoulders drooped and he frowned.

"In our experience," Petra continued, "sometimes vehicles reported stolen are actually *borrowed* by a relative or friend. Any chance this is what happened?"

"Naw," Bradley said, a look of confusion on his face. "I don't have any relatives here. Ronnie Deetz is my best friend, but he has his own truck. He doesn't need mine."

"New Mexico is adjacent to an international border," Cody said. "We do rank pretty high for auto theft, but your pickup doesn't fit the usual target."

"You know, *it is* kind of weird," Bradley said. "My truck's old as dirt and guzzles oil. I always figured no self-respecting car thief would want to mess with it. It only had about an eighth of a tank of gas, so it won't be going far. Maybe someone towed it?" He looked thoughtful, "or maybe hotwired it." He pulled a set of keys from his pocket and jiggled them. "I thought at first I might have left my keys in it, but I got them right here."

"Anyone else have a key?" Petra said.

"Naw." Bradley shook his head, his eyes cast down. "I, um, if you find it, what will happen?" Perspiration popped out in beads on his nearly bald head, and he scuffed a work boot on the thick pile of matted, decades-old shag carpet.

Petra and Cody exchanged looks, their suspicions obviously flowing along the same path. It was not unusual for a reportedly stolen vehicle to turn out to be a case of insurance fraud where the owner needed fast money and either paid someone to steal their vehicle or abandoned it in a remote area. Then, when the insurance company paid up, the owner used the money to pay off the vehicle or pocketed the cash.

"Mister Bradley," Petra said, "if there's something you need to get off your chest, now would be a good time."

Bradley gulped then licked his lips. "I guess you'll find out soon enough." He looked at the detectives, his eyes pleading for understanding. "I don't have any insurance on my truck."

Petra stopped herself from shaking her head. While a confession of complicity in Deetz's activities would have been more helpful, Bradley's agitation at the all-too-common local offense of driving while uninsured allowed a measure of insight into his character. As Cody had said, he came across as a relatively decent sort who just could not get his act together.

"If your pickup *is* found," Cody said, "it will be impounded, and you'll not be allowed to take delivery until you can offer proof of insurance. You can get some fairly inexpensive rates if you shop around."

Bradley started to say something, but his phone rang, and he looked at the caller ID. "It's Ron."

"Answer it," Petra said, "but don't tell him we're looking for him. If you get a chance, ask him where he is."

"Hey, Ron," Bradley said. "What? I can't hear you." He looked at Petra with a what-should-I-do look.

Petra motioned for Bradley to continue talking.

"Where are you?" Bradley paused. "Ron? You still there? Hello?" He lowered the phone and said, "I don't know if my phone dropped the call, but the line just went dead."

Chapter Forty

Deetz smiled as he stood in the middle of Dierdre's living room and studied his handiwork. Short of kicking holes in the walls, something he might do later if he had time, he was leaving relatively few things intact.

He stepped over a smashed rattan chair, picked up a ceramic lamp from a small table beside the sofa and threw it to the floor. The resulting crash not only sounded loud enough to catch the attention of any passersby but pulled him back to reality.

He looked at his watch, surprised to see he had been inside the apartment for nearly an hour. If his math was correct, he had about thirty minutes before the old bag returned.

All too aware that he had not eaten since the night before, Deetz strode to the kitchen. He stepped over broken condiment bottles, opened the refrigerator, and peered inside. A half-filled quart carton of milk and a bowl of the Cheerios he had poured onto the cabinet earlier would tide him over until he got enough money to have a proper meal.

He smiled. Envisioning the look on Dierdre's face when she returned and saw the wreckage, he pulled a chipped cup with a broken handle from the cabinet and used it as a scoop for the cereal. He selected a spoon from among the cutlery scattered on the floor then poured the milk and hastily ate. As an afterthought, he smashed the empty bowl on the floor then sloshed the last bit of milk on top of the broken glass.

It galled Deetz that Lou had run whining to the cops about the bum's missing pickup. But worse than that, it rankled that while Deetz was broke, his *good buddy* had enough money to make a down payment on a new truck, money he had offered Deetz before changing his mind.

While pawning Dierdre's jewelry would bring a few bucks, pawn shops only paid a small percentage of an item's actual worth. Deetz would be surprised if he netted four or five hundred dollars out of the deal.

One option was to wait for Dierdre's return then make her give him any cash she might have in her purse. Or he could force her to go to an ATM. There was no telling how much money she had in her account. Maybe she had *several* accounts, each one filled with money. Mister Z kept four or five.

Once Deetz had the woman's cash, he could deal with her the way he had been itching to do from the minute she plopped his keys onto her coffee table. It would be like rubbing salve on an open wound to hurt her bad, to show her who was boss. By the time she recovered enough to call the cops, Deetz would be in Mexico wooing a lovely young señorita.

However, while Dierdre might be past her prime, she was no dummy. She could have figured he would come back, so took her stash to one of those automatic deposit kiosks installed all over the city. By the time she threw him out that morning, she was looking at him with an expression on her face he had never seen before.

A muffled voice in his head suggested he steer

clear of Dierdre-the-Has-Been. Given that she had thoroughly wiped him off her emotional etch-a-sketch, she would not hesitate to turn him in if she got the chance. The cops would swoop in and haul him off in handcuffs.

Even so, if all else failed, he might chance it. She could be made to disappear the same as that nosey Marcato woman. He still had the key to the scrapyard, and there were plenty of open trunks ready and waiting. There was still one other option, although it was less than perfect.

Deetz sighed, pulled his phone from a jacket pocket, and punched in Lou's number. He was geared up to begin his prepared speech but choked back a bellow when seconds after the doofus answered, his voice was cut off mid-sentence.

Figuring the guy's cheap-o service provider must have dropped the call, Deetz re-dialed. But instead of the ring-back tone that preceded outgoing calls, dead air announced the phone had run out of minutes.

"Dammit!" Deetz threw the pay-as-you-go phone against the wall. The useless piece of junk shattered, sending plastic and glass bits skittering across the floor.

When had the penny-pinching broad found the time to cancel the credit card charge that regularly re-loaded the phone with minutes? Besides having no wheels and no money, Deetz now had no phone.

Muttering invectives, he mulled over a roster of options until, finally, an idea formed itself into a solid thought. He would retrieve his luggage from Lou's pickup and hide it somewhere. Then he would walk the few blocks to the guy's apartment and offer to tell him where he could find his truck in exchange for money and a few hours' head start.

Once Deetz had the chump's cash in his pocket, he would jack another vehicle and get out of the country. Then he would go off-grid and live *la vida loca.* He could almost taste the margaritas and hear the mariachi music.

Deetz took a deep, lingering breath and strode toward Dierdre's back door. Quashing a building sense that he was once again forgetting something important, he retraced his steps through the various back yards and tromped through the ice and snow to Lou's pickup.

Once there, he pulled his suitcases from beneath a grease-stained tarpaulin in the truck bed. He placed the smaller bag on the pickup's hood, opened it, then unfolded a T-shirt and stared at the nine-millimeter handgun inside.

Should he take the weapon with him to Lou's or leave it behind? As a felon, if Deetz were caught with a gun, it could mean jail time. On the other hand, having it readily accessible gave him a sense of security, a feeling of being in control. He had learned early on that people who worked for Mister Z sometimes got hurt.

"Why not," he muttered, reaching for the weapon. "Better safe than sorry."

To ensure he didn't shoot his ass off, Deetz made sure no bullet was in the chamber and that the gun's safety was engaged. Then he stuffed the weapon, barrel first, under his belt at the small of his back.

He hefted both suitcases and hurried to a nearby ravine where he had spotted a dry storm drainpipe underneath the road. He stuffed the luggage inside the two-foot high pipe then pulled a couple of downed tree branches over the opening.

His breath forming clouds in the frigid air, Deetz grimaced as he shoveled ice and snow over the branches with his bare hands.

Once the luggage was hidden to his satisfaction, he rubbed his stinging hands together to stimulate circulation. The friction only intensified the dagger-jab ache in his fingers, and he bit his tongue to keep from hollering.

He stamped his feet to remove the ice and snow caked on his boots. But the warmth from his feet had melted some of the adhering slush, sending rivulets of freezing water through the lace holes. It soaked his socks and pooled inside his boots so he *squish*-ed when he walked. His toes were numb; he was hungry enough to eat anything that didn't eat him first, and he was getting madder by the second.

Deetz had heard of people dying from the cold without even realizing they were in trouble. They got lost in some isolated place, sat down in the ice and snow, then fell asleep…forever.

At least Lou's apartment would be warm; and he would have food and booze. The guy might be a loser-slob, but he could always be depended on to share.

Careful to keep to alleyways and side streets, Deetz started walking.

Chapter Forty-One

Petra escorted Bradley to an interview room and motioned toward a chair. Like a caged animal looking for an escape route, he scanned the room, glancing briefly on the camera and audio recording devices.

"Are you recording me?" Bradley said. "Don't you have to get my permission or something?"

"It is standard procedure," Petra said. "At this point, we're just gathering information."

"I guess that's okay."

"We appreciate your cooperation," Petra said. "The process of downloading your phone will take about twenty minutes; then someone will drive you home."

"Can you tell me what's going on?" Bradley said.

"I can only tell you that we are involved in an investigation."

"Are you investigating me?" Bradley's eyes opened so wide their bloodshot whites resembled a roadmap encircling a mud-filled sinkhole. "I don't think I've done anything."

"As I said, we are just collecting information." Petra offered a reassuring smile.

Another officer entered the room and left with Bradley's phone, and Petra resumed the questioning.

"Has Mister Deetz ever mentioned the names of any of his acquaintances?"

"Naw." Bradley's expression grew thoughtful. "He

did sometimes brag about knowing people who were in the business of making lots of money. I got the feeling they were not what you would call model citizens, if you know what I mean." He paused thoughtfully then added, "I don't know if that means anything, though, because he is always short of cash. And Ronnie is a great one to tell stories."

Petra offered Bradley a cup of coffee and asked a few more questions. The officer returned with Bradley's phone, and Petra escorted him to a car waiting to take him home.

As Petra walked back to the station, she reviewed the interview. Since, other than Mozul, Bradley appeared to be Deetz's only known associate, he remained on her persons-of-interest list. However, based on her years of investigative experience, she instinctively felt that Bradley was innocent of anything more than living a miserable, lonely existence. Like Cody said: *just a sad thirty-year-old who couldn't get his act together.*

Her phone buzzed, and she read a message from Tex. *Finished one quadrant and moving on to the second. So far, Nellie's got nothing.*

No sooner had Petra shot off a response to Tex than her department-issued phone buzzed again, and she automatically read the incoming text.

You have been naughty. Naughty people get punished.

Petra raked her teeth across her bottom lip and considered her response.

While a few of the folks she arrested or against whom she testified in court hurled verbal abuse at her, their anger typically became diluted by virtue of publicly venting it. Most of them recognized they were in enough trouble without adding potential charges of verbal assault against an officer of the law to their resume.

Her phone buzzed again, and she opened the text.

Bet you're wondering if I'm in town.

The flesh on Petra's forearms felt like she had fallen into a bed of fire ants, and the blood drained from her face. The sensation that she was being watched moved from a slight twinge to a full-on warning gong. She swiveled her head and eyed her surroundings as the hairs on the back of her neck moved.

Part of Petra's brain scoffed at the idea that Kent would have gone to the trouble and expense of tracking her to Albuquerque. Another part, the part that housed the horrific images of every murderous assault she had ever investigated, recalled his threats against her as he was arrested and hauled to jail.

How had he found her? She had been so careful to erase her past.

A recollection bubbled up from Petra's subconscious. She remembered a television reporter tried to interview her during a recent serial murder investigation that had drawn national attention. She had waved the reporter off, but not before the young woman's cameraman caught her on tape in time for the evening news.

Again, her phone buzzed.

You'll never see it coming.

Petra clamped her jaws together. The fear she thought she left in Ohio morphed into heat that rose from the soles of her feet and burned through her body like a wildfire.

She had left friends and a decent job to get away from this jackass. Never again. She would not spend the rest of her life looking over her shoulder.

Unable to tamp down the impulse, she texted a response: *You mess with me, and I will defend myself.*

Instantly, her phone buzzed: *Thanks for the heads-up.*

With one last glance around the area, Petra hurried back inside the station.

She would have another law enforcement officer photo and document the texts and call log on her phone, thereby protecting herself against possible future charges of tampering with evidence. From that moment on, she would collect and preserve any bit of evidence that could be used to prove Kent's campaign of sustained harassment. She would do everything in her power to see to it that he was put away for years.

Chapter Forty-Two

Deetz rounded the corner a block up the street from Lou's apartment complex in time to see a cop car pull to the curb in front of the guy's door. His heart rate kicked into high gear, as he slipped behind a Salvation Army donation drop-off bin then peered around the shed-like structure's corner.

Lou got out of the car, stooped, and said something to the driver. He then waved, turned, and walked toward his apartment.

The ice-coated sidewalk proved too difficult to navigate, and he slipped. He performed a jig worthy of a River Dance troupe before his feet flew out from under him, and he fell flat on his can.

The cop powered down his window and yelled an offer of help, but Lou shook his head. "I'm good," he hollered. After several attempts, he managed to get his feet under him and stood. With slow, ballerina-dainty steps, he limped to his front door.

Deetz watched until the cop was out of sight then counted to sixty for good measure before moving from his hiding place. He glanced up and down the street then walked to Lou's door.

Eyeing the busted doorbell's varicolored wires dangling like a mass of dried rat entrails, Deetz knocked on the door.

"Lou-Lou," he stage-whispered with his lips near

the doorjamb. "It's me, buddy. Open up."

Lou pulled the door open, a quizzical look on his face. "Hey, man. You know the cops are looking for you?" He glanced over Deetz's shoulder and into the street.

"Yeah, I know." Deetz pushed his way into the apartment. "I need help, man."

"What kind of trouble are you in?"

"Nothing much. I broke up with Dierdre, and she took it hard." Deetz plastered an embarrassed look on his face. "She kicked me out then called the cops and told them I broke into her place and took some of her stuff."

"Why would she say that?" Lou cocked his head a puzzled look on his face.

"Only thing I can figure is it's one of those *hell hath no fury like a woman scorned* things." Deetz shrugged. "I never thought I'd say this, Lou, but she's pretty desperate for male attention." He grinned. "You might have a shot, now that she's single again."

Lou blushed. "She'd never look twice at me." He got an *aw-shucks* look on his face and stared at his feet.

"I went to the bar and got your truck this morning." When Lou's head jerked up, Deetz took a deep breath and hurried on. "Dierdre took the keys to mine, so I figured you wouldn't mind me picking it up for you."

"It was you who took my pickup?" Lou looked like he had swallowed a gnat. "How'd you get it started?" His eyebrows drew together, and his forehead wrinkled. "Did you hotwire my truck?" Lou said, the closest expression of anger Deetz had ever seen on his face. "You might have permanently messed up the wiring. I got enough trouble keeping Irene running without having to re-do the wiring."

"Irene?" Deetz snorted.

"That's what I call my truck," Lou said, his face scarlet.

"Like I was trying to tell you before my phone died, there's no permanent damage to Irene-the-truck." Deetz felt the expression on his face shift from friendly to offended. "I've wired enough cars and trucks to know how to do it properly."

"Yeah, okay," Lou said. "No offense."

"I figure it's a win-win when you think about it," Deetz said. "I had to run a few errands, and I knew you would need to go get your pickup, so I thought I'd save you the trouble."

"But why would Dierdre keep your keys?" Lou said, his brain obviously unable to move beyond that thought. "She can't sell it; she's not the legal owner." He looked up and studied the ceiling, deep in thought. "I'm not even sure she could drive it without your permission." He looked back at Deetz. "But then, you drove Irene without my permission."

"I think she only meant to keep my apartment key, you know, to evict me or something," Deetz said. "But my truck key was on the same keyring." He shrugged. "Like I said, hell hath no fury."

Lou pondered that tidbit for a few heartbeats, then shrugged and pulled his phone from one pocket and a business card from another. After studying the card, he began punching numbers into the phone.

"What're you doing?" Deetz said uneasily.

"I gotta call the cops and tell them they can stop looking for my pickup."

"Yeah, you should do that," Deetz said

thoughtfully. "But don't tell them it was me that took it, okay? Maybe you can tell them that you just forgot where you left it." Deetz looked up at the ceiling, his mind a swarming beehive of activity. "Apologize all over the place and thank them for being so understanding." He smiled at the sudden shift in circumstances. Lou's pickup would no longer be on the cop watchlist if Deetz played the guy right.

"Good idea," Lou said.

"By the way," Deetz said, "you know that start-up money you promised me?" He generated what he hoped was a disarming smile.

"What about it?" Lou said.

"Since you won't need it for a down payment on a new pickup, you can loan it to me, like you said."

Lou remained silent for several seconds then got a look on his face as though he had just figured out how the earth was formed. He shot a crafty look at Deetz. "I'll tell you what, I'll loan you the two hundred and add another hundred if you help me do some work."

"What kind of work?" Deetz said.

"I gotta load three junkers on the hauler so I can drive them to Ruidoso on Monday."

"I don't have any experience with that kind of thing," Deetz said.

"You don't have to have experience for what I have in mind."

"What *do* you have in mind?" Deetz said.

"I'm no good at driving backward, you know, I tend to reverse into stuff. It's a depth perception problem. I figure you could stand to one side of the junkers where I can see you in the rearview. You can guide me."

"And for this you'll pay me three hundred bucks?" Deetz said, unable to believe his luck.

"I'll pay you one hundred for the work," Lou said. "The other two hundred is the loan for your start-up painting business."

"Oh yeah," Deetz said, "the start-up loan." Although something told him he needed to get away, three hundred in cash would be enough for gas to the border, as well as for a decent dinner. The cereal he ate at Dierdre's had long since worn off, and he could not very well offer a restaurant cashier one of the old bimbo's rings as payment for a meal. Besides, he had no choice but to stay as invisible as possible.

"What do you say?" Lou said cheerfully.

If the doofus were a puppy, his tail would be wagging.

"Deal," Deetz said, "but first, you got anything in your fridge? I haven't eaten since last night." He rubbed his hands together as warmth from the apartment seeped into his fingers.

"Only thing I got is a couple of pieces of bread and a hunk of liver sausage."

"Liver sausage?" Deetz grimaced. "You're kidding. You don't even have a can of soup you can warm up, or maybe some coffee?"

"Naw." Lou shook his head, a look of embarrassment on his face. "I probably should do some shopping."

"Yeah, okay." Deetz wiped a suspicious expression off his face. How did the blubber-ass manage to keep all that belly fat hanging over his belt if he didn't keep any food handy? "You got something to drink? I'd settle for a beer."

"I'm back on the wagon," Lou said, "...but there may be milk in the fridge. There is no guarantee it's not past its use-by date, though."

"Back on the wagon. Right." Deetz felt his upper lip curl into a sneer. "So how many times does this make?"

Lou nodded but remained silent and unmoving, a hurt look on his doofus face.

"Okay, okay," Deetz said. "Sorry about that, Lou-Lou, but I'm in a real bind here, you know? Maybe we should get going."

Lou nodded once and walked to his kitchenette. He pulled a check book and pen out of a drawer filled with junk and sat at the table.

"I can't take a check." Deetz briefly closed his eyes against the headache that was growing in intensity. "What I mean is---"

"No problem. I have cash."

"Perfect. Can't go wrong with cash," Deetz said. He would have money and could even *borrow* Lou's pickup, now that the cops would no longer be looking for it. By the time Lou suspected what had happened, Deetz would be across the border with cash, jewelry, and a free-and-clear pickup. Not a bad haul. "Maybe you should call the cops about your truck before we leave," he said.

"About that," Lou said with an apologetic look. "Here's the thing, I got no insurance. If we get stopped, I'll get a ticket and the cops will impound my pickup. Maybe we should take a cab or one of those Uber things."

"The cops can't pull you over for no reason," Deetz said. "If you drive the speed limit and don't make any illegal turns or pass on a double yellow, you got nothing to worry about." He paused. "Your tags up to date? No smoking exhaust pipe or broken taillight?"

"Naw. I'm real careful about all that, and the headlights are new."

"Then you got nothing to worry about, especially if you stay on side streets. You can always get cheap insurance after Christmas." Deetz smiled. As for himself, he would spend Christmas partying in Mexico. A few *cerveza's* and a pretty, generous-hearted woman would make it his best Christmas ever.

Lou rang the number on the detective's business card. As Deetz had coached him, he spoke briefly, apologized profusely, expressed gratitude, then broke the connection.

"Once we're done with the job, you need to turn yourself in to the cops," Lou said. "It's always best to face that kind of trouble head-on."

"Yeah, I'll do that, I surely will." Deetz squelched a snort of derision.

"You can't outrun cop trouble, you know." Lou turned his eyes upward. "There's no place on earth you can---"

"I heard you the first time," Deetz said. The bum should have been a preacher.

"Hey, maybe you can patch things up with Dierdre, you know, give her some flowers and chocolates." A but-I-hope-you-won't expression on his face, Lou added, "Maybe she'll drop the charges."

"Now, there's a thought." Deetz ground his teeth. He would take relationship advice from a three-time loser like Lou Bradley when NASA finally admitted the world was flat and the moon landing a hoax.

"Give me a second." Lou disappeared down a hallway. A door creaked then drawers opened and closed. He returned stuffing a wad of something into his jeans. "Where'd you park?" he said.

"Heh, that's kind of funny," Deetz said, adding an embarrassed chuckle for effect. "I left your truck parked near Dierdre's. We will have to walk, but it's only a few blocks. I'll explain on the way."

Deetz tried to gin up a warm, best-buddy smile to prevent Lou from over-thinking the situation. Judging by the expression on the guy's face, it had the intended result.

Hopefully, the dumbo would be so thrilled at the idea of getting his pickup back, he would not ask too many questions. By the time they got to the vehicle, Deetz would have figured out a plausible explanation.

"Better bundle up, Lou-Lou." Deetz took a friendly poke at the other man's shoulder. "As my old man used to say, the wind's a-howling."

Chapter Forty-Three

After filling her sergeant in on her history with Kent Fowler, Petra stepped out of his office and headed toward the coffee pot in the breakroom. She had just removed the lid from her thermos and placed it on the counter next to the coffee maker when her phone rang.

"Um, is this Detective Rooney?" the masculine voice said.

"Speaking," Petra said.

"This is Lou Bradley. You remember, Ronnie Deetz's friend? We just talked a little while ago."

"Yes, Mister Bradley." Petra bounced up and down on the balls of her feet as a small shot of adrenaline heightened her senses. Mentally crossing her fingers that Bradley was calling with Deetz's location, she said, "What can I do for you?"

In excruciatingly slow speech, Bradley fell all over himself explaining that he suddenly remembered where he parked his pickup. He apologized for wasting police time and hesitatingly promised not to drive without insurance.

"That's great, thanks for calling," Petra interjected when he paused to take a breath. Something at the back of her brain whispered the whole missing pickup episode was off, but she was working a homicide and an abduction, so a stolen pickup that turned out *not* to be stolen was low on her list. Petra broke the connection and shoved the conversation to the back of her brain.

She was filling her thermos with coffee when Cody strode in, an excited look on his face.

"We may have a break," Cody said. "Dispatch just got a call from an elderly neighbor watching Dierdre Mozul's property. The woman was nearly incoherent, but finally calmed down enough to report someone's broken into Mozul's apartment."

"Could she give Dispatch a description?"

"No," Cody said. "The woman thought she saw movement through a gap in Mozul's blinds, but figured it must be *Dierdre's fancy man*, so didn't pay much attention at first." Cody shook his head. "Apparently, it began to weigh on the old dear, so she finally called Mozul, who told her to call us."

"We'll go in mine," Petra said. "You have Mozul's number handy?"

"Yep." Cody pulled his department-issued phone from its holder. "I'll call her on the way."

Chapter Forty-Four

Dierdre lip synced to music pulsing from her car radio as images of the Ojo Caliente hot springs, spa massages, cold drinks and great food flooded her head. Snowy, frigid weather notwithstanding, she might even pop for a mud bath.

Her phone rang from its in-dash docking device, and she glanced at the caller ID. Her pulse quickened slightly, and she shut off the radio then pushed the Bluetooth button on her steering wheel.

"Hello Iris," she said.

"Hello dear." The elderly woman cleared her throat. "I don't mean to interrupt your vacation, but you did ask me to keep an eye on your place."

"No apologies necessary," Dierdre said, her voice tight. "Is everything okay?"

"Did you give anyone permission to stay in your apartment while you're gone?" She cleared her throat. "Your feller, maybe?"

"I no longer have a *feller*." Dierdre glanced at her phone. When she moved her gaze back to the road, the car in front of her had unexpectedly slowed, forcing her to slam on the brakes and swerve to avoid a collision. Lightheaded at the near miss, she pulled off the highway and onto the shoulder.

"Are you still there, dear?"

"Yes." Dierdre took a deep breath. "No one should

be in my apartment. Please hang up and call the police then call me back."

After disconnecting the call, Dierdre sat staring straight ahead as an internal debate raged. Finally, she opened her phone's screen and punched in a number.

"This is Dierdre Mozul," she said to the receptionist at Ojo Caliente. "I have a reservation for the next two weeks, but I need to postpone it. I'll call back later to re-schedule." She clicked the end-call button, cutting off whatever the receptionist was saying.

Dierdre pulled her vehicle onto the interstate, took the next exit, then merged onto the lane heading toward Albuquerque. She gripped the steering wheel so tightly her arms began to ache.

She could hardly stand the thought of someone going through her things. While her apartment complex was not located in the best part of town, she had never been burgled. In fact, she made it a point to maintain amiable relationships with all her renters, several of whom had formed themselves into an active neighborhood watch group. While most of her tenants were not great money-earners, they generally paid their rent on time. If someone had broken into her place, she felt it wouldn't be one of them.

The morning's final episode in the soap opera that had been her relationship with Ronnie Deetz filled her thoughts. His fear of being spotted by the police had been over-the-top. That, combined with the look he shot at her as he crept around her back yard, had tripped her internal alarm.

Dierdre had dealt with every imaginable kind of male and female over the course of her career in Las Vegas. She had dodged octopus-handed drunks and managed to co-exist with women jealous of her success. By the time she took early retirement, she had learned to recognize and even anticipate a wide range of human, and not so human, emotions and behaviors.

As a result, she had instantly recognized the moment it dawned on Deetz that he was burning his last bridge with her. The look on his face had morphed from rage to disbelief, then to pure desperation.

In Dierdre's experience, rage could be calmed. Disbelief could be nudged in a different direction by offering facts. On the other hand, desperation had no easy remedy. That made Deetz a potentially dangerous man.

He had no money, no vehicle, and no place to stay. The snow and freezing temperatures would compel him to find ways to fill those needs – especially someplace warm to hole up.

Maybe he never left her neighborhood. Maybe he had been sitting in Lou's pickup in the parking lot trying to figure out what to do and saw her leave with packed bags. He was perfectly capable of taking advantage of her absence by flopping in her apartment.

If it *were* Deetz who had broken into her apartment, and if he were still there, he was poised to learn a lesson the hard way. Dierdre would press charges for his every legal infraction.

She chuckled derisively. Since she had taken all her cash and packed most of her expensive jewelry in her luggage, pickings would be somewhat slim.

"So, *nanner-nanner-foo-foo*," she muttered.

Still, a few high-dollar pieces remained in her apartment, along with several special gifts received over the years, things of little intrinsic value but precious because of memories they stirred. When she got home, she would call Detective Rooney in case Iris's call hadn't found the right ear.

What if the burglar wasn't Deetz, but a stranger? What would she do if he were still inside her apartment by the time she got there? Or, what if he saw her and made a run for it? Should she follow him and call the police along the way? What would she do if he had a weapon?

Dierdre's insides jittered with indecision as she passed the Albuquerque city limits and approached the Central Avenue exit minutes from her home.

Her phone rang, jarring her.

"Mizz Mozul?" the masculine voice said. "This is Detective Cody Rankin. I'm afraid I have some bad news."

"I know about the break-in," Dierdre said. "Iris Jenkins called me."

"Ah, okay," Detective Rankin said. "Detective Rooney and I are on our way to your apartment now. You can either meet us there, or if you prefer, you can give us verbal permission to have our investigative team process the apartment in your absence."

"Thank you for the option," Dierdre said, "but I should be there within fifteen minutes or so, depending on traffic."

"Great," the detective said. "It's possible someone is still inside, so when you arrive, you'll need to stay in your vehicle until we have secured the area."

"I'll do that," Dierdre said, relief flooding her midsection.

She tapped the red disconnect icon on her phone. In spite of herself, she smiled at the thought of the cute, chubby detective who had come to her apartment in the middle of the night looking for Deetz. While she did not remember seeing a wedding band on his ring finger, she did notice the way he looked at her. And she remembered that smooth, deep voice -- authoritative, yet velvety. He seemed self-confident and was old enough to have weathered more than a few of life's storms.

Maybe instead of going on vacation after the dust settled from the current break-in drama, she would stay in town for a while. The hot springs at Ojo Caliente were said to have been around for over three thousand years. They could certainly wait a little longer for a visit from Dierdre Mozul.

Chapter Forty-Five

Robin shoved her hands through the jagged rip in the back seat and ran her fingers along the strips of metal anchoring the zigzag springs. As far as she could tell, the manufacturer's assembly-line workers had spot-welded the springs to the strips rather than run a full bead where they intersected. If she were right, mere bubbles of welding wire held the springs in place, tiny balls of metal that could be broken with properly applied force.

Perhaps a few well-placed kicks would do the trick. In theory, once the springs were loosed from their metal moorings, she could separate a couple of them and wiggle through.

Meanwhile, the trunk seemed to be growing warmer. Maybe the weather forecaster had missed the mark. Maybe the sun was brighter and hotter than any of the forecasting models projected. More than one forecaster had been led astray by New Mexico's sneaky weather.

Robin threw the comforter off and started to unbutton her blouse.

You are in moderate hypothermia and your body's lying to you, Robbie Girl. Wrap yourself in the comforter, then kick the hell out of that back seat.

"Shays who?" Robin's tongue felt like a thick, gummy slab of raw bacon.

Your speech is slurred.

"Snot fair," Robin sobbed.

Stop that crying, Robin Marie, or I'll give you something to cry about.

Unwilling to argue with her mother's memory, Robin wrapped herself in the comforter as commanded. She sipped the accumulated water from a moccasin then slid it onto her right foot. After turning onto her left side, she pushed her shoed foot through the slit in the seat backing and kicked against the metal strips. Pain from her knee shot up her leg when the springs bowed but refused to break loose.

Robin gasped and rubbed the flesh along the inside of her kneecap.

"By knee," she said. "I broke sumpin in by knee."

You have another leg.

"Why nod?" Robin said. "Bight as well make it a matched set." Obediently, she turned onto her right side and kicked at the slats with her left leg. Within seconds, she was rewarded by the loud *pop* of a spring breaking free. With a whispered whoop of victory, she wrestled the loosened springs until the resulting gap felt wide enough to squeeze through.

Once she pushed her arms beyond the springs, however, her fingers jammed against the seat's back cushion, a fabric covered pad most likely stuffed with foam.

"Even if I get through duh cushion," Robin whispered, "I can't get through whad will mos' ligely be the outer leather sheat cover, and I broke by glass shhard."

One step at a time, Robbie Girl.

Chapter Forty-Six

By the time Deetz and Lou left the apartment, the wind had picked up. It whipped powdery snow into frenzied eddies that stuck to their faces, numbing their noses, and jabbing ice needles into their cheeks. The windchill dropped into single digits, sending gusts up the duo's pant legs and freezing their backsides. While Deetz ground his teeth and cursed himself for not having the foresight to wear a heavier coat, someone had seemingly plugged in Lou's power cord.

The guy yakked about everything under the sun. He talked about how excited and grateful he was to have been offered the extra work assignment. He said that although the overtime pay would be less than he had offered Deetz, doing the work would prove he was ready for more responsibility. More responsibility would mean better pay. He rambled on about how sorry he was that Deetz and Dierdre broke up, yadda, yadda, yadda. By the time he got around to whining about how tough Christmas would be having no one special with whom to share it, Deetz was ready to throttle him.

There was Deetz, frost hanging off his chin; fingers shooting pains up his hands made blue by the cold wind; toes long since numb, and his back and tailbone aching. And there was Lou, happily trotting along like they were on a summer walking excursion in Yuma, Arizona instead of slogging through snow and slush.

Finally, out of a sense of self-preservation, Deetz tuned out the dolt's ramblings and thought about his future.

He wondered what the temperature would be in Mexico. He envisioned himself wearing designer swim trunks, sitting on a pool-side chaise lounge, wearing sunglasses, drinking some frou-frou designer beverage with a tiny umbrella while thumbing his nose at the rest of the world. He fantasized about starting his own business hauling people from Mexico into the States. Mostly, though, he thought about the stuff he would buy with the money that business would generate.

His first purchase would be a panel truck large enough to hold at least ten people. He would go first class and install a heater and air conditioner in the rear compartment. Maybe he would even install padded seats. Like the late, great Vince Banda once said, *word of mouth would get around*. He would make a ton of money after people learned that relocating with him would be safe and comfortable.

By the time Lou's pickup came into view, Deetz had mentally generated a workable business plan. Now all he had to do was make it happen.

"There she is." Giggling like a seventh-grade girl who just got her first kiss, Lou pulled the key from his pocket. "There's my Irene."

As Lou climbed onto the driver's seat, Deetz slid into the passenger's side.

"Glad to see you, Irene." Lou patted the dashboard.

"It's a truck, Lou," Deetz said, "not a cocker spaniel."

Lou shot a snotty look at his buddy then frowned as he looked at the multi-colored wires dangling from the steering column. Assessing the damage, he stared at the steering column cover and access panels lying in the floor next to Deetz's feet and *tsk-ed*.

"You shoulda called me, Ron. You didn't have to do this to Irene." Like a brain surgeon focused on performing a life-saving operation, Lou slowly and methodically covered the stripped wiring with electrical tape he pulled from the glove compartment, then replaced the access panels and steering column cover.

"I did try to get hold of you, Lou-Lou." Deetz made his voice as conciliatory as his impatience would allow. "I went by your place, but you were passed out. Then I tried to call you, but before I could tell you anything, my phone died, as you may recall."

"What's the rush? You coulda come back later. You coulda called after I woke up."

"You mean I should have known the exact time you would regain consciousness from your drunken stupor?" Deetz said, his effort to keep the disgust out of his voice unsuccessful. "I'm pretty good about figuring stuff out, but I don't have ESP."

Lou sniffed but didn't respond.

"Anyway," Deetz said, "tomorrow's Christmas Eve, and I need the money for gifts."

"So, you *are* going to try to win Dierdre back," Lou said. "I hope that works out, Ron-Ron-duh-doo-Ron-Ron."

"Like you said, maybe she'll drop the charges," Deetz said, then swallowed a derisive snort. *How had the doofus managed to survive beyond puberty?*

Lou inserted the key in the ignition and hooted when the thing fired up. "Let's get to work," he said. He pulled the truck back onto the side street and headed for the scrapyard.

All went smoothly for a few blocks; then, the engine coughed. In another block, it coughed again, then stuttered and died.

"That's not funny, Lou," Deetz said. "Stop with the stupid jokes."

"It's not a joke, Irene's out of gas." Lou's voice sounded wounded.

Deetz cast his eyes heavenward. How many more things could go wrong?

"There's an empty gas can in the back," Lou was saying, "and there's a station about two or three blocks north of here on Broadway."

"Your point?" Deetz said.

"I'm not leaving Irene again." Lou glanced sideways at Deetz, an unusually contrary twist to his mouth. "You never know who might decide to take her for a joy ride."

"Ha," Deetz snorted. "With an empty tank?"

Lou hunched his shoulders and stared straight ahead.

"If you don't go get gas, we're screwed," Deetz said. "I don't even have enough money for a cheap burger, let alone a couple of gallons of gas."

Lou sighed and shook his head. "It's getting late; we don't have time for this." He stepped out of the pickup and yanked the gas can from the truck bed.

A police cruiser, its siren pulsing, flew down the street a few blocks away.

Deetz closed his eyes and slid down in the seat. He sucked in a lung full of air, choked on his saliva and went into a coughing jag as the sirens faded into the distance.

Lou shot an unreadable look at him through the windshield, his face barely discernible through the building frost, then shambled off.

Unable to turn on the engine to power the heater, Deetz wrapped his arms across his chest and hunkered into his jacket. Below-freezing air seeped into the pickup cabin, gripping his face and hands in icy tongs.

He reached under his jacket and tightened his belt. His painfully empty stomach, however, refused to be so easily fooled.

"Hustle, Lou, you worthless meat sack," Deetz muttered.

What was that saying about something not being over until the fat lady sings? With all the delays and unexpected complications that kept dropping out of the blue, Deetz had a sinking feeling the broad was warming up.

Chapter Forty-Seven

Before leaving the pickup to get gasoline, Lou had glared across the pickup seat at Deetz and wondered, not for the first time, how the two had become friends. Now that he thought about it, Deetz had never acted the way a friend was supposed to act.

A real friend did not belittle the other person. Deetz, on the other hand, never missed an opportunity to make Lou feel stupid and worthless.

Friends were honest with each other, but Lou had caught Deetz in countless lies. Sometimes the guy lied when the truth would have made more sense.

While Lou had willingly shared food and money with Deetz, the opposite rarely happened. In fact, he suspected Deetz of taking a couple of things he inherited from his dead mama and hocking them. Admittedly, Deetz bought Lou the occasional beer, but that felt more like the controlling behavior of an enabler rather than of a caring friend.

Sensing a cataclysmic shift in his feelings for the man he had called his best buddy, Lou climbed out of his pickup, reached into the truck bed behind the driver's seat and grabbed an empty five-gallon gas can.

Maybe he would call the police from the gas station and point them toward Deetz. If he showed a willingness to help them with their inquiries, maybe they wouldn't notice he still had no insurance on Irene.

Reluctantly, he tossed that idea aside. If the cops hauled Deetz away before they loaded the hauler, Lou could lose overtime pay as well as the opportunity to score valuable brownie points with Haynie.

While Deetz had blamed Dierdre for his cop troubles, something about his words rang false. Why would Dierdre keep Deetz's beat-up old pickup when she had a late model Lincoln of her own?

On top of that, since Deetz was sitting in Lou's pickup, the cops might suspect them of being partners in whatever the guy was *really* up to. Lou didn't know much about the law, but he could be setting himself up for a charge of aiding and abetting a wanted fugitive.

One thing could lead to another, and he could wind up in deep kimchee. Not only could a police record get him fired, but he would have to fork over hundreds of dollars for an attorney.

By the time the gas station came into view, Lou had decided to let Deetz help load the cars *then* turn him in. Lou would get his overtime and win Haynie's appreciation. He would park Irene at his apartment, wait out the holidays, then buy cheap-o auto insurance. All bases would be covered.

Besides, it would serve Deetz right for being such a lousy friend.

Chapter Forty-Eight

As Petra and Cody drove to Mozul's apartment complex late Saturday afternoon, Cody reviewed her background check.

"Whoa," Cody said. "Listen to this. Dierdre Mozul used to have her own show in Vegas where she rode a Harley Davidson inside a steel mesh sphere." He looked up. "I saw something like that at a circus when I was a kid. An assistant opens a hatch at the side of an enormous metal globe and the rider drives the motorcycle up a ramp and inside. The cyclists start out at the bottom of the globe, going kind of slow, you know, rocking back and forth. Then they rev the motorcycle faster and faster until they're spinning around the sides midway up the ball and perpendicular to the ground. The next thing you know, they're speeding all around the globe, sometimes even upside down."

"I cannot imagine you as a kid, let alone going to a circus." Petra glanced at her partner. "Are you going to go all star-struck on me, or will you eventually give me the salient parts of her background?"

"Right." Cody cleared his throat. "She's not super rich, but not hurting. Her second divorce happened four years ago. No outstanding warrants, no DUIs, no moving traffic violations. Except for Deetz and Bradley, all her known close associates live in Las

Vegas, along with both of her exes. She owns her apartment complex free and clear, so obviously has a good head for business. Even in its rough condition, the complex could be worth a million bucks." He looked up. "I don't get it, Petra. Bradley and Mozul are both decent folks, yet they completely fell for Deetz's line of BS."

"Decent, law-abiding people tend to see other people as decent and law-abiding, until proven otherwise," Petra said, "and crooked people tend to think all people are crooks."

"Where did you learn that stuff?" Cody said. "It's way too cerebral for me."

"Something picked up from a college class a lifetime ago."

The detectives lapsed into silence for the rest of the drive.

As Petra pulled her vehicle into the parking lot in front of Mozul's apartment complex, Cody motioned toward a tiny, elderly woman wringing her hands and pacing up and down the sidewalk along the horseshoe drive. Wearing blue jeans, a knitted cap and matching scarf, she shook her head, seeming to argue with an unseen opponent.

"That must be Mizz Jenkins," Cody said.

When the woman caught sight of the two detectives, she hurried toward them, her steps spry as she ploughed through the snowbanks along the drive's edge.

"Are you the police?" the old woman said as Petra and Cody stepped from the car. After the detectives identified themselves, she said, "I don't think anyone's still inside. At least, I haven't seen any movement since

I called Dierdre. The burglar must have sneaked out the back because I've been watching the front. I would have seen him." She looked down at her soaked, snow-coated cross-trainer tennis shoes. "I guess I should have called earlier."

"It's okay," Petra said. "You did call, that's what's important. I have a few quick questions, then you should go home and get out of the cold. We can talk more later."

"Of course," Miss Jenkins said.

"Can you tell us what you saw or heard that made you suspect someone was inside the apartment?" Petra said.

"I didn't get close enough to *hear* anything," Jenkins said. "But I did *see* something. Dierdre has horizontal blinds on her windows, you know?" She paused and looked expectantly at Petra and Cody. When they nodded in understanding, she continued, "sometimes one of the slats doesn't close all the way and you can see right into her living room. I have warned her a dozen times about it. I mean, you never know who might be watching. Dierdre's an attractive woman and attractive women can *attract* the wrong element." Cody opened his mouth to speak, but Mizz Jenkins plowed on. "I was once disrobing in preparation of taking a shower and forgot to close my bathroom window. I saw movement out of the corner of my eye, and when I looked up, there was someone staring at me through the window with the most frightening look on his face." She distorted her face into a show-and-tell mask then added, "It was horrible. And there I stood, naked as a jaybird." She placed the tip of an index finger alongside her nose and nodded knowingly. "Next day I bought all new window coverings with blackout drapes. No one's going to get a free peepshow from me again."

"So, you saw someone inside Mizz Mozul's apartment?" Cody prompted.

"That's what I'm trying to tell you. I saw someone moving around through a gap in the blinds. It was just a shadow, you understand, so I cannot describe the person, but I got the feeling by the way they moved it was a man, you know, kind of fast-like and aggressive." She swayed and lifted a hand to her forehead. "I'm sorry, but I really need to sit down." Without another word, her eyes rolled back, her body went rigid, and she fell face first into a snow drift.

After a shocked nano-second, Cody turned the woman onto her side to allow her to breathe while Petra called for an ambulance.

"She has a strong pulse." Cody removed his gloves and cupped the old woman's hands in his. "Her fingers are freezing."

"She's been standing outside for at least half an hour," Petra said. "According to the thermometer in my car, it's twenty-five degrees out here." She bent over the old woman. "Iris, can you hear me?"

Miss Jenkins' eyelids fluttered, and she smiled. "You go ahead, Johnathan. I'll feed the cat."

"It's okay, Iris," Petra said. "Help is on the way."

Continuing to gently rub the old woman's hands, Cody looked up at Petra. "Are you thinking what I'm thinking?"

"Probably," Petra said, "but let's hear it."

"I'm thinking Mizz Jenkins saw our man Deetz inside Mozul's apartment. I'll bet you a steak dinner he broke in to get his pickup keys so he can skip town."

"That's possible." Petra motioned toward the rear of the parking lot. "If that's the case, he was unsuccessful, because his pickup is still parked where Mozul left it. I'm thinking he could be inside waiting for her to return. If he's like every people-user I've ever known, he probably has an inflated opinion of himself and figures he can talk her into giving him enough money to get out of Dodge."

"I noticed Bradley's pickup is gone," Cody said. "Is it just me, or is that whole hide-and-go-seek thing with the pickups just a tad dodgy?"

"It definitely smells."

"Then spray something, Johnathan," Iris interrupted, her eyelids fluttering. "Use that nice lilac aerosol."

Within minutes, an ambulance screamed down the street into the apartment complex's parking lot. While emergency medical technicians attended Miss Jenkins, Petra and Cody hurried to Dierdre's apartment.

Her handgun held at the ready, Petra knocked on the front door, identified herself, and shouted for anyone inside to come out with hands raised. When no one responded after the second command, and after determining the front door to be locked, the two circled around to the back.

Silently, Cody motioned toward the broken glass in Mozul's back door. Both detectives glanced down at the concrete step outside the door.

"No pieces of glass on the step," Cody said. "The window was broken in from the outside."

Petra reached a gloved hand to the open door and pushed it wide enough for them to enter. "Careful," she whispered, pointing to red drops on the floor beneath the door's broken window.

The detectives carefully skirted the drops of blood then silently surveyed the kitchen, the expressions on their faces reflecting a level of awe at the sheer magnitude of damage. They looked at each other in unspoken understanding then split up and made their way through the apartment.

"Clear," Petra shouted from Mozul's bedroom.

"Clear here," Cody answered.

"Someone would have to be really pissed to do all this," Cody said as Petra walked into the living room where he stood. "I've never seen a burglar bust up furniture. They get in, get the goods, then get the hell out. This took time."

"Yeah," Petra said. "It feels like a rage-generated rampage geared to leave a message."

"You think Mozul might be in danger?" Cody said.

"That's a possibility," Petra said. "For sure, it's a good thing she wasn't here. Call her and get an estimated time of arrival. Meanwhile, I'll call for a forensics team to process this mess."

Cody retrieved his phone and punched in a number while Petra did the same with hers. They spoke briefly, then broke their respective connections.

"Mozul will be here within three or four minutes," Cody said. "I told her to park in her reserved parking spot and stay there until we can get to her."

"Good," Petra said. "I want to do a walk-through with her before the forensics team gets here."

Careful to touch nothing, the detectives exited the apartment through the back door.

By the time they navigated the snow drifts and icy

sidewalk on their way around to the front of the apartment complex, Dierdre Mozul was pulling her car into her parking space.

Chapter Forty-Nine

Kent Fowler smiled to himself. Had he known how good it would feel to terrify the woman who now called herself Petra Rooney, he would have worked harder at trying to find her.

The whole time he was in jail all he could think about was what he would do to her once he got out. By the time he was released, however, she had disappeared.

Although her friends refused to speak to him, he suspected they knew where she was. The people at her place of employment, however, seemed not to have a clue.

"She dropped out of graduate school and just drove off into the sunset," one woman had said, the expression on her face radiating disapproval.

Then, by a stroke of luck, Kent caught a glimpse of her on television during the evening news. If he had been a superstitious man, he would have said there were unseen forces at play.

When he saw her trying to distance herself from that Albuquerque reporter and her cameraman, it was like the clouds rolled back, the sky opened, and angels sang.

The trip to Albuquerque from Ohio wound up costing more than he had planned to spend. Nevertheless, he still had a couple of thousand bucks in a pre-jail savings account and an old-but-comfortable SUV with plenty of sleeping room. After sharing a six-by-eight jail cell with a three-hundred-pound junkie, the mummy-style sleeping bag and air mattress in the SUV made his sleeping arrangements rank right up there with the Ritz Carlton.

His preliminary phone call and texts to the person he now referred to as *The Woman* had not worked out as he expected. He had hoped to engage her in dialogue on the phone; even wrote a list of the darkest threats imaginable to spew into her ear. But she broke the connection before he could use them.

She had no doubt hoped to frighten him with that answering text, but all it accomplished was to jack him into an adrenaline rush. He was jazzed to the eyeballs.

He learned a lot during his time in jail, most of which he was unwilling to discuss. But two valuable survival skills he picked up were patience and the ability to do what he had to do while remaining invisible. Just like he texted, she would never see it coming.

Kent chuckled and straightened his shoulders. This was going to be fun.

Chapter Fifty

As Petra and Cody approached the car inside which Mozul sat waiting, Petra's eyebrows rose at the change in the woman's appearance. The absence of harsh, penciled eyebrows, fake eyelashes, thick makeup, and black eye liner had left her with a softly mature look. Red, talon-like fingernails had been clipped and coated with clear glossy varnish. While the hair was still red henna, instead of the frowsy hairdo piled on top of her head, Dierdre had brushed the medium length tresses into a becoming pageboy.

Petra glanced at her partner and smiled inwardly. A tough cop who had cried when his border collie died, who had survived a stabbing and a deadly methamphetamine-induced rampage, Detective Cody Rankin stood gawping at Dierdre like a schoolboy staring at his pretty elementary teacher.

Cody sensed Petra's gaze and glanced at her; his face red enough to stop traffic.

"Thank you for making yourself available," Petra said to Dierdre. "We cleared your apartment to make sure no one is still inside. But we would like to do a walk-through with you to determine if anything is missing, or if anything has been left that doesn't belong."

"Of course," Mozul said.

"You might want to prepare yourself," Cody said.

"It's, um, it's been pretty well wrecked."

Dierdre's lips tightened. She nodded her head, stepped out of her car, and pressed the key fob until it chirped. She pulled her apartment key from her purse, unlocked her front door, and followed the two detectives inside.

For the next fifteen minutes, they walked slowly through Mozul's apartment. Other than the occasional gasp and murmured expletive, Dierdre remained subdued.

When she caught sight of the open jewelry box on her bedroom floor, however, she moaned. She swiped at her eyes and poked through the few remaining bits of costume jewelry then turned toward the detectives.

"Nearly everything of real value is gone," Mozul said. "I took most of my nicest things with me, but I left a few expensive pieces behind." A pained look crossed her face. "At least they left some things only valuable because of their memories."

"We'll need a description of the missing items," Petra said.

"I can do better than that." Mozul lifted her chin and looked at Petra. "I took photos for insurance purposes. I keep them on my laptop. I can forward them to you."

"Excellent," Cody said. He reached inside a pocket, extracted a business card, and held it toward Mozul. "Email it all to me."

"I'll do that." Dierdre smiled and put the card in her jeans pocket. She stepped into the hallway leading to the living room, stopped short, and pointed at two pieces of black plastic on the floor. "That's not mine. I don't know what it is."

Cody stooped over the pieces then stepped into the living room and called out, "Here's the rest of it. It appears to be the remains of a cell phone." When the two women approached and stood beside him, he pointed to a triangle-shaped divot in the wall plaster. "Looks like someone threw it against the wall right there."

"It's the pay-as-you-go phone I gave Ron, uh, Mister Deetz," Dierdre said, an indefinable expression on her face. She looked up, muttered something, and strode to the wall opposite the one against which the phone had been thrown. "Just a guess," she said, sarcasm heavy in her voice. "I'm going to go out on a limb here and suggest the culprit is in fact one Mister Ronnie Deetz." She motioned toward a slightly askew electrical outlet cover and growled in the back of her throat. "If you find him, I have a feeling you'll find my missing jewelry. He's the only other person who knows about my bolt money. I would never leave it half open like that." She bent over and reached for the fake cover.

"Stop," Petra said, her voice sharper than she intended. She reached a restraining hand toward Dierdre. "Don't touch anything, please." Startled, Dierdre jerked her hand back. In a softened tone, Petra added, "If there are prints other than yours on that cover, we don't want to smear them."

Dierdre's shoulders relaxed, and she nodded in understanding.

Cody stepped to the outlet, pulled an ink pen from his pocket, and used its tip to push the cover to one side, exposing the hidey-hole behind it. "It's empty."

"Yes," Dierdre said, "as I said, I took all my cash."

"Right," Cody said. "But you wouldn't believe the

strange things left behind after some burglaries."

"We will need to get your fingerprints so we can eliminate them from our investigation," Petra said.

"Happy to oblige," Dierdre said. "Just so you know, you're going to find Mister Deetz's fingerprints all over the place. He spent a lot of time here." She paused and then added, "but neither his fingerprints nor anyone else's should be anywhere near my stash."

"You're certain no one else knew about your hidden money?" Cody said.

"Absolutely. I ordered the complete in-wall unit online and installed it myself." Dierdre shot a smile at Cody that would burn a hole through four inches of steel. "I watch a lot of DIY."

Petra's phone dinged its text message alert, and she opened the screen. "Forensics is here." She turned to Dierdre. "Do you have someplace to stay while they process your apartment?"

"I need to check on Miss Jenkins," Dierdre said. "She gave the hospital my name as her next of kin, and they called me just before I got here." She turned to Cody. "You'll let me know when I can come clean this mess up?"

"I will," Cody said.

"By the way," Dierdre said, the expression on her face serious, "when I spoke to my attorney earlier this morning, I learned that if Mister Deetz decides to report his vehicle stolen, I might be charged with theft if I am holding it without his permission. Do you know if he's done that? I mean, has he reported it stolen?"

"He hasn't at this point," Petra said. "But your attorney is correct about your culpability in the event he does."

"Ah," Dierdre said. "It's nice to know I have a good attorney." She reached into her bag. Metal ticked against metal as she withdrew a set of keys and held them out toward Petra. "My attorney says I should give these to you and offer to help in your investigation any way I can." She motioned toward the keys now in Petra's hand. "That red-tagged key is to Mister Deetz's apartment. It will work for a while, but he is three months past due on his rent, so once my attorney writes up a notice of eviction, I'll be changing the locks."

"Thanks for your help." Petra put the keys into her vest pocket.

"Yeah, thanks." Cody nodded once toward Dierdre, a shy smile on his face.

The three exited the apartment. Dierdre returned to her car, waved farewell in the detectives' general direction, and drove off.

Petra spoke to the head of the forensics team then she turned to Cody. "Let's go take a peek at Deetz's pickup," she said.

"What are you hoping to find?" Cody said.

"I won't know until we see it," Petra said. "But Deetz doesn't come across as the brightest bulb. He might know that without a warrant we can only look at what's out in the open, but I'm hoping he overlooked something."

"Why *hasn't* he reported his pickup stolen?" Cody said. "I mean, he had to be mad as a hornet when Dierdre, um, Mizz Mozul kicked him to the curb, especially after she let him live in the apartment rent-free for three months."

"Yeah," Petra said. "After the first month or two, he would expect a continued free ride. I figure when she yanked that off the table and sent him packing, he decided to pay her back in the style to which he is accustomed; taking her valuables and trashing her place."

"Deetz has no vehicle, and he will soon have no place to stay," Cody said. "All he had to do is call the police and report his pickup stolen to get it back, but he hasn't done that. Both Mizz Mozul and Bradley said the guy was broke most of the time, so that means he likely has little to no money. We have been unable to find any other known associates, and he isn't sleeping in his pickup, so where the hell is he holed up?"

"Your guess is as good as mine," Petra said. "But wherever he is, he can't be too comfortable. It's colder than a polar bear's nose."

"Yeah, and other parts," Cody said.

The two detectives threaded their way through mounds of snow and walked to the rear of the lot where Mozul had parked Deetz's pickup.

"Great," Cody said as the two approached the truck. "It's covered in snow."

"Look at this." Petra pointed to the top inside rim of the closed tailgate free of snow. "Does that look like freeze-dried blood to you?"

"Yeah, it does," Cody said. "It's smeared, like something was dragged across the tailgate."

"Something or *someone*," Petra said. "That's enough to get a warrant."

As the detectives started back to Petra's vehicle, sudden movement from behind a nearby thicket of desert willow was followed by three rapid-fire pops. Splotches of red blossomed on Petra's chest. Her knees gave way, and she dropped onto a mound of snow.

"Rocky," Cody yelled. Palming his handgun, he dropped into a crouch beside her. He reached for her with his free hand, his head swiveling and eyes searching the area.

"I'm okay," Petra said. She dipped a finger in one of the red blobs and held it up. "Paint." Pointing toward the desert willows, she added, "It came from over there."

Cody stood and sprinted for the bushes; his handgun held at the ready.

Petra pulled herself to her feet, disengaged her handgun from its holster, and followed Cody. For several minutes, the two studied the area around and behind the trees.

"Hey Rocky," Cody said, pointing at the ground behind a particularly dense portion of undergrowth. "The snow is trampled here, and footprints lead off toward the street." He nodded his head indicating the direction. "He must have parked over there."

"He's long gone." Petra took a deep, shaky breath. As the two walked back toward her car, she said, "My last date with Kent was to an office party at a paintball gallery."

"Ah, hence the paintball pseudo-hit." Cody's lips thinned.

"He even bragged about bringing his own paintball gun and face guard to the party. He said there was no way he would put a rental mask worn by who-knew how many people with who-knew what diseases anywhere near his face. Before eating the catered meal, he wiped the plastic cutlery with a cloth handkerchief he carries in a plastic baggie in his pocket. He actually lifted the plate of food and sniffed it."

"Controlling *and* obsessive compulsive," Cody said. "That's a great combo."

"I kept telling myself he would not show his face around here, especially after doing time for harassment. Obviously, I was wrong."

"You do realize the guy is escalating, right?" Cody said.

"Yeah. A typical stalker-creep." Petra took a deep shuddering breath.

"Yeah, it *is* typical. That's what worries me," Cody said. "At some point, he won't be content to pull his tricks from a distance. Sooner or later the hit-and-run stuff will stop satisfying him, and all that rage will boil over. He did not come all this way just to play paintball. He'll want to get up close and personal." He shifted his weight from one leg to the other in what Petra had come to recognize as a nervous gesture. "You remember that case we worked last year, the woman whose stalker kept upping the ante until he finally broke into her house late one night and strangled her while her two kids were asleep upstairs?"

"That is one of the many cases that keeps me awake at night," Petra said, her face grim. "The worst part was that she had taken out a restraining order on him the day before." She patted Cody's shoulder to lighten the mood and said, "I don't want you to worry about me. I know the ropes, and I know the kind of guy I'm dealing with."

"I'd feel better if you hadn't just got shot three times," Cody said.

"With paintballs," Petra said. "Come on; let's go get our warrants."

As Petra stepped into her car and buckled up, an

unexpected sense of calm flowed through her. She was not the same woman Kent had harassed two years earlier, and it was more than just a name change. Two years with APD had taught her a lot about human nature and about herself.

If Kent did whip himself into a frenzy and decide to get close enough to try his hand at ending her, she would be ready.

Chapter Fifty-One

Despite a splitting headache, throbbing knee, thick dry tongue, growling belly, and frozen fingers and toes, Robin fought to keep her eyes open. Over twenty-four hours without more than a few minutes of sleep must be playing tricks with her brain, because she kept hearing her brother's model airplane flying around the trunk.

Wasn't there something from a documentary on hypothermia, something she should be careful not to do? Or was it something she *should* do to survive?

Wrap up in that comforter, Robbie. Don't make it too tight, but don't leave any openings. Pull it over your head and face, so it will hold your warm breath inside.

"Tanks, Mob." Robin began to cry. "I never 'pologized for sneaking out ob the hows whed I wuz twelve."

No need. You were just a kid.

"I lub you, Mob." Robin sniffed.

I love you, too, Robbie Girl.

"Gib John a hug frub bee." She drew the comforter completely over her body, taking care to cover her head. She lost the struggle to stay awake, closed her eyes, and fell into a deep sleep.

Chapter Fifty-Two

It was late Saturday afternoon by the time Petra and Cody stood on the county attorney's front porch with an affidavit in support of probable cause to search Deetz's pickup and apartment. Petra described the location of Deetz's truck, the smeared blood on the tailgate, and his potential connection to both Banda's death and Robin's abduction.

The attorney signed off on the proposed warrants, and the two detectives drove to a judge's home. After a few pointed questions, the judge agreed with Petra's assessment and signed off on both warrants.

The sun was going down by the time Petra and Cody started back to the parking lot at Mozul's apartment complex with legal paperwork in hand.

"What if it's not blood on the tailgate?" Cody said. "It could be spilled house paint."

"I don't think so." Petra said. "If it were paint, why wasn't there more of it? We didn't see another smear or drip anywhere else."

After Petra parked, she and Cody palmed their flashlights and exited her car.

They walked around to the rear of the apartment complex and approached Deetz's pickup. Careful to touch nothing with their bare fingers, they began their search.

"Rocky, come here," Cody said. "There's a scrap

of cloth." He pointed his flashlight at a twisted piece of roof flashing barely visible beneath a layer of fresh snow in the truck bed. "It could just be a bit torn from a paint cloth," he added.

As Petra stared down at the patch of fabric, a snippet of her conversation with Robin during their cookie baking marathon popped into her head:

I just bought a new comforter. It's white with splashes of lavender.

"Where was her new comforter?" Petra said.

"Her what?" Cody repeated.

"Robin bought a new comforter, but it was nowhere in her house when we searched it." Petra motioned toward the fabric patch. "She said it was white and lavender. If you were a house painter and wanted to haul a body to a secluded place without anyone paying particular attention, what would you do?"

"I'd wrap it in a bed-cover with a pattern that looks like spattered paint," Cody said. "Chances were slim anyone would see him in the middle of the night to begin with, but from a distance, it could pass as a mound of painting supplies."

Petra called dispatch and requested that Deetz's pickup be towed, impounded, and gone over by the forensics team. Then she pulled the key Dierdre had given her from her vest pocket.

"Let's go take a look at Deetz's apartment."

"What about Bradley's employer?" Cody said. "Do you still want to talk to him?"

"We have a few more pressing things hanging fire," Petra said. "Have you managed to identify the logo on Bradley's shirt?"

"Yup. He works at Haynie's Scrapyard on Broadway."

"A scrapyard," Petra said, her pulse revving. "We need to talk to his boss and any other employees. I want to know how long Bradley has worked there and what kind of employee he is. And we want to know if his buddy Deetz has access to any of the junked cars."

"You want me to do that now?"

"Not yet," Petra said. "Let's check Deetz's apartment first, then we'll catch Bradley's employer."

"My money is on Deetz for being the main culprit in this," Cody said. "Even if he has an accomplice, my innards tell me he's the master cog in the wheel."

"All the signs are he is desperate," Petra said. "You need to call Dierdre and tell her not to go back to her apartment until we find him."

"What about Lou Bradley? Do you want me to call him?"

Petra nodded then said, "Warn him that Deetz may reach out to him. If that happens, Bradley needs to call us immediately. One thing we know from Deetz's police record is that he won't shy away from a physical altercation. If he abducted Robin, he would stop at nothing to save himself. Anyone who knows him is at risk."

Chapter Fifty-Three

Careful to keep at least two cars between his vehicle and The Woman's car, Kent followed her and the middle-aged guy who must be her partner. While clouds covered what remained of the early evening sun, making it tricky to keep the other car in sight, the darkness also gave Kent a sense of security. No one would see him until he was ready for them to.

Were The Woman and her Teddy Bear partner only colleagues, or had their partnership developed into a more intimate relationship?

A word he read in a social psychology book while in jail popped into his head: *propinquity*. Whenever two people were repeatedly thrust into close physical proximity for an extended period, it can lead to what the book called *interpersonal attraction*.

Kent snorted. Such a cold, clinical term for the human dynamic of sexual pursuit. In rudimentary terms, it meant people who lived, moved, and had their being around each other day after day could develop the hots for each other. Like Elizabeth Taylor and Richard Burton; Angelina and Brad; Kurt Russell and Goldie Hawn. The list was endless.

"Has your propinquity with Teddy Bear finally lit your fire?" Kent muttered.

What he liked to refer to as his *season of introspection* during jail time led him to admit that the potent mixture of emotions sluicing in his viscera when in The Woman's presence was pure obsession. Love had nothing to do with it, nor did sexual attraction, oddly enough. While Kent recognized that she *was* attractive, he had not been attracted to her in that way. He hadn't even *liked* her.

She was what his father called *an uppity woman*. It was the challenge of controlling her that held him in thrall; her self-confidence, intelligence, and even persistent refusal to allow him to dictate her behavior.

From the moment they met, he knew he had to possess her. He had even gone so far as to search out a suitable space in which she could be held. But she rejected his attentions, fired up the machinery that sent him to jail, then disappeared.

He had half expected to experience something akin to spontaneous internal combustion upon seeing her again, some Cosmic, world-ending explosion that would kill them both.

But the sight of her had affected him in unexpected ways, and he had revised his goal. He would give her an option: either she would be *his*, or he would kill her Teddy Bear partner.

Based on the terminology Kent had gleaned from the pile of psychology textbooks he read while in jail, he was living out a version of the spurned lover cliché. However, he had no desire to be The Woman's lover. He would much rather be her Lord and Master.

When the Woman pulled her vehicle in front of an apartment complex, Kent drove past, his head turned away in case either of the detectives glanced toward him. Evening was settling in, and it was unlikely they could discern his features. But *careful* was his middle name, another trait he had acquired in jail.

Kent drove his vehicle up the block, turned the corner, then made a U-turn. He pulled behind a van and parked on the street facing the complex.

In less than a minute, unable to sit still, he climbed from his vehicle, zipped up his coat, and walked in the direction taken by the two detectives.

Moving from the cover of one parked vehicle to another, Kent entered the parking lot in time to see The Woman and Teddy Bear walk toward the rear of the complex.

He crept to the building and sidled up to its brick wall. Careful to avoid slipping on the melted snow that was beginning to freeze into sheets of ice, he peered around the corner.

The detectives approached a beat-up old pickup. They moved slowly around the vehicle, shining their flashlights here and there, offering each other a running commentary concerning their finds.

Kent stood immobile for a couple of seconds, then suddenly in the grip of something beyond his control, he returned to his SUV.

He pulled a pair of latex gloves from the glovebox and slipped them on. He retrieved a three- by five-inch spiral notepad and cheap ballpoint pen from the console, along with a packet of anti-bacterial wet wipes. He wiped the pen and notepad to destroy any fingerprints, then scrawled a message on the first page.

His blood sizzling through his veins, he scribed a note all in capital letters, each slanted so far to the left as to be barely legible, therefore untraceable. He read his words then smiled.

A sense of urgency making his hands shake, he

tore the note from the pad, folded the page in half, and stepped out of his SUV. Pretending to be out for a late-afternoon constitutional, he sauntered to The Woman's vehicle.

When a glance around the area indicated no one was watching, he lifted the wiper blade on the driver's side, placed the note underneath, then strolled back to his SUV.

Within minutes, The Woman and Teddy Bear returned to her vehicle.

Kent drummed his feet on the floorboard when she spotted the note and pulled it from behind the wiper blade. He mentally pounded himself on the back in approval of her obvious agitation. And he nearly whooped aloud as her body language shifted from relaxed to combat mode.

The Woman dropped into a crouch. She said something to Teddy Bear and pulled her handgun from its holster.

As she began to turn her head in Kent's direction, he lowered himself in his seat. Under the cover of the evening's darkness, and with only his eyes and the top of his head showing above the dash, he watched the unfolding milieu.

"What are you thinking?" Kent murmured. "Are you afraid for yourself, or for Teddy Bear?"

What if The Woman recognized his van? While she had never ridden in it, she had seen him driving it at least once. Even though he had it painted brown upon his release from jail, The Woman had grown intensely vigilant those last few weeks before sending him to jail -- vigilant and sharp-eyed.

Her gaze slid past Kent's van, and he smiled.

Standing under the flickering light from a dying streetlight, her jerky, fierce movements reminded him of an old black-and-white silent movie.

When she and Teddy Bear finally holstered their weapons, Kent breathed in a long, satisfied breath.

"Perfect," he whispered. "Do you think you're safe from the Boogey Man now?"

The impromptu note had been an inspiration. If there was one thing on which Kent prided himself, it was his ability to seize the moment.

When The Woman started her engine and drove away, Kent made no move to do likewise. He knew where to find her and was loathe to end the contented afterglow from her reaction to his note.

He chuckled. Whistling "Twinkle, Twinkle Little Star," he fired his engine and pulled into the street. Time to begin phase two.

Chapter Fifty-Four

Robin awoke groggy and disoriented. Her head throbbed with every heartbeat. As usually happened after a nap, she took a second or two to remember where she was and how she got there. Images from a terror-filled dream slowly evaporated as her body jerked and twitched inside the freezer that was her prison.

How long had she slept? Maybe she hadn't been asleep, but unconscious.

Were her vital organs beginning to shut down? Her shivering had stopped, and she was finding it harder to think and reason. Was it nearing the time to consider taking herself out of the nightmare?

Robin rolled to one side and lifted a corner of the carpet square. Gingerly, she moved her fingers across the bits of glass from her broken phone in search of the largest remaining shard. She selected a piece about an inch long and half an inch wide, gripped it in one hand, and ran her thumb along its sharp edge.

"That one could work," she murmured.

Carefully, she placed the glass on the floor next to the metal wall where she could easily find it. While not quite ready to make that final choice, she found comfort in knowing the means was available.

Robin squinted at her watch. While the phosphorescent glow-in-the-dark face had long since given up its fight, the timepiece still regularly beeped out its pre-set alarm commanding her to stretch her muscles.

She pushed the button to stop the alarm's beeping and reflected on the irony that since the watch was fully charged, it would continue to run, even in total darkness, for at least six months. If nothing intervened, the watch would likely live long after Robin's life had faded into history.

Her eyes strained, hoping to determine the time of day by the hair's width ray of sunlight filtering through the tiny pinholes. Somehow the importance of knowing what time it was had assumed monumental proportions.

Where there had been rays of light before her nap, now there was only darkness.

Had she slept through Saturday night and into Sunday morning? Was it Christmas Eve?

Christmas Eve, and all over the world, people would be singing *Deck the Halls*. Kids would be shaking packages hoping to glean some clue to their contents. Moms and dads would be strategizing how best to keep their hyper-vigilant kids from learning who really eats the cookies and drinks the milk.

Glad to see you got some rest. Now get back to work. If a task is once begun, never leave it 'til it's done.

Obediently, Robin assumed her work position at the widening hole in the back seat. She slipped her trembling hands through the opening and resumed digging and pulling.

Chapter Fifty-Five

After Petra and Cody finished searching Deetz's pickup, they started back to her car. They talked excitedly about the feeling that progress was being made in their investigations.

As the detectives neared Petra's vehicle, a flutter of white drew her gaze to the windshield.

"Cody," she said, "he's been here."

"Who?" Cody's initial look of confusion quickly morphed into anger. "Kent."

"He's following me." Petra pulled her handgun from its holster.

She crouched behind her vehicle, and Cody followed suit. Using the car as cover, the detectives scanned the surroundings.

Nothing moved in the frigid Saturday evening darkness. Other than traffic noise, no sound floated on the icy breeze.

"He's playing you," Cody said. "If he really wanted to take you out, he could have done that just now."

"Then what *does* he want?"

"In my opinion?" Cody said.

Petra nodded.

"He wants to scare the beejeebers out of you before finishing what he came to do." Cody looked at Petra. "He's getting his jollies by watching you squirm."

For the next few minutes, the two studied the surrounding area. Petra peered into the dark alleyway and up the empty street.

"You could hang meat out here," Cody said. "He's not likely to be walking around any longer than he has to."

Once the detectives agreed the immediate danger had passed, Petra lifted the wiper blade and retrieved the note. As she read the message, Cody pulled a plastic evidence baggie from inside his vest pocket, opened it and held it toward his partner.

"Your face is white, even in this dim light," Cody said.

Petra silently placed the note inside the baggie and motioned for Cody to put it into his pocket.

"Are you going to tell me what that says?" Cody said.

"It says: *Would your Teddy Bear take a bullet for you? If you care about him, you'll talk to me.*"

"Teddy Bear?" Cody repeated.

"I'm so sorry you're being dragged into this mess," Petra said. "It looks like you've been added to Kent's to-do list."

"Yeah?" Cody said. "He's been on mine ever since you told me about him." He turned and looked earnestly at his partner. "You can't make any deals with this man. You know that, right? That would be playing right into his hands."

"I know." Petra sighed. "But I can't ask you to risk your life. Maybe you should go back to the main station and help search the traffic cams."

"That's not happening. You are stuck between two high-pressure situations. You're lead detective on a murder *and* an abduction." Cody took a deep breath. "No offense, but you're distracted. I'll wear my vest to bed if I have to but I'm going nowhere. So, what's next?"

"Next, we search Deetz's apartment," Petra said.

"Teddy Bear?" Cody muttered.

Once the two were inside Petra's car and buckled up, Petra impulsively retrieved her phone and sent a text to the number associated with Kent's earlier messages. Then she fired up the engine.

"You going to tell me what you just did?" Cody said.

"Yeah, I texted Kent and told him to go get stuffed."

"That's the Rocky I've come to know and respect." Cody chuckled.

Petra smiled at her partner but inwardly, she cringed. If she had made the wrong choice, she could be putting both herself and Cody in Kent's crosshairs. She was not so worried about herself, but Cody had become like a big brother to her. She would have a hard time living with herself if he were to get hurt because of her.

Chapter Fifty-Six

Search warrants in hand, Petra and Cody drove to Deetz's apartment. Following the standard protocol of identifying themselves and giving anyone inside the apartment a chance to answer, Petra used the key Dierdre had given her to unlock the front door. Heads turning from side to side, ears tuned to the slightest sound, the detectives drew their handguns and stepped into the semi-dark front room. Light from a nearby streetlamp sifted through sheer window coverings, offering just enough visibility to enable the detectives to move about freely.

"APD," Petra yelled. "If anyone is here, you need to come out now with your hands above your head."

As always, when no one spoke or moved after two more commands, Petra moved one hand along the wall beside the front door and flipped on the lights.

The first thing that struck her was the absence of anything personal. Unlike Bradley's spartan in-house camp site, Deetz's apartment contained an assortment of furniture, most of which appeared to have come from cheap motel garage sales.

There were no family photographs, either on the side tables or on the walls. No knickknacks accumulated from past vacations. The wall art consisted of boiler plate prints, probably the same ones that came with the frames. A mass-produced calendar displaying dates two months old hung from a nail driven into the wall, the plaster around which was cracked and chipped.

In the bedroom, a feeling of hurried escape was nearly palpable. Bureau drawers had been emptied of their contents and left hanging open. The closet contained a few white plastic hangers and a worn, paint-spattered pair of bib overalls. Other than a small, filthy hand towel dropped onto the floor, the bathroom had been cleared. No shaving gear, toothbrush, or shampoo had been left behind.

"Rocky," Cody called. "There are two nine-millimeter bullets on the kitchen floor. It looks like he spilled them from the box but didn't want to take the time to pick them up."

"Call in a BOLO for Deetz," Petra said. "Tell Dispatch he is presumed armed and dangerous."

"Will do." Cody pulled his phone from its holder.

"Did you get hold of Mozul to warn her to stay away?" Petra said after Cody broke the connection with Dispatch.

"I did," Cody said. "She's going to sit with Mizz Jenkins then get a motel room."

"Good," Petra said. "Deetz angry, cold, hungry, and broke is one thing. Deetz all of those things *and* in possession of a firearm is a whole new strata of bad news."

Cody yawned loudly and scratched his chin where salt-and-pepper colored beard stubble was beginning to sprout.

"You're wiped out," Petra said.

"We both are." Cody stifled another yawn. "I know you don't want to hear it, but we need to grab a few

ZZs. We can't help anyone if our brains turn to mush."

Reluctantly, Petra nodded.

Her phone buzzed and she looked at the screen.

Bringing pastries and coffee to the main station. Be there in fifteen.

"What's up?" Cody said.

"Quil O'Farrell's bringing goodies to the station."

"It's Quil now, is it?"

Petra's face grew warm at Cody's speculative expression, and she threw a punch at his arm. "He's bringing them for everyone."

"Whatever you say, Rocky." Cody grinned then yawned.

"Let's catch some rest," Petra said. "First thing tomorrow I want to talk to Bradley again. I can't shake the feeling there was something hinky going on with all that stolen-not-stolen pickup thing."

"Agreed."

"Set your alarm," Petra said as the two exited Deetz's apartment. "I want to get an early start."

Chapter Fifty-Seven

Lou trudged through freezing mounds of snow and ice toward the gas station. By the time he reached his destination, his face was stinging, and his feet were numb. In response to the handwritten note taped to the pump commanding customers to pay before pumping, he walked inside the convenience store and passed a twenty-dollar bill across the counter.

"Are you going to fill that up?" the young station employee said, nodding toward the gas can.

"Naw," Lou said, "just half." He could easily handle a couple of gallons, but more than that and the can would weigh too much to carry over three city blocks of snow and ice. Once he got Irene up and running, he could drive back to the station and fill her up the rest of the way.

"That's two and a half gallons on pump number two," The employee said. He rang up the charge then pushed Lou's change across the counter.

Squelching the desire to stay inside the warm station long enough for a cup of coffee, Lou stuffed the change into his pocket and shuffled toward the exit. Along the way, he passed the hot food display case. His mouth watered at the sights and smells of hotdogs rotating inside a rotisserie, bean burritos, hamburger patties, and his all-time favorite: chimichangas.

Maybe he would stop by for a snack after loading

the hauler. If there were a rest stop on the way to Heaven, it would offer chimichangas to traveling pilgrims.

The sun was going down, and the slush on the road was in the process of refreezing. If he did not get to the scrapyard within the next half hour or so, it would be too dark to load the cars on the hauler, even with Deetz's help.

Postponing the work until Sunday morning would be fine with Lou, but probably not with Deetz. And without his help, Lou could easily back the steel trailer into one of the cars Haynie was paying him to haul. He would not only lose the overtime, but Haynie would make him pay for damages.

"Merry Christmas to me," he muttered sarcastically, repeating Haynie's words from the morning's phone call.

Lou hefted the half-filled can and started back to the pickup. Along the way, trucks and cars shot past him, their drivers unable to see where the road ended, and its snow-covered shoulder began. Some ploughed so near to him, he could have reached out and raked snow from their fenders as they passed. His warm breath turned into frozen clouds that drifted onto his cheeks, eyelashes, and eyebrows. With every inhalation, icy air jabbed pins into his lungs.

He was within a block of the pickup when he stepped onto a slick patch of black ice and lost his balance. His arms flapped like a flag in a high wind, and his left leg shot from under him. After dropping the gas can, he fell into the headlights of an oncoming car.

Lou heard more than felt a *whump,* and his body was catapulted into the air. He thought he heard someone yell, then everything went dark.

Chapter Fifty-Eight

Lips thin, Deetz sat in Lou's pickup flapping his arms and bouncing his legs on the balls of his feet to stay warm. He looked at his wristwatch for the umpteenth time, wondering how long it could take to fill a gas can. Maybe doofus Lou filled the gas can to the brim. Carrying five gallons would be like carrying a half-grown kid.

"That's so typical," Deetz said. He blew on his hands and rubbed them together then peered through the frost-covered windshield into the gathering darkness. He swiveled in the seat and looked out the pickup's rear window.

Still no Lou.

Walking the three blocks to the station, even in snowy conditions, couldn't take more than ten or fifteen minutes. Add to that a couple of minutes to fill the gas can and another twenty or so for the return, and the bum should have been back, even if he had to drag the can over the snow and ice like a sled.

The sound of sirens made Deetz's pulse rate spike, and he hunkered down in the seat. Sweat beaded on his upper lip and forehead. The salty liquid seeped into the corners of his mouth and burned his eyes. A second siren whooped, and every muscle in Deetz's body tensed. Had Lou decided to tell the cops where to find him? He had been none too pleased with Deetz's refusal to get the gasoline.

As the sirens faded into the distance, Deetz took a deep breath and sat up. He fought a nearly overwhelming urge to get out and run, but of course, he had nowhere to go.

He couldn't return to Deirdre's place. She would long since have returned home, figured out who trashed the apartment, and called the cops. He couldn't get into his own apartment, and he couldn't haul ass out of town in his own pickup truck. Not only did Dierdre have all his keys, but every cop in the country would have memorized his description and made a note of his truck's tags. There was probably a cop parked outside his apartment right then.

Without winter gear, Deetz couldn't even hike to the Bosque and camp out. People died in this kind of weather.

He tried to comfort himself with the thought that perhaps Lou decided to take a leak at the gas station and was late starting back. Maybe he was flirting with the counter help, probably a middle-aged woman; the guy wasn't choosey.

Another possibility was that Lou might have decided to pay Deetz back by taking his sweet time. Maybe he realized it was too late to get to the scrapyard this evening, so was lollygagging inside the warm gas station leisurely drinking coffee and eating something from the grill. Deetz's mouth watered.

When Lou hadn't returned in another ten minutes, he pulled the keys from the ignition then stepped out of the pickup. He shoved his hands into his pockets and started walking in the direction Lou had gone.

In less than a block, he came upon what appeared

to be the aftermath of a traffic accident, the obvious destination of the sirens he had heard earlier.

Strobing ambulance lights cut through the darkness. Paramedics squatted next to a bundle on the ground while a kid paced back and forth in front of a late model sportscar, its engine running, lights on.

Deetz slipped behind a snow-mounded bush. He bent over, pushed a branch to one side, and peeked through the resulting gap.

"It was an accident," the kid was saying. "One second he was walking at the side of the road then it was like he jumped out in front of me." He pointed at his car. "He busted my windshield. My dad's going to kill me."

Deetz swallowed a frustrated yell. The doofus must have gone and got himself killed. Now he would be carted off to the morgue, along with Deetz's cash.

Paramedics rolled the gurney to the rear of the ambulance. Light from inside poured into the surrounding darkness, bringing into stark relief the faces of paramedics and cops, along with the kid's dented car, and the snow-covered underbrush beside the road.

Lou moaned and tried to sit up. The paramedic murmured something, and he collapsed onto the gurney.

Relieved that his chance at Lou's money might be only delayed rather than dead in the water, Deetz fought down the nearly overwhelming urge to stride onto the scene and demand Doofus give him his money. Even so, the part of his brain that was still functioning kept him rooted in place. With cops and firemen milling around the scene, any action on Deetz's part would be the equivalent of walking into a police station and handing himself over.

The good news was that unless the dumbass's injuries were life threatening, he could be treated and released instead of spending any real time in the hospital.

The ambulance doors closed, and the vehicle drove off into the night. Within a few minutes the firetruck and cop car did the same.

Deetz stood behind the bush, unable to decide what to do. Wrapping his arms tightly across his chest, he ground his teeth as his brain sizzled and popped with questions and speculations.

No money, no food, no vehicle, no one left to hit up.

His random gaze fell beyond the accident site to a patch of bright red atop a roadside snowbank. Every nerve in his body fired simultaneously at the sight.

"I got me a vehicle, after all," he said with a satisfied grin. "It's a start."

With one last glance around, he stepped across the road, hefted the gas can, and started toward the pickup. Gasoline sloshed with each step; the sound more soothing to Deetz's ears than a Grammy-winning song.

He had a pickup, he had gas, and he had Doofus's keys. Life was looking up. Now all he had to do was get his hands on some cash.

Deetz was certain Lou had retrieved the cash to pay for his help from his bedroom earlier. Maybe, like Dierdre, he had his own stash of ready cash for use in emergencies.

If there was folding green anywhere inside the guy's place, he would find it. Depending on how *much*, Deetz would not only get something to eat, but he would fill Lou's pickup with gas and happily put Albuquerque in the rearview mirror.

Deetz emptied the gasoline into Lou's gas tank, tossed the can into the truck bed, then climbed into the driver's seat. He turned the key, pumped the gas pedal until the engine fired, then drove to Lou's apartment.

Chapter Fifty-Nine

When Robin awoke again, her breaths were coming in shallow fits and starts. Her heartbeat was erratic. Her head and arms felt too heavy to lift.

So, this was what it felt like to freeze to death.

Suddenly, she was standing in a meadow of rolling hills as far as her eyes could see. Lush green grass bespangled with proud wildflowers swayed in a gentle breeze. Smiling, she breathed in the herbal fragrances of sage brush, and juniper. The sun warmed her face, and a handful of fluffy white clouds floated lazily through delicate blue space.

Across the meadow, two familiar figures walked toward her. She cried out and ran to them.

"John?" Robin threw herself into her husband's arms and covered his face with kisses.

John smiled and hugged her tightly but remained silent.

She turned to her mother. "Mom?"

"You have to go back, Robbie," her mother said.

"No," Robin cried. "I want to stay here with you and John."

"It's not time, Darling Girl," John said. He reached out a hand and gently touched her face. "I would love for you to stay, but it's important that you go back."

"There are things left undone," her mom said, "things only you can do, children who need what you have to offer."

"I don't understand," Robin said.

"You will," John said.

John's image dimmed and faded, as did her mother's. Robin tried to hold onto them, but her grasping hands met only air.

Chapter Sixty

Quil O'Farrell eased his van into the main police station parking lot at the same time Detectives Rooney and Rankin arrived. He waved at the officers as they approached his van then slid the passenger's side door back and reached for a box of pastries.

"Hello, detectives," Quil said. "Good timing."

Something about the expression on Rooney's face tugged at his heart. Not only was she obviously exhausted, but she was expected to execute her duties impartially and professionally, even though her close friend had been abducted, and time was flying.

"You need a hand?" Detective Rooney said.

"Thanks," Quil said. "I brought a couple dozen pastries: scones, fruit tarts, and cinnamon rolls." He nodded toward the van's interior. "Your breakroom probably keeps a pot of coffee going, but I had a fifty-cup urn brewed, so I brought that rather than toss it out."

"That's very kind of you," Detective Rankin said. He glanced at Petra and added, "Fifty cups sound about right for me, but it looks like everyone else is going to have that brown sludge lovingly referred to as *breakroom coffee* with their pastries."

Quil pulled a wheeled cart from his van. He unfolded the cart and loaded the coffee urn onto it.

"I'll get the pastries." Detective Rankin reached for

the two stacked boxes. "The crew is going to love this," he said. "It's a generous thing for you to do."

"It might even get you added to someone's will." Detective Rooney smiled.

The three laughed, and something shifted in Quil's spirit, something he hadn't felt in a long time.

Chapter Sixty-One

Lou sat slumped on an examination table in the hospital emergency room. His head throbbed, and his chest felt like he had been thrown down two flights of stairs.

"You'll need to take it easy for a few weeks," the emergency room doctor was saying. "You are lucky your injuries are not worse. You have no broken bones, but the four stitches in your scalp and three cracked ribs are going to take a while to heal."

Lou took a shallow breath and grimaced.

"I'm going to give you something for the pain," the doc said. "You can take up to four tablets over a twenty-four-hour period, but if your pain becomes too severe, call and I will prescribe something stronger. Don't try to tough it out. Pain is more manageable if you take something before it gets really bad." The doctor motioned toward Lou's chest. "Your ribs should heal within six weeks or so, but you should put ice on them and limit your activities."

After the doctor left, a nurse pushed a wheelchair into the curtained space. She smiled and steadied the chair as Lou slowly lowered himself into it. Once he was seated, the nurse handed him a plastic bag containing everything that had been in his pockets when he came in, then she offered him a handful of sealed packets with the words *Extra Strength* on the front.

"Is there someone who can come get you?" the nurse said. "Someone to drive you home?"

"Naw," Lou said. "It's just me."

"We can give you a bus pass or chit for a taxi," the nurse said.

"A cab would be great." Lou said, careful not to move too quickly. As the nurse wheeled the chair toward the waiting area, he pulled his wallet from the bag and checked its contents, grateful to find his cash still there.

He was glad to be going home. Although his pickup and apartment keys were still in his truck, he had a duplicate house key hidden under the welcome mat in front of his door.

He would be warm and comfortable. Deetz, however, was sitting inside what amounted to an icebox waiting for Lou to return.

Deetz hadn't eaten in twenty-four hours, had no phone and no money. And as far as Lou knew, not another person in the world gave a rat's ass about him.

Lou glanced at his wristwatch. Nearly three hours had passed since he left the pickup. Hopefully, Deetz would have found his apartment key on the truck's fob and walked back to Lou's apartment.

The taxi pulled up to the patient pickup area. Moving slowly, Lou slid into the back seat and gave the driver his address.

As the taxi pulled into traffic, Lou used his in-phone app for a local pizzeria. He ordered a large everything pizza and a two-liter soda delivered to his apartment.

It was no more than he should do for a friend, even a lousy friend.

Chapter Sixty-Two

Kent Fowler drove a late model compact car out of the airport rental car lot and pulled it onto the interstate. While he wasn't too happy about renting the vehicle, he had a feeling it was necessary. His van's Ohio tags might as well be a flashing neon sign with the words *Herein sits the guy you seek* written in capital letters. Maybe The Woman remembered the van, or maybe she didn't. He couldn't take the chance.

Once he completed his mission, he would return the rental car, pay the airport long term parking fee for his van, and go home. Alone. The Woman had made her choice.

Chapter Sixty-Three

With the pickup's heater on full blast, Deetz drove through the parking lot outside Lou's apartment. Like a barn owl searching for a snack, he scanned the area for any sign of a staked-out cop. A shorting streetlight blinked, giving the mounded snow and dark vehicles a surreal appearance, but no cop was visible.

"Home free," Deetz murmured when the few vehicles in the lot proved empty, their windshields ice coated. Maybe all the cops were inside their cozy homes watching television, drinking beer, and waiting for their supper.

He drove to the rear of the apartment complex and pulled the truck into the parking slot farthest from the street. Keys jangled as he withdrew them from the ignition. By the time Lou left the hospital, Deetz and Irene-the-pickup would be dust in the wind.

Maybe Deetz would buy himself a steak dinner before leaving town. Or maybe he'd buy the whole cow. The thought made his mouth water and his stomach complain.

Pretending to be just another tenant returning home from work, he walked to Lou's apartment and unlocked the door. Warm air poured through the opening, and Deetz wrinkled his nose.

"The doofus has no pride," he muttered as he hit the light switch next to the front door.

At least the heat was on, and the bathroom was functional.

Deetz removed his jacket and tossed it onto the floor beside the front door. He strode to Lou's bedroom, skirted the mattress with its unwashed quilt piled on the floor beside it, and hustled to the small bureau against one wall. Beginning with the top drawer, he rifled through stained T-shirts and holey socks, every movement making the rickety piece of furniture's joints squeal and move. Everything in the place appeared to be on the verge of falling apart.

Mentally shuddering, Deetz ran his hands through the man's underwear drawer.

Paper crinkled. With a short-lived hoot, he wrapped his fingers around what was left of Lou's stash.

"Twenty bucks? That's it?" Deetz cursed, stuffed the bill into his pants pocket, then re-checked the drawers. Nothing, not even pocket change.

"Dammit," Deetz roared. He punched the wall beside Lou's bureau then shook his hand and flexed his throbbing fingers to determine if he'd broken any bones.

His chest tight, he sucked at the blood oozing from his scraped knuckles. He stormed through the other rooms of the single bedroom apartment; his search made easy by the lack of furnishings.

He checked the orange plastic chair in the living room in case Doofus had taped a bagful of money to its underside. He looked inside the cardboard boxes used as end tables. He searched the water tank in the bathroom, hoping a plastic bag filled with money had been duct taped inside. He rifled through the medicine cabinet, but no rolled bills had been stuffed inside plastic prescription bottles, nothing but a half-empty bottle of generic aspirin.

"Not even a name brand," he muttered.

Deetz stomped to the kitchen. Drawer after drawer proved empty of anything but greasy wadded up fast-food menus and receipts, rubber bands, logo-etched ink pens from local businesses, and dust bunnies.

On the off-chance Lou had lied about having no food in his apartment, Deetz opened the fridge. A nearly empty, plastic gallon milk jug sat beside a partially wrapped cylinder of some pulverized meat product. Deetz shook the jug of milk then opened it and sniffed.

He gagged and poured the chunky semi-liquid down the sink then stepped to the pantry. A fistful of dry cereal, or even a few saltines sounded good, anything to tide him over until he could figure out a plan of action.

He pulled back the accordion-style door and surveyed the small enclosure. A broom and mop leaned against the wall beside a yellow plastic, wheeled mop bucket. A thick, obviously old spider web ran from the cleaning supplies to the pantry's corners, crisscrossing the entire inside space. The only thing that seemed to have been disturbed recently was a pile of oily rags on the floor just inside the door.

But there was no food. Not even a can of sardines.

Deetz strode to the living room and plopped into the ugly orange plastic chair.

Since tomorrow was Christmas Eve, no pawn shops would be open. That meant Deetz could either use Lou's twenty bucks for a few gallons of gas or food. It was not nearly enough to get across the border. Either way, he was going nowhere.

A knock on the front door echoed through the empty apartment, sending Deetz's pulse into overdrive. He jumped up from the chair, strode to the door, and squinted through the peephole.

Lou, his head swathed in a bandage, chatted with a kid carrying what appeared to be a large pizza. Steam rose from the box into the cold air.

Drooling, Deetz opened the door.

Chapter Sixty-Four

Lou took a drink of soda, belched, and patted his belly. He looked across the card-table at Deetz who had already managed to pack in over half of the giant pizza. Throughout dinner, Lou had grown increasingly uneasy about the way Deetz avoided looking him in the eye.

"Are you pissed at me about something?" Lou finally said.

"Now why would I be?" Deetz's gaze slid to the wall behind Lou's shoulder. "You couldn't help getting hit by a car, could you?"

"I feel bad about having to wait until tomorrow morning to go to the yard."

"You know what they say," Deetz said between chews. "Stuff happens."

"The doc said I'm supposed to take it easy," Lou said. "But I really need that overtime, and you need the three hundred."

"That's for sure." Deetz glanced up at the ceiling, a strange look in his eye. "I don't suppose you'd be willing to front me another hundred or so."

"I wish I could," Lou said. "But three hundred is all I have until payday. I could loan you another hundred then, but that's not for two weeks."

"Two weeks, huh?" Deetz shot an unreadable look at Lou then glanced at his watch. "So, what do you do to pass the time, you being on the wagon again and all?"

"I got a laptop," Lou said.

He disappeared into the kitchen and returned with a heavy, antiquated laptop.

Deetz's head jerked up. "I didn't see, I mean, I've never seen you use one."

"I keep it in the kitchen broom closet under a pile of old rags," Lou said, mentally thumping his chest.

Deetz shook his head and muttered, eyeing the laptop.

"I bought it off a scrapyard customer who upgraded to something more expensive. I get Netflix if you wanna watch something."

"Why don't you pick out something?" Deetz yawned.

"You're welcome to stay here tonight, since Dierdre's locked you out and all." Lou glanced at his buddy then grabbed another slice of pizza. "I have a sleeping bag with its own air mattress. That's pretty well all I got out of the last divorce."

"Sounds like a plan." Deetz finished his soda, an indefinable expression on his face.

"First light is about six," Lou said. "We can go any time after that." He started to stand then winced and sat back down. "Do me a favor, Deetz, and bring me one of those packets of pills on the floor by the front door."

Deetz started to say something then stopped himself and a weird look flashed across his face. A cold shudder skipped across Lou's scalp.

Once the pizza was gone, and the men had watched an episode of some mystery or other, Lou pointed Deetz to where the sleeping bag and air mattress were stored.

Within a few minutes, Deetz was snoring

convincingly. Lou, however, was unable to fall asleep for several hours. When sleep finally came, it was fitful and uneasy.

Chapter Sixty-Five

Early Sunday morning, perspiration dripped down Deetz's cheeks despite the icy wind and blowing snow. He rubbed his freezing hands together and shifted his weight from leg to leg as Lou unlocked the junkyard gate.

During the night, Deetz had considered rifling through Lou's pockets for the money he knew was there. He had even toyed with the idea of knocking the doofus out with the butt of his gun and taking off in his pickup.

Sometime around two in the morning, though, he decided his best course of action was to let the current scenario play itself out. At least by going along with Lou's plan, Deetz had a chance of sneaking out of town with his pockets full of cash and jewelry.

But by robbing Lou, he would effectively paint an even brighter target on his own back than was there already. Lou would call the cops and tell them he was assaulted then robbed and his pickup stolen. A full-scale manhunt would roar through the state like a wildfire. Roadblocks would be set up, and the border to Mexico would be watched. Within less time than it took to think about it, Deetz would be found and hauled off in handcuffs.

Nonetheless, the feeling that his chance to escape was rapidly growing slimmer made his muscles twitch and jerk all night. Deetz was relieved when the emerging light of dawn sifted through the grimy windows.

After the two men stepped through the junkyard gate and into the enclosure beyond, Lou re-engaged the lock then turned to Deetz.

"It's that big boy over there." Lou pointed to a snow-covered car-hauler. "We need to load the junkers on it."

"No problem," Deetz said, trying unsuccessfully to keep his voice level, surprised at how returning to the yard was affecting him. From the time they got into Lou's pickup, the nearer they got to the yard, the harder it had been for him to breathe. And now, every nerve fizzed. "Which ones are we supposed to load?"

Lou pulled a dirt-smudged piece of lined paper from his pocket and held it up. "Haynie said to load these three." He tapped the paper with an index finger. "The nineteen-eighty Fiat Spider, the nineteen sixty-five Ford Mustang, and that old Cadillac Cimarron."

"Is there only one?"

"Only one what?" Lou said.

"Cadillac Cimarron," Deetz said. His voice sounded high-pitched.

"Yep. It's been sitting there for thirty-five years. I never thought it would sell. The whole time I've worked here, no one has pulled a single part from it. Old man Haynie nearly peed himself, he was so excited about selling it off." Lou shot a quizzical look at Deetz. "Are you okay? You're looking kind of pale."

"Yeah." Deetz cleared his throat. "Can we get going?" He rubbed his hands together to warm them. "The quicker we get done here, the quicker we can wrap ourselves around breakfast."

"Anxious to get your hands on that start-up money," Lou said. "I gotta hand it to you; I never figured you for an entrepreneur. I kind of thought I'd like to start my own business sometime."

Lou's droning voice faded into the background as Deetz's brain sizzled and popped.

What the hell had he been thinking by agreeing to help the bozo? If he had started hitchhiking as soon as he knocked over Dierdre's apartment, he might have been near the border by now. Truckers were known for their lonely willingness to pick up hitchers. But his brain had seized up, and all he could think about was getting his hands on enough money to eat and get away from the crew of cops who must be scouring the city for him.

He comforted himself with thoughts of the three hundred bucks he would have in his hands within a few minutes. As a bonus, the junkyard was within spitting distance of a truck stop.

Impulsively, Deetz shoved his hands into the jacket's deep pockets where he fingered Dierdre's jewelry. Today was Christmas Eve, and while pawn shops in the States would be closed for the next two days, he could hock the jewelry in Mexico. He might even get a better payout there.

"Let's start with the two at the front of the lot," Lou was saying. "We can load the Caddy last."

"You got my cash on you?" Deetz said, eyeing Lou speculatively.

"Yeah," Lou said. "But you know what they say, no payola until the job's done." When the jerk chuckled like he had said something worthwhile, Deetz could barely keep from backhanding him.

The get-the-hell-out-of-here part of Deetz's brain bellowed: *Knock him into next week, grab the money, and split.* Then the don't-be-stupid part kicked in: *Just do the work and take the man's money.* By the time the guy in Ruidoso gets around to working on the Caddy and discovers what is left of Marcato, Ronnie Deetz will be the missing person.

Deetz stood next to the first car to be loaded as Lou stomped toward the hauler.

"Damn, damn, damn," Lou hollered. "The hauler's got a flat." Grimacing with every step, he slogged through drifted snow toward a stack of wheels located next to a metal building. "How about lending a hand, Deetz?"

"I don't change flats. You do it. You're the one stewed to the eyeballs with painkillers," Deetz hollered through tight lips. "Let me know when you're done."

Moving in slow motion, Lou squatted stiffly in front of the blown tire. As he moved, his phone fell from his back pocket and plopped into the snow next to his right foot.

Deetz waited to see if he would notice, but the doofus never missed a beat. He replaced the blown tire with a spare then, peppering the air with mournful moans and groans, finally managed to crank the jack until all four of the trailer's tires rested on the ground.

Lou stood and kicked the jack aside then tossed the jack handle onto the hauler's flat, snow-covered fender. Moving slowly, he climbed into to the hauler driver's seat.

"He's definitely hammered on pain pills," Deetz muttered.

"We're all set," Lou hollered through the open window.

"Just a sec," Deetz yelled. "I got something in my boot." He stooped, snatched up Lou's phone, and stuffed it inside his jacket pocket.

When the first car was loaded, Deetz fought the urge to make a run for the gate. By the time the second car was loaded, he had bitten the inside of his cheek hard enough to taste blood.

With dragging footsteps, he walked toward the rear of the lot where the Cimarron waited with its Christmas surprise. Strangely unwilling to look directly at the Caddy, he swallowed against the knot in his throat, and his chest began to tingle.

When Lou's phone rang from inside Deetz's pocket, he gasped and nearly choked on his saliva. His brain froze up. Should he answer the phone, or just let it ring? If it kept ringing, Lou would hear it and question where he had managed to get a phone when just a few hours earlier his had died mid-conversation.

He glanced toward Lou, relieved that the guy was sitting in the hauler, head bowed, studying something in front of him. Deetz took a deep breath, pulled the phone from his pocket, and pushed the answer icon.

"Hello," he said in his best imitation of Lou's voice.

"Mister Bradley?" the male voice said, "this is Detective Rankin. We have just received information that leads us to believe Mister Deetz might try to get in touch with you. It is possible that he is armed and therefore dangerous. Please do not go anywhere with him or let him inside your apartment. If you see him, call this number."

"Okay," Deetz mumbled, the flesh on his arms rucking up. "Thanks."

The detective broke the connection, and Deetz's stomach took a dive toward his boots. The cops were closing in, and he was still wandering around with his head up his backside.

A new thought entered Deetz's overheated mind. What if in his rush to get rid of Marcato's body he had not completely closed the lid, and it was slightly ajar? Lou would freak out to catch sight of a frozen body. He might even put two and two together and figure Deetz was somehow connected with it. At the very least, he would tell any cop who would listen that his best buddy sometimes came by the yard at odd hours, especially if the copper finger of suspicion should point toward the doofus himself.

What if some quirk in the trunk's locking mechanism had kept it from engaging when Deetz closed it, and the thing was sitting there half-cocked? The bumpy ride to Ruidoso could make it spring open.

Deetz envisioned the trailer hitting a bump in the road and sending Marcato's mummy-wrapped body onto the highway in front of a station wagon carrying a mom, dad, and three kids on Christmas vacation. By the time the car finished thumping over the body in the road, the family would have lost their stupid minds.

"Yo, Ron," Lou shouted from the open window of the hauler's tractor as he began backing toward the Cadillac. "Get a move on, man. I'm freezing.

"Yeah, yeah." Deetz gritted his teeth and scraped some of the snow off the Caddy's trunk, then casually pushed down on the lid. Almost giddy with relief when it proved to be tightly closed, he stepped into position.

"So, what's the hold up?" he yelled.

A thumping sound from inside the trunk caused Deetz's breath to catch and the hair on the back of his neck to flutter. At first, he thought he must be hearing things, but when the sound was repeated, he knew either something had climbed in with Marcato and was feasting on her remains, or she was still alive.

Deetz's brain spun. If the woman were not dead, he had to finish her off. Then, of course, he would have to deal with Lou. The question was how to get the trunk open without a key?

He glanced at the part of Lou's head visible through the rear window of the hauler then at the rusty jack handle on the trailer's fender where the doofus had tossed it earlier.

"Hold up Lou," Deetz yelled. He picked up the curved steel bar and lifted it. "You don't want to lose this; you'll need it if you have a flat on your trip to Ruidoso."

"Yeah, thanks." The sap stuck his hand out the open window and gave Deetz a thumbs up then slowly began to reverse the trailer toward the Caddy.

With only seconds to determine a course of action, Deetz yelled. "Hey man, I think something's moving around inside the trunk."

Lou shut down the engine. He opened the door, painfully stepped down, and carefully waded through drifted snow toward the Cimarron. "Probably a feral cat," he said. "Mister Haynie had to call animal control two or three times in the last six months. People bring their tabbies out here and dump them. You know a yowling cat sounds just like a crying baby…makes the hair stand straight up on the back of my neck."

His vital organs juiced on adrenaline; Deetz licked his lips and tightened his grip on the tire iron. For several seconds, he mentally struggled over whether it would be better to shoot Lou or just cold cock him with the bar.

While shooting him would be easier, quicker, and less messy, a pistol shot could be heard a long way in this cold, still air. The nearest residential area was only a few blocks away. What Deetz did *not* need was for someone to call the cops and report hearing shots fired. He would be caught with two dead bodies. Case closed.

Besides, who needed a pistol when he was holding the perfect multi-purpose tool. He could whack Lou, pop the trunk, then finish Marcato off…all with the same steel bar.

Although it might be a tight squeeze, he could add Lou's body to the trunk. The doofus would finally get up close and personal with an attractive female who would not gag and shove him away. Too bad he would never know it.

"Wham, bam, thank you ma'am," Deetz murmured.

"What's so funny, Ron?" Lou looked expectantly at Deetz, a goofy grin on his face.

"I just remembered a joke." Deetz said.

"So, you going to tell me, or what?"

"Sure, Lou-Lou, I'll tell you." Deetz smiled and nodded. "You need to come closer for it to make sense. It's one of those what-do-you-have-in-your-hand jokes." His smile widened as the other man stepped to within striking distance.

Chapter Sixty-Six

By the time Petra got to Tex's office, her head was pounding, verifying an often-visited chiropractor's diagnosis that she carried stress in her neck and jaws. As Tex had promised, the drone's recorded video was cued up, the frozen image on his monitor awaiting Petra's arrival.

"What do you have?" Petra skirted Tex's desk and stared at the screen.

"Once Nellie finished all four quadrants, I went back over her recorded footage and found something I missed the first time around." Tex said. "See that?" He pointed to the picture of an old car sitting among dozens of similar vehicles. "This is from the first section I taped. I just spotted it a few minutes ago."

"I don't…" Petra squinted and moved her head closer to the monitor.

"Unless I'm wrong," Tex was saying, "those small circular spaces on that trunk were made by melting snow." He tapped the screen. "And it seems to me the rear window is slightly fogged up."

"Where exactly was this taken?"

Tex pointed to a diagram on which he had drawn an X in red. "It's a junkyard."

"Haynie's Scrapyard." Petra's voice rose and her heart pounded as she hovered an index finger over the melted circles. "What are those dark areas surrounding the melted spots?"

"Let me zoom in." Tex manipulated some buttons and the image enlarged.

Petra's eyes widened. "That looks like blood."

"Yup, it does." Tex looked up at Petra. "And it doesn't appear to be the result of one animal preying on another. It's too symmetrical."

"Does the drone have a speaker or a microphone?" Petra said. "Can we talk to Robin if she's in that trunk to let her know we're coming? Can we hear her if she answers?"

"Drones don't have audio," Tex said. "The noise of their own engines would drown out any other sounds. But see there?" He pointed again at the screen. "It looks like something's moving in and out of one of those small holes."

Petra's pulse rate shot through the roof. She licked her dry lips, grabbed the phone from her vest pocket, and punched in the dispatch number.

"Beckie," Petra said, "I need a K-9 unit and ambulance at Haynie's Scrapyard on the corner of Broadway and Industrial Parkway. And I need you to call the owner and ask him to meet us there to let us in."

"I'm on it," the dispatch operator said.

Petra called her team members. She gave them the scrapyard's address, requested their help in securing and processing the scene, then sprinted for her car.

"Hold on, Robin," she murmured. "God, please don't let us be too late."

Chapter Sixty-Seven

Robin jabbed an icy index finger into the fabric-covered, foam-filled padding beyond the back seat's zigzag springs. She gasped when the fabric unexpectedly and easily ripped. With renewed energy, she dug at the filling, her progress impeded by numbness in her fingers and hands. She tore handfuls of foam padding from the seat and packed it into the corners of the trunk until she made a hole that she estimated was large enough for her to squeeze through.

Robin's skull seemed to be stuffed with mud. Her body had grown so warm she repeatedly had the urge to throw off her comforter and remove her clothes. Each time she began, her mother's voice interrupted.

Keep the comforter in place, you hear me? Hustle, you are almost there.

Unable to think beyond the need to persevere, Robin brought her knees to her chest then rolled over. Kneeling, she faced the back seat and inched headfirst through the slit. She moved past the zigzag springs and into the void from which she had removed the foam padding. If the Universe were kind, the leather seat cover would be brittle from decades of exposure to the sun. However, if she were destined to learn some cosmically induced life-lesson, she would be back at square one.

Robin made a right-handed fist and jabbed the seat

cover's taut back. Again, and again she punched, telling herself surely the next thrust would tear the covering loose from its moorings and open a flap wide enough for her to crawl through.

Her hand could have been made of butter for all the effect it had on the seat cover.

"Maybe the end vor bee, Mob," Robin said through numb lips. She sighed and rubbed her icy hands together.

How much do you weigh, Robbie?

"Wad?" Robin said.

Energy equals mass times speed.

"Izz thad all you god, an Einshhtein mishquote?"

Remember the kid up the street who used to tease you?

"Yesh."

What was his nickname for you?

"Bonehead."

You have a hard head; you have mass; and even in this small space you can generate a level of momentum.

"Ah," Robin said, a new thought like an invisible lightbulb suddenly flashing above her head. She got back onto her knees then moved her head and shoulders through the slit. Again, the seat's fabric closed itself against her body, seemingly unwilling to allow her entry.

"Reenacting by birth." Robin giggled, the sound near maniacal in the icy darkness. "God, pleasz doan led bee lose by mind."

She mentally shook herself then lowered her head. Like a battering ram and with all the strength she could muster, she propelled herself forward between the bowed springs, beyond the seat padding void, and against the seat cover.

Instead of breaking through the cover and into the back seat, however, the impact with the taut leather forced her head backward, jamming it against her vertebrae. A lightning bolt of pain shot down her spine and, disoriented, she started to reverse out of the slit.

However, seemingly manipulated by an unseen hand, the springs closed around her head, scraping the dried blood from the scalp wound inflicted by her abductor. The air whooshed from Robin's lungs, and bright flashes of light popped like fireworks against the darkness of her vision. Sticky liquid oozed down her cheek.

Her suddenly rubber arms folded at their elbows. She dropped to the trunk floor where she lay gasping, her body half in and half out of the slit.

Robin gagged, then wiped the sour vomit from her lips and chin with the back of her hand. She forced herself to breathe slowly and deeply until her insides stopped heaving.

An old hymn from her childhood flowed through her head, and she drummed her fingers on her thighs, mentally playing a piano.

"Swing low sweet chariot, coming for to carry me home. Swing low…."

The sound of distant voices caught at the edges of Robin's consciousness, instantly returning her to the cold dark trunk.

She mocked herself for thinking the outside voices were real then held her breath as they grew louder.

Chapter Sixty-Eight

"You have to come a little closer," Deetz said to Lou. "It's one of those interactive jokes."

"I like a good joke," Lou said. "I never can remember them, though." He closed the distance to Deetz, an expectant smile on his doofus face.

"You'll remember this one," Deetz said. He whipped the tire iron from behind his back and lifted it above his head.

"What are you doing?" Lou's eyes opened wide. He instinctively threw up his arms, his face registering disbelief.

Deetz brought the iron down on Lou's raised arms, and a loud *crack* split the icy air. Lou yelped as Deetz raised the bar for a second strike.

One arm dangling uselessly at his side, Lou lifted his unbroken arm in front of his face. He stepped backward onto a mound of snow, lost his balance, and fell onto his back as the swinging bar whispered through the air inches above his head.

Deetz cursed, leaned over Lou, and raised the iron. "Sorry, Lou-Lou; it's you or me."

Lou growled and rolled to his right in the nick of time. The iron bar ploughed into the snowdrift where his head had been.

Before Deetz could bring the bar up again, Lou was on him like a mad man. Unable to use his left arm,

Lou gripped the bar in his right hand. Face to face, the men danced in a tug of war next to the Caddy's rear bumper. Beyond reasoning, they did battle in what each instinctively knew would end one of them.

It was then that the back door of the Caddy slowly opened.

Chapter Sixty-Nine

Robin's breath caught. At least two men must be walking around within earshot of the trunk, men who might have bottles of water or a thermos of hot coffee, men who could help.

Robin opened her mouth to call out. But the words died in her throat when a familiar voice spoke.

"Yo, man, something's moving around inside the trunk."

Gorge rose in Robin's throat. Her hands clenched into fists as she imagined pounding the man into a puddle of red gelatin who killed Vince and tried to kill her.

With a strength she did not recognize as her own, she lowered her head, moved into the slit, and threw her body against the back seat cover. With a loud *pop*, a portion of leather pulled away from the staples and stitching holding it in place.

Robin's head and upper body shot through the slit, past the padding void, and across the newly detached leather seat cover. Stunned, she lay face down on the floorboard's hump with the lower half of her body and legs still inside the trunk.

Move, Robbie Girl. Move now!

Robin pulled herself into a sitting position on the back seat. Movement and sounds of scuffling drew her attention, and she peered through the side window.

Grunting and cursing, two men danced in a macabre wrestling match beside the rear bumper, struggling to gain control of what appeared to be a tire iron.

While Robin did not recognize one man's face, the sight of the second drew a whispered battle cry from her lips.

Adrenaline pumping like a fire hose, she marshalled her strength and shakily pushed the rusty back door open. Oxidized hinges squealed like a monstrous beast, the sound loud in the frigid early morning air.

Mouths gaping, eyes wide, the men swiveled their heads toward Robin.

Chapter Seventy

A cross between a moan and croak come from the Caddy's back seat, but Deetz did not dare look toward the sound. Still gripping the tire iron with one hand, he reached with the other behind his back for the handgun stuffed under his belt. If he jammed the gun against Lou's fat belly, the shot's sound would be muffled.

A repeated low-throated growl from the Caddy's back seat caused the hair at the nape of Deetz's neck to shift. Both men froze and simultaneously turned their heads toward the sound.

Like a scene from a horror movie, the Marcato woman, shoeless, bloody hair hanging in ropes from her bleeding scalp, hands covered in blood, eyes wild, and lips pulled back in a snarl; the woman Deetz had presumed dead, opened the back door.

Chapter Seventy-One

Robin's abductor swung his head toward her. When their eyes made contact, he gasped and took a step back.

Mouth open, eyes wide, he slipped on the snow and ice. After a frantic struggle to regain his balance, he fell face down onto a mound of snow inches from Robin's feet.

Holding the tire iron in one hand, the other man gawped at Robin.

Robin slid off the Caddy's back seat and plopped onto her abductor's back, pressing him deeper into the heaped snow beneath his body.

Deetz struggled as she ground her teeth into his neck and shoulder. He yelped and tried to shake Robin off his back, but she wrapped one arm around his neck and clung to him with all her strength. She pulled his hair, and weakly pummeled his head with her fists.

"Get her off me," the man yelled. "Help me, Lou-Lou. She's crazy."

Fully expecting the second man to turn on her with the iron bar, Robin glanced up at him.

"Shut up, Ronnie," the other man said. "You hurt her, and I'll brain you for sure." He looked at Robin. "I got you covered, lady."

Chapter Seventy-Two

Sirens screaming and lights pulsing, Petra drove her car into the scrapyard's parking area. A K-9 unit and ambulance pulled in beside her and waited for her to give them orders.

A middle-aged man paced back and forth in front of the gate. His head bent, he repeatedly ran his fingers along his collar, his movements jerky.

The two detectives got out of Petra's car and approached him.

"Mister Haynie?" Petra said.

"I've been going crazy waiting for you," the man said. "I thought I heard someone yell from the back of the yard, but you said to wait out here." He motioned toward the gate. "I unlocked it for you."

"Thank you," Petra said. "Please go back to your vehicle and wait there."

Petra motioned to the K-9 team then pulled the gate open and stood to one side as the German Shepherds and their handlers hurried through.

The handlers spoke to their dogs then removed their tethers, giving them free reign. Ears pricked up and eyes focused straight ahead, the dogs shot across the scrapyard and, within seconds, began snarling and barking.

With handguns drawn, Petra and Cody followed the animals through the gate, past stacks of junked cars to the back of the yard.

At the sight of the armed detectives, the dog handlers called their animals off and stood down.

Barely recognizable as human, Robin lay prone on a man's back as he lay trapped face down in a mound of snow. Like a beast out of the jungle, she bit at the back of his neck, thumped his head weakly with her fists, and pulled his hair.

Lou Bradley stood off to one side and stared down at the scene, mesmerized. Holding one arm bent at the elbow and tight against his chest, he dangled a crowbar from his other hand.

"APD," Petra yelled, "Drop the crowbar and get down on your knees with your hands behind your head. Do it now, Mister Bradley."

Bradley glanced at Petra, a look of surprise on his face. He dropped the bar and raised his good arm. "I wasn't going to hurt her," he said. "I was trying to help."

"Get that woman off me," the man on the ground yelled. "She's biting and pulling my hair. She thinks I'm someone else."

"Robin," Petra said.

Robin raised her head and stared into space, seeing something no one else could.

"Robin," Petra said, "look at me. You need to get off him."

Robin shifted her gaze to Petra, a dawning look of recognition on her face. "Mom said you would come." She paused to catch her breath then gestured to the man beneath her. "He killed Vince. Then he broke into my house and kidnapped me."

Robin's eyes closed. She dropped her head onto

Deetz's back. Her arms fell from around his neck and into the snow where they lay unmoving.

Petra immediately motioned the all-clear to the paramedics.

Carrying their jump kits, the medical team hurried to Robin. They gently lifted her from Deetz's back and onto what looked like a surfboard.

"Get on your knees with your hands behind your head," Cody yelled at Deetz.

"Okay, okay." Deetz struggled to right himself. "I'm freezing, man, can't I just---"

"The sooner you do as you're told, the sooner we can all get warm," Petra said through gritted teeth.

Deetz got on his knees and raised his arms. "I want to press assault charges against that woman. She bit me at least a hundred times. I think she pulled out half my hair. That's assault, right?"

"My left arm's busted," Bradley said. "My ribs are on fire, and I think my stitches came loose." He grimaced and his face grew ashen. Perspiration broke out on his upper lip as he struggled to continue to hold his unbroken right arm high.

"Lower your arm if you need to," Petra said to Bradley. "But stay on your knees."

The paramedics assessed Robin's condition then hooked her up to an IV. They lifted her onto a gurney, covered her with warm blankets, and put her into the ambulance.

One paramedic stayed in the ambulance with Robin while the other hurried to Bradley. He immobilized Bradley's broken arm in a sling and taped a patch of gauze to his head wound.

As Cody covered the two kneeling men with his

handgun, the paramedic stepped to Deetz and studied the bite marks. He applied ointment to the broken skin, suggested Deetz get a tetanus shot as soon as possible, and gathered his equipment. Lights flashing, the ambulance drove away.

Bradley turned toward Deetz. "I thought we were friends. I was going to loan you money, and all. I even bought you a pizza."

"Friends?" Deetz lifted his lips in a sneer as he glared at Bradley. "You don't have any friends except for a bunch of halfway house losers. You're a drunken, filthy slob."

Cody glanced at Petra, awaiting instructions.

"Search them," Petra said, remembering the bullets Cody found in Deetz's apartment.

Cody squatted behind Deetz, reached under his jacket, and pulled out a handgun. "That's gonna cost you," he said. "What part of its being against Federal law for convicted felons to be in possession of firearms do you not understand?"

"Mirandize Mister Deetz, Detective Rankin," Petra said. "Then take his statement."

"I know Miranda," Deetz said with a sneer. "One word: attorney."

"Your choice," Petra said. She nodded at Cody.

"*You have the right to remain silent*," Cody began.

"He tried to kill me with that tire tool." Bradley grimaced and adjusted his broken arm's position closer to his chest. "If that woman had not climbed out of the Caddy and gone all Valkyrie on him when she did, I'd be a goner for sure."

"He's lying," Deetz said, his previous threat to remain silent obviously forgotten. "It was the other way around. He was trying to kill me. I hit him in self-defense."

"*Anything you say may be used in against you in a court of law,*" Cody continued.

Deetz licked his lips then glared first at Cody then at Petra.

"Ask her. Ask that woman in the ambulance," Bradley was saying. "She saw it all."

"I got an alibi for Friday night," Deetz said. "That's when that woman was abducted, right?"

"Where did you hear she was abducted Friday night?" Cody said, glancing first at Petra then back at Deetz. "For that matter, how do you even know she *was* abducted?"

Deetz's face paled and he gulped audibly. "She screamed it in my ear while she was assaulting me. She could have permanently damaged my hearing." He lifted one side of his mouth in a smile, pleased with that bit of reasonable doubt. "But it couldn't have been me; I was in a bar drinking with my buddy Friday night." He nodded toward Bradley. "Ask the bartender at the Cacahuate Bar. He'll remember. We were there until about midnight."

"*You have the right to an attorney. If you cannot afford an attorney, the court will appoint one…*"

"We were drinking," Bradley said, "but he didn't get there until after ten." He turned toward Deetz. "And I'm not your buddy."

"*Do you understand your rights as stated?*" Cody said to Deetz.

"Yeah, yeah, I've heard it all before," Deetz said, his shoulders slumped.

The K-9 officers packed up and left; then Petra and

Cody herded Deetz and Bradley to waiting patrol cars. Deetz was loaded into one back seat, Bradley slowly edged into the other.

"Take Mister Deetz to the police main station," Petra said to one officer. "Put him in a holding cell and keep an eye on him to make sure he doesn't hurt himself or try to escape." She strode to the car holding Bradley. "Take this man to the emergency room but stay with him. I'll be there shortly to interview him."

After giving the forensics team the all-clear, Cody held the scrapyard gate open as they trooped in with their crime scene investigation equipment. He was pulling crime scene tape across the gate when Haynie scrambled from his car a strode toward him.

"Hold on, hold on," Haynie shouted. "What are you doing? I have three cars to deliver on Tuesday, and they have to be loaded."

"Once forensics are done, you can get back up and running," Cody said. "That Cadillac Cimmaron will be impounded, though, and the area around it taped off since that's where Mizz Mercato spent the better part of the last thirty-six hours. It may be a while before you get the Caddy back."

"Look," Haynie said, "I'm sympathetic to all this, I really am. But if I do not get that Cimmaron to Ruidoso by Monday, I'm going to lose the sale."

"I understand your situation," Cody said, "but your scrapyard is a crime scene, and we are required by law to deal with it as such."

Lips compressed, Haynie nodded in reluctant acceptance. He stood immobile, his eyes staring into space.

Petra could almost hear the gears in the scrapyard

owner's brain grinding out ways to capitalize on the situation. When a demi-smile began to play along one side of Haynie's mouth, Petra suspected that within hours, he would be online advertising the Cadillac as a one-of-a-kind crime scene. Human nature being what it was, someone would be willing to pay big bucks for the satisfaction of owning it. The splashes of blood and fingerprint dust would only add to the vehicle's value.

Haynie's gaze drifted toward the back fence. "Is that one of your guys? What's he looking for? There's nothing on the other side of that fence but weeds."

Petra followed Haynie's line of vision. No one was there, and nothing moved beyond the six-foot high, chain link fence.

"He's a tall guy, maybe six one or two." Haynie looked at Petra.

Petra studied the thicket of brush outside the fence. Where the heavy snow on the bushes formed a nearly solid mass of white, one side of the largest bush was bare where something had brushed against it.

While Haynie could merely have seen a lookie-loo, Petra's instincts discounted the idea. As she knew all too well, Kent was smart, sneaky, and persistent. He could be anywhere.

"You'll get a receipt for anything that has to be removed," Cody was saying. "But for the next few hours, you should go home and enjoy your holiday."

"Of course," Haynie said, obviously barely able to refrain from rubbing his hands together in glee. "You folks do whatever you need to do. If there is any way I can help, just let me know." An expression on his face like a wealthy relative had died leaving him sole heir, he climbed into his car and drove off.

The violent crime team members assembled in the scrapyard parking lot. Cold, tired, hungry, but pleased and relieved, they nodded and spoke to each other.

"Well done," Petra said to her teammates. "Thank you for all your hard work."

The team drifted away, some to their homes for a bit of rest before returning to their own caseloads, and some to the station and whatever paperwork they had yet to finish.

"You should go home," Petra said to Cody. "Your part of the paperwork can wait until tomorrow."

"Yeah, maybe," Cody said. "But Deetz, Bradley, and Mizz Marcato still need to be interviewed. Why don't I take Deetz's statement while you go to the hospital and see to your friend and Bradley? My car is still at the station, so it's a two-birds-one-stone thing."

"Thanks, Cody. Much appreciated." Petra took a deep breath and scanned their surroundings.

If the person Haynie saw outside the scrapyard fence was Kent, he had apparently decided against trying anything in the presence of so many officers. It seemed that she and Cody would most likely be safe if they stayed in a crowd.

The trouble was, sooner or later they each had to go home alone.

Chapter Seventy-Three

Kent parked his rental hatchback up the block from the police station where he had followed The Woman and Teddy Bear. Periodically glancing at The Woman's car to ensure he didn't miss her departure, he jotted thoughts in his spiral notebook and plotted his next move.

Thoughtfully, he stroked the butt of a rifle on the seat next to him. With all the broo-ha-ha about guns nowadays, he was ecstatic when he caught sight of the thing inside a pickup parked at the rest stop where he spent the night. He glanced inside the vehicle on his way to the public restrooms and saw it in the floor on the passenger's side. A quick smash and grab while its owner visited the toilet ensured that he had the means to administer justice whenever it suited him.

He had been relieved to discover the weapon loaded with twenty rounds. If he couldn't take care of business in less than twenty rounds, he didn't deserve the second-place ribbon he won in a paint gun contest a lifetime ago.

The two detectives burst from the station and ran to The Woman's car. While Kent was too far away to discern the expressions on their faces, their body movements were tense and hurried.

A vicarious thrill pulsed through him. He fired up the hatchback's engine and followed.

When The Woman's vehicle pulled into a scrapyard's parking lot, Kent drove on. He circled the scrapyard, pulled onto a dirt road at its rear, parked, and made his way to the back fence.

He crouched behind mounded snow atop a bush at the rear of the scrapyard and pushed a heavily laden branch aside for better view. Wet snow plopped from the branch onto his feet, but he didn't care.

Excitement stirred in response to the screaming police and ambulance sirens, the growling and barking dogs, images of the bloodied writhing creature atop some yelping guy mashed into a mountain of snow. He smiled as he took in the milieu.

Shouting orders, with her handgun drawn, The Woman stormed onto the scene. Within minutes, she gained control of the chaos.

Barely able to refrain from roaring in excitement, Kent hugged his arms against his body as his gaze remained riveted on the action.

The Woman was again proving how right he had been to pursue her. After getting rid of Teddy Bear, he would take The Woman to a beautiful, secluded spot and the two of them would leave this world together. A perfect, poetic exit.

One of the men in the scrapyard looked directly at Kent. The guy pointed toward him and spoke to The Woman, compelling Kent to let go of the branch and hurry back to his rental.

He hurriedly pulled the rental onto the road and parked in a secluded spot where he could maintain visual contact with The Woman's vehicle.

Kent patiently waited while the ambulances, firetrucks, and dog handlers left. Then he followed The

Woman to the police station. Teddy Bear climbed from her vehicle and hurried into the station as she drove away.

The targets had split up. Kent had to revise his plans.

For a nano-second he considered waiting for Teddy Bear to exit the station but thought better of it. That way lay certain failure. Nothing like attacking a cop to set the hounds of hell onto one's heels.

Careful to keep The Woman in view, he followed at a distance.

She drove to a hospital, parked, and hurried into the emergency entrance. Most likely checking on the well-being of the bloody creature she had seemed to know, she could be in the hospital for hours. Kent turned the engine off and leaned the seat back.

No longer necessary to Kent's plan, Teddy Bear had been given a reprieve.

But The Woman would be his.

Chapter Seventy-Four

Yawning, Petra walked into the hospital emergency room. She identified herself to a nurse behind the counter then moved around the circular hallway until she spotted two officers standing guard outside two curtained cubicles. Voices from behind the curtains indicated Robin and Bradley were being treated, so Petra approached the guards.

"I'll interview Bradley first," she said to one officer. "Depending on what I learn, I may need you to bring him downtown and put him in a holding cell."

"Yes, ma'am."

Petra turned to the other officer, who stood from the plastic chair in which he had been sitting.

"Stay with Ms. Marcato after I interview her," Petra said. "We haven't yet unraveled everyone who's involved in this case, and she may still be in danger."

The officer nodded in understanding then returned to his seat.

Petra stepped inside the cubicle where Bradley was being treated. A forlorn look on his face, he reclined on the bed and stared at the wall.

"Mister Bradley?" Petra said. "Are you ready to give me a statement?"

Bradley slowly turned his head toward her. He started to nod his head, but grimaced and froze. "Yeah," he said. "You got a couple of hours?"

"Take all the time you need," Petra said. "Start with everything you can remember, especially from Friday night on."

Slowly, in a monotonous voice, with several repetitions, Bradley recounted his and Deetz's interactions over the past two days. When he finally stopped speaking, Petra asked a few questions to fill in some gaps then turned to go.

"I may need to talk to you again," she said over her shoulder as she pulled aside the curtain.

"I'm going nowhere," Bradley said. His shoulders drooping, he stared down at his empty hands atop the blanket.

An emergency room doctor stepped out of Robin's cubicle, and Petra approached him.

"Okay if I talk to Robin now?" Petra nodded toward the curtain.

"She's awake but seriously dehydrated and suffering from hypothermia," the doctor said. "We have yet to determine the full extent of her injuries, so it would be good if you could make it short as possible."

Petra engaged her body cam then nodded, pulled the curtain aside, and stepped into the small enclosure.

Robin lay under a thin blanket, the upper half of her body slightly raised into a semi-sitting position. An IV dripped clear liquid through a tube into in her arm. One side of her scalp had been shaved and bandaged. Her unexpectedly bright eyes peered out from under heavy lids.

"How are you feeling?" Petra said.

"Better," Robin said. "I keep hoping this isn't a dream, that I won't wake up still inside that trunk."

"Can you tell me what happened?" Petra said.

Between periods of silence to catch her breath, Robin recounted everything she could remember from the moment she witnessed Deetz tinkering with Vince's air compressor. As the story unfolded, Petra repeatedly found herself shaking her head.

As Petra had done with Bradley, she asked a few questions to fill in the sequence of events.

"I'm having trouble remembering everything," Robin said. "Some of it's pretty sketchy."

"That's to be expected," Petra said. "Not only do you have a head injury, but you've also been put through a day and a half of hell in some of the worst weather we've seen here in years."

"I figured I was done for." Robin smiled wanly.

"I'm curious about something you said at the scrapyard," Petra said. "…you said your mom told you I was coming?"

A faraway look in her eyes, Robin nodded, but didn't answer.

"I don't understand," Petra said.

"Neither do I." Robin glanced up. She smiled, took a deep breath, shrugged. "It was probably just a memory from when I was a kid."

Chapter Seventy-Five

Ronnie Deetz sat in the holding cell. His mind churning, he jumped at every sound. He tried to comfort himself with the knowledge that his every move was being watched. Cameras recessed in the ceiling were sending his picture to some cop sitting behind a desk staring at him through a monitor…no one could get to him…

Deetz swiped at the perspiration beaded on his forehead and upper lip. Maybe he could cut a deal. He had a pile of information about Mister Z's multiple streams of income. He could trade names and locations for a new life. While the stuff on Vince's laptop wouldn't offer enough evidence to guarantee the cagey Mister Z and his cronies would be convicted and put away, it would strongly point the cops in their direction.

Witness protection, that was the way to go.

Deetz sat on the cell bench, his heart beating so hard it felt like it could jump through his ribs. He had run out of options.

Chapter Seventy-Six

Petra walked toward the hospital exit. At the same time, a nurse pushed a wheelchair bearing Lou Bradley toward the same exit, the attending officer beside them.

"Hello again, Detective," Bradley said.

"Hello, Mister Bradley," Petra said. "How are you holding up?"

"My arm's shattered." Bradley lifted his arm, now encased in white plaster. "But the doc gave me something for pain, so I'm okay." He held a business card-sized paper up, a look of surprise on his face. "The nurse gave me a voucher for a taxi so I can go home. That's nice, you know?"

"Is there anyone who can help out until you get back on your feet?" Petra said.

"Yeah, my AA sponsor offered to drop by every so often." Bradley squared his shoulders. "I figure it's time to make some changes." He studied his feet. "I should have called you when Ronnie showed up on my porch, but all I could think about was getting my pickup so I could make a few extra bucks." He snorted and shook his head. "Now my pickup will be impounded, and I've lost the overtime to boot." He shook his head then his gaze moved beyond Petra. "Hey, what's that guy…" His eyes widened and his mouth flew open.

Before Petra realized what was happening, Lou jumped from the wheelchair and threw himself in front of her. Two pops sounded, and instantly two red splotches appeared on Lou's chest. With a surprised look on his face, he dropped to his knees on the icy drive as thick red liquid pulsed from his wounds.

Shouts and screams erupted as people who had been milling around the hospital entrance and parking lot dodged behind trash cans and parked vehicles.

Two orderlies ran from the emergency room. They reached under Bradley's arms, lifted him onto the wheelchair, then hustled him back through the hospital's pneumatic double doors.

Petra sprinted to an empty van for cover. Palming her police radio, she squatted on her haunches and called Dispatch.

"Beckie, if there's a SWAT team available, I need them, and the on-duty K-9 unit sent to my location. We have an armed and barricaded suspect. Shots have been fired."

Petra crept around the back of the vehicle and looked around the bumper.

The *pop-pop* of a semi-automatic weapon sliced through the cold air, and the window above her shattered. Bits of safety glass peppered her head and ticked onto the asphalt around her.

Movement behind a biohazard waste removal truck caught Petra's attention and, handgun at the ready, she ran in a serpentine pattern from the van to the parking lot's six-foot tall, brick entrance sign. She crouched with her back against the sign's rough façade and looked around its corner.

A shadowy form darted from behind the waste removal truck and headed for a stand of cottonwood trees at the rear of the lot.

"Now that I have your attention, have you checked on your Teddy Bear lately?" Kent yelled. A maniacal laugh pulsed through the darkness.

Petra shivered as if someone had just dumped a bucket of ice water over her head. She clicked on her radio and tried to raise her partner. No answer. Frantically, she tried again. When Cody still didn't answer, she called Dispatch.

"Beckie, I need you to send someone to check on Cody at the main station. He should be in an interview room questioning a suspect. Let me know if he's there."

"Will do," Beckie said.

More rapid-fire shots sliced through the darkness. Chunks of brick exploded from the sign behind which Petra crouched. Debris stung her face and neck.

"Hey, woman," Kent yelled. "I'm talking to you."

Silently, Petra scanned the parking lot for straggling bystanders. Where dozens of people had been milling around just seconds earlier, the lot seemed empty of anything other than parked vehicles. She took a grateful breath and blew it out through pursed lips. She relayed Kent's approximate location to Dispatch.

"Cody's okay," Beckie said. "He said to apologize, but he was so focused on getting Deetz's statement, that he put his radio on silent mode and didn't hear it buzz."

"Thank God," Petra said as air whooshed from her lungs.

"I'm coming for you," Kent yelled, his voice nearer than before. "You and I have an appointment with death." He laughed, the sound making the hair on Petra's arms move.

Petra mentally shook her head at what was either the man's stupidity or arrogance. Did he not realize that with every word and every shouted epithet, he was effectively announcing his position?

She crouched and ran from vehicle to vehicle, closing the distance to the area she'd pinpointed as Kent's location.

A shadow moved from behind a minivan within a few feet of Petra. She raised her handgun and took aim.

Pushing a terrified female hostage ahead of him, Kent walked into view.

"Please don't hurt me," the woman cried. "I have two children."

"You hear that?" Kent yelled. "If you don't show yourself by the time I count to ten, I'll pop her, and her sweet little kiddies will be without a mommy."

"You don't want to hurt her, Kent," Petra said. "She has nothing to do with this. This is between you and me."

"Too late," Kent said. "One, two…"

Sirens screamed into the parking lot. Officers wearing jackets that identified them as members of a SWAT team poured from a van. Dog handlers and their canine charges exited units marked K-9.

"Three, four…"

The canine team released their dogs. The well-trained animals shot across the parking lot and into the cottonwoods toward Kent and his hostage.

"Five, six…"

The woman's knees buckled. She unexpectedly dropped to the ground and lay still a millisecond before the dogs attacked Kent.

Growling and snarling, the dogs moved quickly, their bodies like furry blurs as they scrambled to subdue the target.

Kent screamed and unsuccessfully tried to escape the animals' snapping teeth. But their jaws, once locked, would remain so until the handlers gave the release command.

As Kent was handcuffed and escorted away, Petra ran a trembling hand across her face. She would have to write a report and give a statement. Then she would have to testify during Kent's trial. The whole mess of her previous life would be made public. She sighed. The next few months were going to be tense.

If Kent were released on bail, he might take it as a sign it was okay to escalate his campaign against her. He was obsessive compulsive, controlling, as well as superstitious.

However, he would be charged with stalking with intent to cause physical harm as well as attempted murder of a law enforcement officer, so the judge might not allow bail. By the time Kent gets out of prison, if he ever does, he will be an old man.

Petra squared her shoulders. Perhaps she would finally manage to leave the past where it belonged and embrace her present.

Once the SWAT officers and K-9 crew loaded up and left the scene, Petra hurried back to the emergency room where the ER staff would be working feverishly to save Lou Bradley's life.

After learning Bradley was still in surgery, Petra checked on Robin. Pleased to see her friend sleeping peacefully, she went to the gift shop and bought a couple of thick magazines and a paperback mystery. She stopped in at a coffee kiosk in the hospital corridor for a large black coffee then headed for the waiting room.

Petra had thumbed through both magazines and started the mystery when she sensed someone's approach.

"Is this seat taken?" Quil O'Farrell said.

"Hello." Petra returned his smile.

"You are all over the news," Quil said. "I'm so glad you found Robin."

For the next four hours, between frequent coffee refills and the occasional update on Robin's and Lou Bradley's condition, Petra alternately shared her past with Quil and listened to his.

"Seems we have an awful lot in common," Quil said.

"So it would seem." Petra smiled.

Chapter Seventy-Seven

Sunday afternoon, Deetz and three other prisoners were marched from their cells to the prison library where they would be arraigned. The prisoners sat in chairs facing a large television monitor.

A judge sitting in a courtroom appeared on the screen. He addressed each of the prisoners by name then proceeded to advise them of their bail amounts and court dates.

Deetz nearly swallowed his tongue when the judge set his bail at half a million dollars, ...*because of the severity of the charges and the element of flight risk.*

Once all the prisoners had been arraigned, they were escorted back to their cells.

Deetz sat on the cot and thought about how best to spin his story. He had a couple of things going in his favor.

First, Banda's death had been an accident. Deetz would simply claim to have innocently misjudged the tightness of the air compressor's valve, and no one could prove otherwise. Because of *reasonable doubt,* he would skate on those charges.

Second, Marcato had not died. Although assault, kidnapping, and a couple of other charges could be brought against him, they wouldn't include murder. Even if he got jail time, he would be a model prisoner and get out early. Prisons were jam packed nowadays, and the courts were always looking for ways to lighten the load.

Maybe he was going to be okay after all. Especially since Mister Z's threat that he would not survive long enough to be arraigned had proven empty.

Two men approached Deetz's cell; one was the guard, the other a stranger.

"You've been bailed," the guard said.

Deetz smirked. So, Dierdre had come through after all. He must be addictive as hell.

The guard motioned toward the second man and said, "Mister Douglas here is a bondsman. He'll explain the rules."

Douglas? Deetz studied the man's face. Where had he heard that name before?

The cop turned a switch and the cell door slid back far enough to allow the bondsman entry.

Deetz proffered a hand, but the bondsman pretended not to notice. Instead, he opened a briefcase and retrieved a small box from which he extracted an ankle monitor.

"You'll have to wear this when you leave." The bondsman spent the next few minutes explaining the device and its workings. "You'll be expected to charge it every few days, as the batteries will run out."

"Yessir," Deetz said. It would be easy enough to cut that thing off once he was out. A quick convenience store heist, and he'd be smoke.

"You are expected to make all court appearances promptly and without fail," the bondsman said in a bored voice.

"Yessir." Deetz studied Douglas's familiar face, trying to place him.

Once the ankle monitor had been attached, the guard handed Deetz his clothes and stood to one side of the cell door.

Deetz dressed, offered a mock salute to the cop, strutted out of the cell, and followed the guard to the main gate. No one tried to stop him, and no one called to him as he stepped through the gate into the street beyond.

With Lou's twenty dollars in his pocket, he could take a city bus to the nearest truck stop. By the time anyone realized the ankle monitor was defunct, he'd be well on his way.

As Deetz walked toward the nearby bus stop, a black sedan pulled around the corner. When he stopped, the sedan stopped. When he ran, the sedan sped up.

The blood drained from Deetz's face when the sedan's driver pulled to the curb and stepped out.

Deetz ran, but Flash was faster.

Chapter Seventy-Eight

One half of her head shaved, and wearing a hinged knee brace, Robin carried a platter of steaming barbecued baby back ribs to her dining room table where Petra, Quil, Cody, and Dierdre sat amiably chatting.

"That smells wonderful," Petra said. "Are you sure you don't need any help in the kitchen? I'm fairly certain your doctor told you to stay off that leg so it can heal properly, not to mention the sore arm where you got a tetanus shot."

"Thank you, no, thank you, and yes, she did." Robin chuckled. "But there's not that much to do. With your hot German potato salad, Dierdre's grilled broccoli, Cody's crudité platter, and Quil's cherry pie, all I had to do was put the ribs in the oven." She sat at the head of the table and looked each of her guests in the eye. "I am so pleased that all of you could come."

"I wouldn't miss such a feast," Cody said. "Attendance at church potlucks and all variations thereof was duct taped to my DNA at birth." He glanced at Dierdre, and blushed when she returned his smile.

"I called the hospital," Petra said. "Lou Bradley is sitting up and flirting with the nurses." She sighed, a somber expression on her face. "I owe him."

"His picture is on the front of today's paper,"

Dierdre said. "His smile was so wide it barely fit on the page."

"The mayor visited him at the hospital to award him a medal of heroism," Petra said. "Bradley says he wants to go back to school to become a counselor for people suffering from addiction. Evidently, University of New Mexico has offered him a scholarship."

"I stopped by the hospital to see him this morning," Quil said, "I gave him a laminated, wallet-sized certificate good for a cup of coffee and pastry every day for the rest of his life." He threw a warm look at Petra, who returned it with a half-smile. "Life is too short to put off following your heart."

"What about Deetz?" Robin said to Petra.

"The chewing gum found in your bathroom as well as the specks of blood on your rug match his DNA, so he can be placed at the scene," Petra said. "The scrap of fabric we found in the back of his pickup is from your comforter, so there is plenty of evidence against him for your abduction." She looked at Dierdre. "The blood on your kitchen floor is his, so he's definitely the one who broke into your apartment. That, along with the smashed phone and his possession of your jewelry sealed the deal on that set of charges."

"I can't get the image of his face out of my head," Robin said. "He showed a complete lack of emotion when he decided to kill me."

"Have you called that number I gave you?" Petra said. "It'll help to talk things over with someone."

"Yes. I have an appointment this coming Thursday."

"Good," Petra said. "You'll be interested to know that my sergeant called just before I left home to come here. Before Deetz was bailed, he approached the district attorney hoping to make a deal. He told the DA where to find Banda's laptop as part of a plea deal. He said it holds information tying Zephyr Enterprises to various rackets across two states. He was hoping to go into witness protection."

"We've been after old man Zephyr for years," Cody said. "It would be great to nail him. But a deal with Deetz?" He tsked. "That rankles. If anyone ever deserved hard time, it's that bum."

"Evidently, the plea deal was put on hold after he was released on bail," Petra said.

"What?" Cody's head jerked up. "How could he make bail; the guy was flat broke."

"You remember when we first interviewed Bradley, he told us Deetz bragged about having rich friends?" Petra said. "Looks like that was true. Someone posted bail to the tune of half a million dollars."

"I don't understand," Dierdre said. "If Ronnie, um Mister Deetz had access to that kind of money, why would he have to borrow a few bucks every so often? He couldn't even afford to pay his rent."

"Good question," Petra said.

"Who paid his bail?" Quil said.

"We have our suspicions, but your guess is as good as ours," Cody said.

"You mean there's no way for you to find out?" Robin said.

"Not until after the trial," Petra said. "Then the case becomes a matter of public record." She paused then added, "I have a feeling the FBI is going to be called in, though."

"Why?" Robin said. "I thought the FBI only worked on federal cases."

"They do," Petra said. "But Zephyr is suspected of all kinds of interstate and intrastate criminal activity." She took a sip of iced tea. "Deetz missed his court date, so there's a warrant out for his arrest. But he disappeared almost the minute he was bailed."

"Like a puff of *un*holy smoke," Cody said.

"Maybe someone posted his bail then helped him leave the country," Quil said. "He's probably huddling in some freighter headed to Hong Kong as we speak."

"That doesn't fit with what we know of Zephyr's modus operandi," Petra said.

"I'd say it's more likely that Deetz had to be silenced," Cody said. "If he had business dealings with the Z-Man as he claimed, he's probably compost by now."

"It's tougher to lay hands on a prisoner than most people realize," Petra said. "Posting their bail is a quick work-around."

"At least we have the laptop," Cody said. "Hopefully, Deetz didn't lie about its evidentiary value."

"I'm just glad to get my jewelry back," Dierdre said. "Funny how you think you know someone, then learn you didn't have a clue." She looked at Cody and added, "I much prefer to be around the *what you see is what you get* kind of people."

Cody grinned and shot a sly look at Dierdre. The air between them crackled.

The group sat in thoughtful silence for several seconds.

"Have you decided where you want to go from

here?" Quil said to Robin.

"That's one of the reasons I invited all of you for dinner," Robin said. "Besides thanking you for your support, I want to ask for help. I have decided to set aside one day a week to offer piano lessons to underprivileged kids who cannot afford to pay." She looked at each face and added, "If you know any kids who need calm, instructive, adult attention for one hour a week, let me know."

"What a lovely idea," Dierdre said. "I've heard that learning music helps with brain development, especially in the area of mathematics."

"I might know one kid who could benefit," Petra said. "He lost his mom last week to an overdose."

"That's a start," Robin said.

After various comments, plaudits, and expressions of support, the group fell silent.

"A toast," Robin said, raising her glass. "Here's to new friends and new beginnings."

"To new friends and new beginnings," everyone said in unison.

Good for you, Robbie Girl. Good for you.

A word about the author…

Olive Balla makes her home near Albuquerque, New Mexico with her husband Victor and their bossy dog Dazee. When not writing, she makes sawdust in her woodshop. http://omballa.com